DELTA CROSSROADS

A Novel from the Delta Jade Collection

Michael Cravatt

ISBN-10: 149362573X
ISBN-13: 9781493625734
Library of Congress Control Number: 2013920641
CreateSpace Independent Publishing Platform
North Charleston, South Carolina

Delta Crossroads

Preface

*D*elta Crossroads is a fictional novel packed full of suspense, mystery, romance, intrigue, and heart-pounding action as Michael Cravatt's newest heroine, Delta Jade Colton, finds herself in seemingly endless and unpredictable dangers and dilemmas.

Jade, a Greenwood, Mississippi-born beauty is a very distant descendant of a great Choctaw Indian chief. To Jasen Prospero, her strongly principled and equally vulnerable next door neighbor, she was to become the temptress and seductress who would exploit his weaknesses and send him spinning out of control down a pathway of infatuation, admiration, confusion, and secrets. Her concealed life was all about nightmares and demons, and Jasen had dared to enter the innermost, darkest recesses of it. Their relationship was as mysterious as her past and her remote lineage to the Choctaw Nation's chief. She was the poster child of every man's fantasy, and she would become Jasen's partner in a terrifying trip back into her past. Sorting fact from his fantasy consumed his journey into her world. Their relationship existed only in Jasen's mind—or did it? She was the epitome of Southern female strength and possessed an uncanny gift of survival against seemingly impossible odds.

To Jasen Prospero, she becomes the synthespian of his hidden desires... like a synthesized heroine in a computer game...addicting, alluring, challenging, and always just a click away from being his.

The book opens in 1828 in La Guairá, Venezuela, in the midst of Venezuela's struggle to secure independence from centuries of rule under imperial Spain. Manuel Sanz, a freed slave, and his wife, Maria, embark on an ill-fated journey to America on a Yankee merchant ship, fleeing retribution from the ruling government because of their daughter's relation to the deposed dictator Simon Batista. The two-thousand-mile voyage does not go as planned, but upon arrival in the United States, Manuel encounters a Choctaw Indian who becomes the unexpected and gracious beneficiary of Manuel's sole possessions.

Two years later, the Choctaw Nation's principle chief, Colonel Greenwood LeFlore, sets out on his historic mission to Washington, DC, to convince President Andrew Jackson to reconsider his stubborn resolve to relocate the entire Choctaw Nation to the unknown Oklahoma territory, dubbed "The Great American Desert." LeFlore returns to Mississippi and uses his position as principle chief of the Choctaws to persuade his fellow chieftains to agree to the infamous Indian Removal Treaty with amendments that was signed on September 27, 1830.

In an ingeniously crafted attempt to secure justice, honor, and lasting trust from the US commissioners present at the signing, LeFlore demands a ceremonial smoking of a rare solid gold effigy peace pipe. In LeFlore's mind, the gold pipe will cement a binding contract between the Choctaws and the US government. During the dangerous return to his home, the priceless treasure is secretly hidden away by LeFlore, who fears the priceless instrument of peace will be stolen or fall into the wrong hands and be lost for eternity. Unexplainably, he carries his secret to his grave, having left a hidden, coded message that he hopes will ensure that the priceless relic will find its rightful and sacred place in the history of the Choctaw Nation.

Over a century and a half later, Jade Colton is haunted by her tragic past, and she still wonders about her mother's demons that had forever changed their lives. Jade had reluctantly inherited her mother's magnificently preserved and very rare Venezuelan Amerindian rooster, a taxidermist's masterpiece. From its roots on another continent, it had serendipitously become the property of Greenwood LeFlore and had stood watch as the sentinel dining room centerpiece in Malmaison, Colonel LeFlore's magnificent plantation home ten miles outside of the town named for him. The incredibly beautiful rooster had become Jade's silent guardian, possessing a secret apparently known only to the great Choctaw chief.

After Malmaison burned to the ground in 1942, the rooster had mysteriously fallen into the hands of sinister Jake Luther, the racist boss of Jade's mother, Jean. Little did Jade and Jean know that the secret kept by the rooster would ultimately send Jade cascading down a treacherous trail back to her roots in Greenwood where revenge was lurking unsuspected in the Delta shadows of a small town and its prominent leaders, who had secrets of their own.

And who could have known that fate was about to deal a shocking hand to Jade and her handsome neighbor and lover in the intimacy of a bitterly cold and stormy winter night? A major winter storm was approaching on a night that was supposed to be the beginning of a new journey for both of them. In the privacy of that stormy yet ironically perfect night, in the darkness of that bliss, a shadow stepped from the edge of the past and forever changed everything. But it would be the rooster that would plunge them even deeper into the oblivion of Jade's past in Mississippi and into a secret world of conspiracy, danger, intrigue, and shocking surprise. Mother Nature had brewed up a midsummer Delta storm, a devastating tempest that would cast them into a seemingly hopeless encounter with some of Greenwood's most unsavory citizens.

The gargoyles of injustice, obsession, greed, hate, and desire had been released from their inner sanctums. Jade Colton and Jasen Prospero had hoped for a new beginning but were totally unprepared for what came next. The secret hidden away by the great Indian chief for more than a century in the Mississippi Delta would propel them into a world of unimagined dangers, harrowing escapes, and hidden treasures.

The book's heroine, Delta Jade Colton, is sure to win the admiration and respect of any reader who has faced some of life's most unpredictable challenges and survived. *Delta Crossroads* is Cravatt's first fictional novel and adventure/thriller fans' introduction to Delta Jade's roller coaster adventures and misadventures. Fasten your seat belt!

Delta Crossroads

*"There are moments in our lives when we find
ourselves at a crossroads;
afraid, confused, without a roadmap.
The choices we make in those moments will define us for the
rest of our days…."*

--one tree hill

Prologue

CHAPTER ONE

The Anne McInn

La Guairá, Venezuela
1828

Manuel and Maria Sanz stepped onto the deck of the imposing triple-mast merchant sloop that was docked in the small port of La Guairá, near Caracas. They both turned simultaneously and tearfully looked back at the serene little fishing village where they had lived and raised their three children while eking out a meager living, Manuel as a day fisherman and Maria as a house servant to nobleman Jose Morales in Caracas. They were both *pardos* (freed slaves) and tended to blend in with the locals, many of whom were also *pardos*. They had never been mistreated. Politicians often formed alliances with the *pardos* in exchange for increased popularity and any chances of gaining political power. Juntas and military rivalries were a dime a dozen as ambitious and greedy leaders raced to gain control and ultimate dominance in a new Venezuelan government.

Venezuelans were on the verge of independence from the long-ruling Spanish imperial power that had proliferated in South America in the seventeenth and eighteenth centuries. Spanish armies and eventual colonization had conquered native Indian tribes and dominated the enormous southern continent of the Americas. Organized conspiracies against the colonial regime in Venezuela were not new. As early as 1797, the French Revolution had inspired locals to pursue independence.

The seeds were sown as European events like the Napoleonic Wars and the Spanish-American War mushroomed. Venezuelans were hungry for independence and longed to shed the colonial chains that had shackled them to the whims and fancies of many despicable Spanish tyrants.

Manuel held Maria in his arms.

"We will be fine, Maria," he reassured her. "I have heard good things about the great city in America that they call 'The Crescent.' New Orleans is very far away, but I think we can find safety and perhaps opportunity in the American states." He knew that Spanish authorities might retaliate against his family because of his daughter Concita. An extremely beautiful girl with warmth and charms that would tempt any man, she had become the mistress of the embattled leader of Gran Colombia, Simon Batista. A self-declared dictator, Batista barely escaped assassination by rival army leaders with Concita's help. With assassinations occurring almost daily around the struggling Venezuelan provinces, Batista's escape infuriated the power-hungry general Jose De la Rosa who was the next of many-to-come *caudillos* (strongmen) poised to assume control of an independent Venezuela. De la Rosa had issued official orders to hunt down and capture or kill the hated dictator. Batista and his lover secretly retreated to the Colombian coast hoping to leave Venezuela in safe exile. A mysterious illness consumed the wanted leader in a matter of days and he died suddenly at age forty-seven.

When De la Rosa heard about Batista's death and Concita's role in his escape, Concita and her family became prime targets for De la Rosa sympathizers. Concita disappeared into anonymity somewhere in the Colombian countryside. The remaining Sanz children, two sons, had married and relocated to Peru and north to Colombia several years back. Manuel and Maria had heard many stories about De la Rosa's propensity for revenge against anyone who opposed him. Manuel had hastily arranged for safe passage out of La Guairá and to somewhere far removed from De la Rosa's reach. The only ship in port was sailing for New Orleans with a generous load of Venezuelan cocoa for American markets along with precious imports from China, and he had paid the captain a generous sum for passage. Captain Henrique Valdez was sympathetic considering all the horrors and injustices that he had heard about De la Rosa, whose notoriety had spread far north. The Sanzs were welcomed aboard to join Valdez and his ten-man crew.

It was very early, and the new morning sun had not yet débuted above the seemingly endless eastern horizon of the vast sapphire Caribbean Sea that lay calm and deceiving in the quiet dawn. The resupplied and well-stocked *Anne McInn*, a four-hundred-ton-capacity cargo clipper that was a sleeked-down version of the Baltimore Clipper line, would be embarking soon. She was a strikingly beautiful ship with a frame of live oak and mahogany. Originally designed to accommodate twelve brass cannon, the *Anne McInn* had scaled back to only six to increase cargo capacity. She was a new design in merchant ships and was known for her speed and endurance in choppy seas.

The Sanzs had stowed below deck their meager possessions, which consisted of two large and tattered burlap sacks of clothes, extra sandals, and a few odds and ends. Manuel had also convinced Captain Valdez to let him bring his caged rooster and two hens on board. He had brought a small sack of corn that would be plenty for the birds to eat on the voyage, which he was told would take ten to twelve days, weather permitting and winds favorable. The hens were layers and would provide eggs that could be shared with the crew.

Valdez had looked rather curiously at the brilliant-colored rooster and pressed Manuel for details. "That doesn't appear to be any ordinary farm rooster, Sanz," observed Valdez. "I have never seen one with such magnificent colors and a wattle like that. Where did you get him?"

Manuel looked at his rooster proudly and then back at the captain. "It was a gift, Captain Valdez, from a very special friend, Juan Mariches. He was an Amerindian, a direct descendant of a famous native Indian leader named Tamanaco, who was brutally executed by the actual founder of

Caracas, Diego de Losada, two centuries ago. Juan told me about this rare species of roosters that had been bred for hundreds of years by early Indian inhabitants of our land.

"These roosters were like no others in the world because of their mix of amazing colors and their extraordinary combs and wattles. They were coveted also because of their virility and dominance over other animals. They brought good fortune to all who possessed them. Juan said that they are even more magical and powerful than the famous Portuguese O Galo de Barcelós (The Rooster of Barcelós), a dead rooster that was roasted and served up on a judge's banquet table and then suddenly crowed, saving a condemned Spaniard from a sure death by hanging."

"Quite a story, Sanz," Valdez said, intrigued. "Better keep that creature safe down below. I don't think you want the crew getting any notion about a savory rooster meal! And maybe he *will* bring us good fortune on the journey."

"Please, sir," pleaded Manuel. "You must respect my rooster. He may be the last of his kind. I have to protect him."

"Relax, Sanz," Valdez smiled. "He'll be safe."

At the first hint of the rising orange globe at the edge of the distant eastern horizon, the crew of the *Anne McInn* released her bulky hemp hawsers and bolt ropes from the giant wooden bollards and drifted seaward with only her mizzen lofted. The wind was gentle but adequate to resume the long journey that began eight months earlier in China.

The well-built clipper had sailed eastward and southward around the southern tip of the continent with a fresh cargo of Chinese teas, spices, linens, and silks. The weather had been kind to Valdez and his seasoned crew, even meeting unexpectedly favorable conditions as they rounded Cape Horn and traversed the unpredictable and typically unforgiving Drake Passage. They had battled and survived treacherous howling winds and deep swells on previous runs. Valdez felt confident and rested as he left the Venezuelan coast and sailed north into the Caribbean Sea.

Just as Valdez was preparing to order full sails and the unfurling of the mainsail, a lookout in the crow's nest bellowed a loud announcement.

"Ship astern! Ship astern!"

Valdez immediately pivoted 180 degrees at his command post on the bridge and stared at a distant ship with sails that were reflecting the now brilliant morning sun. He reached for his looking glass and studied the ship. It was a Spanish military sloop, and it was moving toward them under full sail. He had a sinking feeling that someone might be in pursuit of the Sanzs. He commanded a merchant ship and was not equipped sufficiently for a sea battle against a twenty-cannon military sloop. But Valdez was no novice on the sea. He felt no panic. The Spanish sloop was relatively small, but its wide bow lent it a disadvantage when it came to speed. The *Anne McInn* was built for speed and for cutting through choppy seas.

It had now cleared the shallow straits several miles out, so Valdez ordered full sails from all three mastheads. They had just passed the Pearl Islands, now in the distance off starboard. The well-engineered and sturdily built clipper immediately caught the increasing prevailing trade winds and soon was up to a respectable eight knots. The cargo holds were nearly at capacity, and Valdez was not convinced that he could get more speed. But even for a heavy cargo ship, the *Anne McInn* was not sitting as low as most merchant ships did with similar loads. The Spanish ship had now narrowed the distance and was closing within cannon range. Valdez was now seriously concerned about the ultimate winner of this high seas race. He needed more wind. He *had* to have more wind.

Just as the leathered-skinned captain had feared, a cloud of black smoke appeared, followed almost at the same time by a jarring boom as the pursuing ship fired in the direction of the merchant clipper. The cannon's projectile collided with a wall of ocean water just five yards off the starboard side of the *Anne McInn* and drenched Valdez and his first mate with a soaking curtain of cold sea spray.

"Too close for comfort," Valdez mumbled to the first mate. The next lob would be closer or on target.

Valdez was suddenly startled to see Manuel Sanz poke his head from the cargo hold just in front of the bridge and climb up the steps and onto the deck. Manuel held his prized rooster by the handle on top of the rooster's small wooden cage.

"What in God's name is he doing up on deck and of all the craziness carrying that rare farm bird?" Valdez screamed silently to himself. "Sanz! Get back below deck. We are under attack by the Spanish military. If we can't outrun them, we're sitting ducks. Now get below!"

"Captain Valdez," Manuel said, aware of the threat of the pursuing ship and knowing it was sent by De la Rosa to extract his revenge, "I told you that this rooster will bring good fortune to us. I brought him on deck so that he could see the enemy."

"Sanz, you are trying my patience, and you are acting in an outrageous and insane manner! We are about to be blown out of the waters and splintered into kindling if they fire again. Please, get back down below with your wife and brace yourselves."

Manuel turned, holding his prize to the level of his own eyes, and facing the menacing sloop, he disappeared back down into the hold to join Maria.

Valdez and his crew were beginning to reconcile themselves to the fact that surrender might be the wisest of their choices, considering the obvious intent of the Spanish ship with its loaded cannons. Valdez glanced back at the sloop and decided to give his first mate the order to drop sail and come to.

Suddenly, before he could bark the command, a tremendous gust of wind rushed past him in what seemed like multiple directions all at once and caught the main sail of the *Anne McInn*. The clipper lurched ahead, causing Valdez to lose his balance and fall backward into the bridge railing. Acting on reflex, he straightened his large frame and tightly grabbed the helm as his ship skipped across the open sea at a speed he had never experienced before. He felt the magnificent wind against his face and thought of the treacherous Drake Passage winds that he had fought more than once. He turned and looked astern and could not believe the sight of the disappearing silhouette of the sloop behind them. Soon the Spanish ship had evaporated below the horizon. The *Anne McInn* had won the race. They were safe.

The rolling, choppy waters were nothing out of the ordinary for experienced sailors and voyagers, but for Maria Sanz, they were the worst experience of her life. The sudden surge in the ship's speed as it cut across wave after wave in the white-capped Caribbean Sea quickly began to take its toll. Manuel was a fisherman and easily adjusted to the ocean's assaults of deep, rolling swells and occasional house-sized waves of foam and salty water that slapped like a giant sledgehammer against the bow and at times washed across the deck.

Days passed as Maria fought a losing battle with the unrelenting and unmerciful sea, weakening from her continuous bouts of gut-tightening nausea and painful retching and vomiting. Manuel sat with her head in his lap and held her by the waist each time she leaned over to gag and empty what little juices she still had in her stomach into a wooden bucket that filled the stale cargo hold with a sharp, acrid stench that burned Manuel's nostrils.

Finally the waters grew calmer, and a crewman said that they had entered the Gulf of Mexico. They had been sailing for five days. Maria was listless, severely dehydrated, and starving, in spite of Manuel's desperate attempts to get her to drink water and nibble at dried bread.

"Maria," Manuel softly pleaded into her ear. "Wake up, my love. The waters have calmed. Please, wake up. Maria, please talk to me."

She could not open her eyes, but her cracked and bloody lips tried to respond. No sound came. She took in a final long, deep gasp of the hot, putrid air and then fell completely limp in her husband's arms.

"Maria! Maria!" He knew she was gone, consumed by the demons of the sea. He had been helpless to protect her. He drew her closer in his arms and leaned over and kissed her cold, parched, and bleeding lips. He sobbed and rocked her back and forth.

"No-o. No-o. I won't let you have her!" he cried as if the sea could hear him. But Maria was gone. Manuel was alone.

He looked at his caged companion and did not understand what had happened.

"Damn you, bird! You were our protector. You have forsaken me. Where is your justice? "

His face was drawn and defeated. He could only embrace Maria and sob. The rooster stared at him as if he understood but did not care.

The next day, Captain Valdez and his crew prepared the body. In his final farewell to his lifelong soul mate, Manuel, with Valdez's help, pushed the sailcloth-wrapped body over the leeward side of the *Anne McInn* and watched the sea swallow her into its watery grave. The remaining four days of the voyage to a new beginning would be without his love. He slept mostly and ate only small bites at a crewman's urging. He could see no more good fortune in his life. He had only brief thoughts of what fate might have in store. He really did not care anymore.

On the last morning of the two-thousand-mile journey, Manuel was startled awake by a rhythmical pounding against the ship's thick wooden hull and deck. It was a torrential tropical rainstorm, and the ship suddenly began pitching and rolling violently. Safety was so close and now an unexpected storm had surrounded the merchant ship, which was limping the last few miles toward the port of Orleans so that Valdez could deliver the precious goods from China and Venezuela. Valdez had sailed over twelve thousand miles in six months and was weary beyond words or description and ready for a long rest on dry land. The sea gods were not being kind.

Valdez had halfheartedly credited the rooster for their good luck in out-sailing the Spanish sloop, and if it was really true, then the *Anne McInn* could outlast this final attack on her also. But then the vicious winds began to circle the ship and howl and screech like a beckoning Aegean siren maiden calling for Ulysses. The ship was at the sea's mercy. The white-capped walls of water swelled and repeatedly lifted the clipper thirty feet or higher onto wave crests, only to drop her again and again like dead weight into a valley of foaming, spewing seawater.

Valdez fought the wheel at the helm but could not control the rudder. The sails had been partially ripped from the violent winds before the crew had rolled them in. Luckily the mast beams had not broken. The fierce wind pushed the ship more and more eastward, away from its intended destination. For the next three hours, the storm's attack was unrelenting. The ship was tossed around like a tiny toy in a vast ocean. Lightning flashed from every direction and kissed the sea's surface in a spectacle of jagged spikes as deafening thunderclaps roared through the dark morning skies. Manuel and the crew had tied themselves to the beams below deck as they rode out the maelstrom.

Finally they sensed an easing of the hurricane-like winds, and the rain and hail were mercifully replaced by a gentle, warm shower. There was a glimmer of hope in their eyes, but just as they released their secure bindings, the *Anne McInn* lurched sharply over on its side, and with a loud, ominous creaking and then a thunderous snap of the hull, it stopped. The crew knew at once. Their ship had slammed into a sandbar or a reef and was dead in the water. They had shipwrecked and were not near New Orleans.

Manuel and the crew crawled up to the deck, which was now awash in ocean water. The sea had started to pour into the cargo hold. Manuel looked through the light rain and fog and saw land. Rays of hope returned. They had wrecked on a sandbar very near the shore. A crewman called out for Valdez. There was no response. He called again. Nothing came back. Valdez's fate was unknown. Had the sea claimed their captain?

The *Anne McInn* was on her side and half-covered by the turquoise-green seawater. Abandoning her was their only choice. Manuel started to follow the crew who had leaped into the waist-deep water and were sloshing ashore. He stopped just before jumping and turned back to the open hold. Floating in the salty water that was now flooding the precious cargo from faraway worlds was the wooden cage with his rooster.

"You have brought us bad fortune!" he shouted scornfully at the wet bird. The rooster was a curse, he said to himself. "Drown, evil bird, drown!"

Suddenly a blinding flash of lightning lit up the heavens over the wrecked ship. At that very instant, he thought he could see his friend Juan Mariches hovering in the haziness above the doomed ship. Fear and confusion cast a dark shadow over him. He got down on his belly and stretched his arm into the hold and retrieved his rooster, who seemed quite calm and totally unperturbed by the tragic end to their voyage. Cage in hand, Manuel plunged into the chilly waters and waded ashore.

He found the crew and Captain Valdez safely on dry ground and sitting in the sand. Just as he started to join them and thank God for sparing them, three figures dressed quite smartly in full native Indian regalia of beaded and tasseled deerskin costumes and multi-colored feathered headdresses walked from the palmetto brush beyond the dunes and moved toward them. The drenched and weary survivors of the *Anne McInn* were defenseless and could only stare at the Indian warriors coming toward them.

One of the Indians, a tall and imposing man, spoke first. They were amazed. His English was polished and distinct.

"We saw your ship slam violently into the sandbar and turn onto its side. You are very fortunate to have survived the fury of such a ferocious storm. We are Choctaws. You have landed on the shores of our territory, which we call Mississippi. Nearby is our former village that we called Bilocci (Biloxi). Our brothers from the tribes of Choctaws, Pascagoulas, and Acolapissas have gathered there for a festival to celebrate the fall harvest. We were here many years before the French and British settlers. Please. Come with us and we will tend to your needs, give you dry clothes, and provide food and drink."

The speaker turned, and the three Choctaws headed back into the palmetto brush and onto a narrow trail.

"Well, men." Valdez took charge again. "Don't just sit there. Get up off your soggy, dead arses and follow them. They mean us no harm. I have met Choctaws before. They are gentle and peace-loving farmers. Let's go! God has saved us. Make your weary bums move!"

The Choctaws were quite hospitable and did just as the tall leader had said. The next day, the leader arranged for a mule-drawn wagon to carry the shipwrecked travelers to their original destination of New Orleans. It would be a two-day journey, they were told. Valdez had lost his ship and all of his cargo, but he and his crew were alive. The Indian leader promised Valdez that he would send tribesmen out to the wrecked ship to see if anything could be salvaged. If so, he would send what they could save to the New Orleans port. Maybe there *was* a glimmer of good fortune for which to thank the rooster.

Manuel had decided to go on to New Orleans with Valdez and his ten hands. Without Maria he had no idea what fate might be in store for a Venezuelan *pardo*. His dark skin would not be an issue in New Orleans, he was assured by the Indian leader. The South had many freed coloreds, though many were still slaves. Manuel was a free man. Valdez would speak for him.

Manuel was about to climb into the wagon and continue his journey when he turned and saw the tall Choctaw leader looking satisfyingly, arms folded, at what was left of the *Anne McInn* shipwreck. Manuel, with his caged rooster in tow, walked over to the Indian.

"I'm sorry. I did not get your name. Your kindness is beyond any words that I can muster in my useless and melancholy condition. My wife died on board during our voyage. I am very thankful to you and the Choctaws. Here, I want you to have this rooster. I thought it was our curse, and I offered it to the sea, but I was reminded by God of its purpose. It is very special and is said to bring good fortune and perpetual happiness to its owner. I have nothing else to give."

The tall Indian hesitated briefly, then reached out and grasped the wooden handle of the cage. "I am honored to receive such a generous gift. May many blessings from God and better days be with you. I am Greenwood LeFlore, chief of the Mississippi Choctaw Nation. Your gift will find a good home on my farm north of here near the beginning of the river called Yazoo, where the Tallahatchie and Yalobusha come together. Maybe someday you will visit me there. Safe travel, my friend."

"Thank you, Chief LeFlore. I am Manuel Sanz. Peace and justice be yours always."

As he started to climb into the uncovered wagon with the others, he heard LeFlore call after him. The chief had noticed something tied around the rooster's neck. "Manuel, wait! There is a leather pouch tied around the rooster's neck. You must have forgotten it."

Manuel continued to board the wagon. "Good chief," he said with a flashing grin of his very white teeth, "it is part of my gift. It now belongs to you also. Farewell."

The wagon driver flicked his whip at the mules, and as the wagon jerked forward, Manuel began a new and unchartered journey alone without his Maria. He waved back at the hospitable Indians and tried to imagine his future life in America.

CHAPTER TWO

Nacoochee

Washington, DC
Summer 1830

The trip from the Mississippi Delta where his Choctaw tribes had flourished peacefully for many decades was a long, tedious, and tiring sojourn for the Choctaw chief. The August weather was unusually mild and not as humid that year, a godsend for travelers in the South. His beautiful handcrafted carriage was one of the South's finest and a well-deserved tribute to his title of chieftain. But the long trip had tired him considerably. He worried about his chances of convincing "Old Hickory" that the unjust demands and underhanded dealings of US agents were risking an outright war with the Choctaw Nation and civil unrest between the district tribes. Colonel Greenwood LeFlore had finally exhausted all local negotiations and felt compelled to meet face to face with the president.

Andrew Jackson stormed into the greeting hall of the White House as soon as he received notice of LeFlore's arrival.

"Colonel, so happy to have you in Washington again." He stared into the chief's eyes. "The last two chiefs who tried to make the journey to Washington City to see me died en route, I sadly learned. Apuckshunubbee and Pushmataha—great chiefs, both of them. Good fortune must have been with you, Colonel."

He approached the tired traveler and blurted out, "My God! Greenwood, you look damned spent! Reminds me of how I felt after whipping those stubborn British redcoats in New Orleans fifteen years ago. Most physically draining campaign of my career. Come on down to the new north portico and we'll commandeer the Jefferson sitting room. I'll have the butler find something to wet your whistle."

"Thank you, Mr. President. Remember, no alcohol for me. Hot tea would be fine."

The chief followed the president and an apparent bodyguard down the broad, red-carpeted corridor into a small receiving room and then through another doorway into the spacious sitting room.

"Please, Greenwood, make yourself at home on the sofa," Jackson said, pointing to the solid crimson camel-back sofa that had been a favorite of Martha Washington.

The butler glided silently into the beautiful round room with its eighteen-foot domed ceiling and sat the silver serving tray down on an ornate mahogany piecrust table to the left of LeFlore. He poured from a highly polished silver teapot into a small teacup with presidential embossing and handed the cup to the chief.

"Thank you," he said and immediately took a sip of the steaming tea.

Waving the butler from the room, the president wasted no time with idle chitchat or boring questions about the long trip from Mississippi.

"OK, let's have it, Greenwood. I think I know why you are here. Mighty bold of you to try and run my agents out of your tribal council meetings. They had strict orders from me, in case you wondered."

"I never doubted that, sir. I know how you have resisted interfering with the treaty negotiations, but I also know you told Major Eaton's and

Colonel Coffee's agents your desires. I think they quoted you—'Fail not to make a treaty!'

"Mr. President, you are surely aware that I am opposed by the majority of tribal leaders in my position that it is inevitable that the Choctaws must cede the remainder of their homelands to the federal government and to the white settlers staged at our very doorsteps.

"You also know that I am not full-bloodied Choctaw, and that alone has angered my opponent council chiefs, who have stated to you that I do not represent the Choctaw Nation. I was elected tribal chief of the Choctaw Western District when I was only twenty-two years old, and that was thirteen years ago. I have earned much trust and respect from the Choctaw Nation since that time because I have always stood up for my people. I am now principle chief of all Mississippi Choctaws. My success has been in part due to my mother being the niece of the departed great Chief Pushmataha, who was on a mission to challenge your recently passed Indian Removal Act. Surely, sir, you have not forgotten how Pushmataha and my Choctaw brothers provided strategic advantage for you during the Creek Rebellion and again over the British you referenced in New Orleans?"

"Yes, of course, Greenwood," Jackson snapped back, patience now wearing thin. "You needn't remind me. So let's get to your point."

"Mr. President, I am quite aware of your personal support of the Indian Removal Act legislation passed this very year and how this will affect my beloved nation. Your agents have not been transparent with our council leaders about finalizing a treaty that will uproot our noble and peace-loving tribe and send them to the western lands of the Great American Desert, a land unknown to them. They must sadly leave the sacred burial mounds of their fathers, grandfathers, and ancestors that settled our great land. I am only asking that the Choctaws be dealt with fairly and justly. Removing your agents is my request, indeed, my *demand*! Your commissioner is a damn liar! And you have been unduly persistent in resisting me."

The president was indignant. "Colonel, do you realize that you're speaking to the president of the United States?"

LeFlore did not flinch; instead, he was stiffening with a surge of ego and confidence. Pounding his fist against his large, barreled chest, he stood and was quick to respond.

"And do *you* realize that you are speaking to the chief of the Choctaw Nation!?"

He walked over to Old Hickory and stopped within a tea-scented breath of Jackson's face. With grim determination he stared undaunted into the eyes of this battle-tested soldier and great leader.

"Mr. President, I demand *justice!*"

The president knew almost immediately that he had met his match. Seconds passed. Neither blinked. More seconds passed as the silence became much too awkward. Finally Jackson took LeFlore by the hand and with an almost painfully firm grip conceded.

"Greenwood, we have been friendly too long to fall out now. Justice *shall* be done."

Colonel LeFlore held his head high as his tall, commanding frame left the White House, walking slowly and victoriously to his grand carriage. He sat back in the heavily padded leather seat and leaned his head against the soft crimson velvet headrest. He knew that the task ahead would be taxing if not impossible, but earlier that year he had been elected principle chief of the Choctaw Nation, and he certainly intended to see that justice was done. Closing his weary lids, he exhaled a long, content sigh and smiled proudly to himself.

***

Almost to a man, the Choctaws had opposed any treaty that would displace them from their cherished ancestral homeland. In mid-September 1830, the United States commissioners had arrived near the council grounds called Chukfi-Ahihla Bogue (literally, 'where the rabbits gather to dance') by the Choctaws. Dancing Rabbit Creek Springs was a traditional gathering place of the Choctaw people and the site of many past councils of district tribes. It was also a famous hunting ground of the Choctaws. So it was no coincidence that the council grounds, so familiar to all Choctaws, was selected as the treaty signing site.

Between six and twelve thousand Choctaw men, women, and children gathered in the camps around Dancing Rabbit Creek that historical September. Nearly five hundred whites mingled with the Indians, some offering bribery in the form of trinkets and alcohol if they would sign the treaty. For the next ten days, daily council meetings failed to garner any support for a treaty from the Choctaw chiefs, mingoes, and captains. Not one single leader had spoken in favor of a treaty. When Chief Killihota finally stood and spoke in support of executing the treaty, coined the Indian Removal Treaty by the Choctaws, many of those present stood and openly threatened Killihota. One elderly woman even charged at the chief flashing a butcher knife. The elder Choctaw women were respected in their matrilineal society as the primary decision makers, controlling all access to governance and families. As such, most of them strongly opposed ceding their ancestral lands to the US government.

Greenwood LeFlore had secured the promise from President Jackson that justice would be done, and now was the time to call due that promise. He and several other chiefs had met secretly with the government commissioners and had crafted a tempting compromise that would hopefully convince the chiefs of the futility of continued opposition. In the manner of a true statesman, he stood and addressed the large gathering of council chiefs, mingoes, captains, commissioners, other officials, and many defiant warriors of his great nation. Other tribal chiefs had previously sent word to Washington that LeFlore did not represent the Choctaw Nation. LeFlore had even had a stand-off with Chief Mushulatubbee, with war-painted warriors, rifles, and threats of attack. Thus it was a tense moment at Dancing Rabbit Creek.

"My brothers and sisters of the noble and great Choctaw Nation, honorable commissioners, and revered chiefs, mingoes, captains, and warriors. For over twenty years we have witnessed other treaties signed by fellow tribes who have reluctantly agreed to relocation to the vast lands west of the Father of Waters. Have you forgotten the treaties of Fort Adams, Hopewell, Hoe Buckintoopa, Mount Dexter, Fort St. Stephens, Fort Confederation, Washington City, and Doak's Stand? We have seen our destiny. Those of us who have personal experience with US government mandates and land procurement methods know that removal from our homeland is inevitable. Our only other choice is war. We are a peaceful farming people. We do not want war or violence. Our own district tribes are on the verge of civil war. The forces of the federal government are formidable.

"I have made a visit to the United States of America's capital and counseled with the great president. He looked me in the eyes just as I am looking into your eyes and assured me that we would have justice. I believe he told me the truth.

"Our great nation will be given new lands in the southeastern part of the Great American Desert to the west of the Great River—lands that are forested and fertile with flowing rivers and lakes, unlike most of that Great Desert. I have insisted on modifications to the proposed treaty that provides that those of our tribe who possess land sections and who desire to remain in this territory and become US citizens will have the privilege of doing so. You will be given land, food, supplies, and compensation. The United States commissioners that are here today are prepared to amend the treaty with these changes. I urge you to accept the new future and new terms of the treaty. We are a proud nation. Let us secure a future for those that follow us. The Choctaw Nation must be preserved."

There were many district chiefs who listened to the colonel with scorn and anger. Many had threatened to kill him. LeFlore was not a full-blooded Choctaw and was resented by some leaders in the camp at Dancing Rabbit Creek.

Finally three other chiefs and several other respected leaders rose in what seemed like rehearsed unison and asked to address the council. The chiefs said that they had been moved by LeFlore's address and urged the acceptance of the terms as amended. Feeling betrayed and suspicious of a secret deal, many tribesmen were stunned.

The two commissioners, Major John Eaton, the secretary of the US War Department, and Colonel John Coffee had appealed to the Indians' hopes and fears, and finally secured an affirmative vote when they reminded the huge crowd of the "Great Father General Jackson's" sincere interest in the Choctaw people. Some murmured and scoffed at this, knowing that President Jackson had pledged in his presidential campaign to not rest until all Indians were relocated and corralled onto reservations. It was a tense climax as the time for the signing approached.

So with LeFlore's amendment, tribal fears of bitter consequences, some polite intimidation, and outright bribery in terms of land awards and annual cash payments, and gentle coercive pragmatism, the entire Choctaw Nation agreed to sign the treaty. Their lives would never be the same.

Colonel LeFlore had one more trick up his sleeve to help guarantee the justice he had demanded from Jackson. On the day of the treaty sign-ing, September 27, 1830, Greenwood had brought with him to the his-toric event a very valuable and well-known peace pipe. The integrity of peace agreements between the Choctaws and the US government was highlighted by the traditional smoking of the peace pipe. Only on rare and highly important occasions was LeFlore's effigy pipe used. The pipe was made of solid gold in the shape of the head of a great warrior bird with an elbowed short tube for attaching a wooden pipe and inhaling the *hakchuma*, or tobacco smoke. It was considered a rare and priceless possession. It had been a gift to the Choctaws from a Cherokee chieftain of a Georgian tribe in the Nacoochee region. Choctaw treaties executed with this particular effigy pipe were considered sacred and irreversible to the parties involved.

In demonstration of the justice promised by the president, LeFlore, holding the gold pipe, sat down in the innermost of the traditional Choctaw three concentric horseshoe-shaped powwow semicircles. The innermost horseshoe was composed of chiefs, high-ranking council members, and seven elder women. The two commissioners sat on a large wooden log facing the Indians and separated by a central fire pit. Their interpreter and other agents sat along the right side of the horseshoe.

"My brothers, sisters, and honorable commissioners, I hold in my hands the sacred Cherokee peace pipe of Nacoochee. It was given to the Choctaw Nation by the Cherokee as a symbol of unity and brotherhood of all Southern Indian tribes. Before this treaty is signed, this pipe will be passed to all seated at the council. The words of this treaty will be trusted and followed with honor by all at this great council and by all of the Choctaw people. The vapors exhaled will carry your words upward to the Creator. Your words and the words of this document will be eternal."

Attaching an extended wooden smoking pipe into the elbowed end of the effigy, LeFlore put flame to the *hakchuma* and passed the heavy pipe to Chief Mushulatubbee, his stubborn opponent, who was seated to his left. Next, he passed the pipe to his right to Chief Nittucachee.

All of the other Choctaw chiefs and delegates were seated in the three horseshoe-shaped semicircles as LeFlore had instructed, and after all delegates and the US agents had inhaled and then exhaled the vapors upward toward the heavens, the Treaty of Dancing Rabbit Creek was signed. Major Eaton, Colonel Coffee, Chief Mushulatubbee, Colonel

LeFlore, Chief Nittucachee, and all the other Choctaw chiefs and captains signed the twenty-two articles and four amendments that comprised the text of the treaty that September day at the ceremonial council.

The Choctaws' sovereignty had yielded to white supremacy. Another great tribe that had been the undisputed owner of a vast portion of the territory of Mississippi had been conquered by the white man with a stroke of a pen and ink, relinquishing all of the remaining lands east of the Mississippi River. In the months and years to come, the Choctaws would set out on a long, melancholy march to the lands west of the Mississippi, away from all they had ever known.

***

Greenwood was entrusted with the security of the golden pipe Nacoochee, which had sealed in perpetuity the words of the treaty for all generations to follow. He did not remain at Dancing Rabbit Creek for the ribald dancing, gambling, drinking, and grand celebration that went on for days after the signing. His mission had been accomplished, and he settled into the comfort of his majestic horse-drawn carriage (in reality, a fancy stagecoach) for the trip from the Noxubee area westward back to Carrollton.

His thoughts and emotions were mixed and often somber as he felt every jaw-snapping, tooth-clacking jolt from the potholed frontier roads stretching across the north central Mississippi territory. He took out Nacoochee and reflected on the foreseen historical significance of the gold bird pipe. Visions of robbers and curiosity seekers flashed repeatedly and nervously through his mind. He felt that he would have to find a secret resting place for the pipe, at least until all of the publicity around the treaty signing had subsided. Before the Dancing Rabbit Council, he had kept it in his nine-foot-tall mahogany French china cabinet trimmed in gold inlay. Something more secure was needed, he decided. It would be a secret known only to him until he felt it could be safely transferred to a more official location for future generations to admire, respect, and comprehend its significance to the Choctaw Nation and to the United States.

After a brief rest stop at French Camp, where his father, Louis, operated a small trading post, LeFlore resumed the final leg of his journey home. He closed his eyes as the tandem horse-drawn coach plodded through the mostly unsettled Mississippi frontier forest and on toward Carrollton. Exhaustion clouded his thoughts, and he began to drift off into a fitful sleep.

Suddenly a startling report cracked through his sleep-dulled senses, and the carriage lurched forward with an unexpectedly jarring force that propelled him first backward then just as rapidly forward into the facing seats. Pulling his well-conditioned, muscular bulk back onto the plush seat, he looked quickly outside. He saw two horsemen, one on each side of the carriage, waving rifles in the air, firing skyward again and demanding that the coachman stop. The carriage slowed and quickly came to a complete rest on the dark, densely forested trail.

Greenwood LeFlore was not unprepared for such surprises, having suspected that he would be followed from Dancing Rabbit Creek with the now-priceless Nacoochee a prime target for scoundrels and thieves. He reached quickly for his twin pepperbox revolvers, imported from Europe and presented to him as a gift by President Jackson. He had kept the new percussion cap pistols holstered and loaded just in case they were needed. He simultaneously pointed the weapons out either side of the coach. He was an expert marksman and aimed for the rifles held in the hands of the would-be robbers. In less than a second, and with precise execution, he had incapacitated both with a single shot from each pistol into their trigger hands. Robberies along remote frontier trails were not uncommon, but Greenwood's lightning reaction had caught the attackers by surprise.

Both horsemen screeched loudly as the exploding bullets tore into the sinew and bones of their hands. The weapons dropped to the ground like hot iron weights as both men pulled reflexively on their reins and jerked their horses away from the carriage, galloping away before the colonel could aim and fire again. LeFlore threw open the carriage door and stepped down onto the road, revolvers smoking and readied again to continue to defend life and property. The thieves did not look back as they escaped like whipped hounds and faded around a bend in the trail into the early dusk of the evening. Satisfied, LeFlore stared after the disappearing cowards and confidently holstered his guns. He turned and looked up at his driver, who had cowered down under his coachman's seat in the hopes of escaping sure death or at best being wounded. The driver, pallid even beneath his dark skin, realized that his master had won an uncontested victory and slowly crawled back onto his seat.

"I guess you showed them scalawags a thing or two!" beamed the driver, a loyal black coachman named Aaron. "Do you think they'll be back?"

"Not if they know what's good for them!" LeFlore reassured his man. "Move over, Aaron. I'm riding shotgun until we are out of the forest. Let's be removed from this ambush and get on to Carrollton with haste. I think we are close to Tuchula, so we don't have much more distance to travel."

Aaron slid over and made room for the colonel. As the spooked horses perked back to their task, the carriage lurched ahead with both men silently wondering if more trouble lay ahead. LeFlore was more alert than ever, ready for whatever might spring out at him from any darkened hiding places along the forested trail.

Another hour passed and the threat of danger became more and more distant. Carrollton was close. Greenwood, now more relaxed as safe refuge was near, returned to his plush coach seat and reflected back on the treaty signing and questioned his own actions—had justice really been done for his people, or would fate cast him as the enemy of his own brothers? He felt he was an honorable chief and a fair, just man. But sadly he knew what would come next for his Mississippi Choctaws.

The long march westward into lands unknown would become theirs and many, many more Native Americans' "trail of tears." He had no idea at the time that the danger-filled journey would bring death to almost three thousand of his Choctaw brothers and sisters and to tens of thousands from other tribes. He painfully debated with his conscience: would history paint him as a patriot of the great United States of America or a traitor of the great Choctaw Nation? He needed redemption.

He would have to leave final judgment to the historians, he concluded as he continually scanned his surroundings. For the moment he had forgotten the extreme exhaustion brought on by the tenseness and historical significance of the past ten days. Soon he would be safely back in his home and would find a sanctuary for Nacoochee.

The carriage turned off the main trail just two miles north of the Carrollton settlement as darkness enveloped the Mississippi countryside. The horses had slowed to a comfortable trot as they climbed the fifteen-degree incline up to the estate atop the crest on Point LeFlore. The LeFlore main house was just two hundred yards up the winding, well-worn trail that was much smoother than the rough frontier highways in the distance behind them.

Aaron pulled hard on the reins and directed the twin horses around the semicircular entry and gave his command. "Whoa! Whoa!" The carriage came to a gentle stop. The loyal driver secured his coachman's whip and hustled down from his driver's perch, but before he could plant both feet on the ground, a dark-skinned man in an old tattered straw hat carrying a candle-lit lantern came bounding around the left side of the house and hurried to the carriage before Aaron could make his way to the carriage door. The dark-skinned man was unknown to LeFlore's coachman, whose initial reaction was to attempt to block him from approaching. Too late. The man put his hand on the door handle and opened it to the surprise of the chief who was just beginning to rise from his seat to exit after his long and intense journey from Dancing Rabbit Creek.

The man was smiling with a bright set of white teeth flashing in sharp contrast to his dark ebony skin. He extended his hand toward LeFlore and spoke. "Welcome home, Chief LeFlore. I know you must be very weary. The house servants have prepared a hearty meal for you. It is so nice to see you again."

Greenwood braced on the man's arm as he stepped down, easily extracting his bulky torso from his grand but now very dusty carriage. He looked at the man and was somewhat surprised.

"Why, if it isn't Manuel Sanz! My goodness, it's been two years since your ill-fated voyage and shipwreck. I surely thought our paths would never intersect again. So good to see you looking so much healthier." He took Sanz's hand and gripped it firmly, shaking it generously and with much delight.

"Thank you, Colonel. I had no difficulty locating your estate. You are well-known around here and I just followed the River Yazoo like you said. I am hoping to find work. Maybe you could help me," Sanz said hopefully.

LeFlore was gracious and kind as he responded, "Why, Manuel, I am sure we can accommodate another farmhand or some other position that may suit your desire. You have journeyed a vast distant from your homeland and tragedy followed you. You are more than welcome in my house. I am honored to assist such a courageous and determined man like you. We will talk more tomorrow after I have revitalized my very tired and achy bones."

Manuel smiled and nodded his head. "So nice of you, Colonel. Thank you. Thank you."

LeFlore, already advancing toward his front stoop, stopped and turned back to face Sanz again.

"Manuel, you need to know that I still have your gift. Sadly, the bird was killed by a hostile predator which attacked in the dead of the night. I never forgot what you conveyed to me about his rare vintage and his apparent ordained control over his owner's destiny. I employed a master restorer to preserve the rooster for my family and for any future generations which may be charged with protecting him. He has become our talisman. I am sure he is responsible for my Choctaws' justice and for our perpetual friendship. Thank you again for your gift. I have also saved the contents of the leather pouch. Someday this unselfish gift will bring mountains of good fortune to a chosen one."

He turned and disappeared into his candle-lit house.

Manuel smiled with only a hint of sadness about his rooster. If not for God's command and his friend Juan Mariches, the rooster would have become bait for the sharks of the sea.

The rooster was still a puzzling mystery to him. God's gift or the devil's curse? He did not know. Now it was dead but, alas, preserved for eternity. He walked off to the slaves' quarters behind the main house trying not to think about his sad and tragic sea voyage, his love for Maria, and the rooster that had brought "justice" to Greenwood LeFlore's Choctaws.

Part One

CHAPTER ONE

The Beginning

Gwinnett County, Georgia
1995

S ometimes on the Journey of Life, we encounter certain people or events that profoundly change our destiny, and afterward things are never the way we could have ever imagined. This was one of those nights on an unsuspecting and complexly intertwined couple's journey.

It wasn't the kind of night that Southerners are accustomed to—or could *ever* get accustomed to. The wind was beginning to howl like a timber wolf in heat and swirl in all directions at once, and its razor-sharp bite was a shocker to anyone who dared to venture out. Cold weather in late January in the Deep South was not all that unusual, but seldom did it linger long enough to make life so hatefully miserable. Two consecutive weeks of temperatures never above freezing was almost a freak of nature for Georgians. And now, to make matters worse, the weather service had just issued a winter storm watch for the Southeast, with expectations that a winter storm warning was forthcoming if the computer model predictions materialized before the night was done. It was, after all, another year of El Niño, predicted to be even more merciless to world weather than the 1994 phenomenon. From devastating record one-hundred-year floods to parching and killing droughts and everything in between, El Niño was a global reminder of nature's dominance over that mortal creation called humankind.

Frantic citizens would soon besiege the local supermarkets and just as soon every grocer in town would be sold out of milk and bread. No matter that there had been many false alarms from the weatherman in winters past. Predictions of six or more inches of snow, only to get a light dusting or none at all. Didn't matter. In the South, if snow is forecast, you go buy milk and bread.

This night seemed different. The prolonged cold snap and the ominous low-pressure system speeding out of the southwestern US corridors toward the South were a perfect match for the unbelievably frigid arctic air blasting its way in from Canada and a moisture-laden low-pressure system brewing in the Gulf of Mexico.

Indeed, there was something very different about this night. It was an opportunity that had been a long time coming. It was time to finally separate fantasy from reality. Jasen Prospero had struggled to find the emotional strength to face each new day. Jade Colton, the mysterious beauty and his next door neighbor, was the forbidden fruit, and she was finally waiting for him on that dreary, unpredictable cold night.

"Timing is everything," he had told her over and over.
Go slow. Be patient. What was she thinking? Was this a new beginning or an end?

Jasen showered in anxious anticipation, using his favorite shower gel, Pacific Breeze. The scent was refreshing and lingered on his skin. He wondered out loud, "She probably won't even notice, much less care."

As he brushed his teeth and swished with spearmint Scope, he kept one eye on the portable TV reflected in the beveled-glass bathroom mirror. There were frequent weather updates as the threat of an unprecedented snowstorm continued to increase.

He thought about his wife, Caitlyn, who had left the night before for a three-day convention of major insurance firms being held in Pensacola.

He knew that she would be fine that far south of the storm. She most surely wasn't disappointed to be missing the biggest winter storm of the century, as Richard Vance, the Channel 11 weather anchor, was calling it. She hated cold weather. He knew that she would probably be worried about him being home alone. And he wouldn't dare tell her that he forgot to get some milk and bread! She would call at 8:00 p.m., just as she said. She was always prompt. He would convince her that everything was fine…no problem. He could handle it. No worry.

The Prosperos' daughter, Ariel, wouldn't be a worry either. She was home for a short break from Mississippi State University in Starkville, Mississippi, where she had started her freshman year six months earlier. She had already departed for a weekend at her best friend's, Ernestine "Teenie" Marshall, parents' country estate—an impressive ten-thousand-square-foot home on Lake Sydney Lanier, thirty miles north of Suwannee. If she got stranded there in the storm, she'd be OK. Teenie's family had everything that ten families could possibly need or ever want.

If your father was CEO and president of the South's largest grocery chain and had a net worth of fifty million dollars, you didn't lack for much. And you could bet *they* would have milk and bread!

And Jasen? He was just focused on convincing Jade that there just might be a chance for them. A chance for what? He didn't exactly know. There were so many unknowns. His life had become consumed with fantasies and obsession. She seemed to have cast some type of spell on him and he could not escape. Why did she even care? Questions, questions, questions. He had too many. Answers, answers, answers…he had none. Maybe he would finally begin to understand her tonight. He looked into the mirror again. "What in the world are you doing, Jasen?" he asked himself. His thoughts were suddenly interrupted.

The phone call came exactly at 8:00, and it was as he had predicted… worry, worry, worry. "Her middle name should be Worry," he quipped aloud. He rationalized what he had accepted and tolerated for nearly nineteen years…or was it just stupidity…or simply gentle craziness?

As he hung up the phone, it briefly crossed his mind that she hadn't called collect as she usually did. And he had briefly felt a chill of distance in her voice. He dismissed the thought. He did not think to look at the caller ID to see where she was calling from.

The house was warm and secure. He wasn't worried about leaving it in a snowstorm. After all, he would just be next door. As he walked toward the front door, he began to wonder how he had survived the mental torment of the past eleven months since he had moved next door to someone who consumed every thought of his waking day. Luckily it was really not apparent to anyone else. He was a master of hiding emotions. At least, he thought so.

As he locked the front door, he felt the first drop of sleet on his warm earlobe. It stung like a dull, overused junkie's needle. The screaming wind was colder than he had imagined. He knew that it would be snowing soon.

His thoughts suddenly turned to another cold and blustery day that past February, when he had first met this strange and alluring person named Jade Colton, who had since become his mission to conquer.

He covered his head with his navy-blue Nautica jacket and sped across the lawn to her front stoop. All of his fantasies over the past eleven months played like the rewind of a DVD in his mind. Every detail was still so clear…crystal clear. He could not explain it, but he sensed some chapters of her life had not been revealed to him. He tried not to think about that. He told himself tonight would be special.

CHAPTER TWO

The Winter Storm

As he reached her front door on that unpredictable Friday evening, all of their brief times together raced again through his anxious mind. To Jasen, it seemed as if years had passed since he had met her. It had only been a few months. And he remembered every detail of those few nights. The memories were cast in stone in his heart. As he rang her doorbell, he was not certain what to expect. He longed for something. He was not sure what exactly.

She opened the door, and he felt his heart skip several beats. She was more beautiful than he had ever seen her. Her radiant smile captured his soul. He flashed briefly back to their very first meeting at the mailbox, and he knew he would be her prisoner forever. Tonight she was dressed in a long silk gown that touched the floor. The striking crimson color complemented her stunning jade eyes. For the first time, he realized how her name fit. Her feet were petite and bare, but the house was warm. Her dark auburn hair fell below her shoulders and lit up the room with its shine. She wore no obvious makeup—she really didn't need any on her perfect skin. Her lipstick was a light reddish-pink. She rarely used a dark color. Jasen thought he could detect the fragrance of Romance by Ralph Lauren. He remembered her saying that she hated strong, lingering perfumes or body lotions. She smelled so alive.

"Hello, stranger. Looking for some company on a cold, snowy night?"

"Hi, Jade." Dummy! he thought to himself. That's the best you can come up with? He struggled for the right words as he followed her into her den.

He stopped near her sofa. She turned and came to him. He reached for her with both arms, and she fell into his embrace and put her arms around his back. He squeezed her tightly. He should have done this a long time ago, he thought to himself. Their lips met, and an intense energy of many weeks of bottled emotions was released as they shared a very long and impassioned kiss. All Jasen could think about at that point was never losing her. She did not really know what she had done to his life. He had never told her. Her powers and magnetic hold on him were mysterious but real.

Jade pushed back slightly and looked into his soft brown eyes. She had never really studied him from so close. She looked at him as if they were meeting for the first time.

Physically, Jasen was quite a looker from the female perspective, with muscular arms and calves from his almost addictive dedication to weight lifting. With well-defined bone structure and broad shoulders, his sculptured arms were not intimidating or uninviting, but it was clear he could pack a punch if necessary. The shape of his biceps, triceps, and deltoids could easily be seen through his shirt. His trunk was slender for a somewhat tall man at six feet two inches, and he carried himself well. An elegant and slightly tanned face with a chiseled jaw complemented his dark brown, barely combed hair, made eye-catching by a few lighter-colored highlights in the front. The generous full head of soft hair always seemed to attract mesmerized stares from admiring females. His amazing smile underscored his gentle, kind features and suggested a warm and caring inner soul. The few, like Jade, who had managed to lock onto his warm brown irises also saw a mysterious and guarded side that seemed to contradict his outward appearance of charming ease. On rare occasions, he could muster a penetrating look that felt as if he was reading your mind.

Jade was not sure if he was reading her mind at that moment, but he looked at her with extreme satisfaction, if not relief. She wondered if he felt what she was feeling. Sometimes love is a feeling that is not logical. When it happens, it happens. It is not always definable or understandable. But if it is real, you know. Jasen had known for a long time. He thought he was finally where he belonged. Jade was suddenly aware of a similar feeling. Her heart was liberated and alive again.

Jasen glanced toward the window. Light snow was falling. The wind was agitating and swirling in blustery gusts. If the meteorologists were correct, it would a very stormy night. The thought of being snowbound with Jade was an unexpected dream come true for Jasen. He had call-forwarded his home phone to Jade's number. If anyone called, he was OK. Nothing would stand in their path on this perfect night. So he thought.

They sat down on the carpet in front of the fireplace. Jade had started a fire earlier, and the logs were burning with a bluish-orange glow. She loved to burn real wood, not gas logs. She loved the smell of oak burning and the abundant heat it generated. Jasen thought it added such a perfect touch to the wintry maelstrom churning outside and to the romantic mood unfolding inside. Jade had already poured two glasses of white wine, and she handed him a glass as she took a sip from hers.

He placed his left hand on her thigh, and they stared into each other's eyes. He tried to understand what she was really thinking behind those penetrating green eyes. Her smile told him that she had really wanted this moment for as long as he had. She gently placed her head on his shoulder as she sat her wine glass on the cocktail table. It was the first time that they had truly been alone and unrushed and were not worried about the time or being discovered. There was no need to hurry. Time was now on their side.

She was the first to speak and arouse him from his mesmerized state. "Are you hungry?"

"Not for food," he confessed. "I ate some leftovers earlier. But if you're hungry, go ahead. I'll be OK. We have all night, and more, if we get snowbound."

She laughed softly. "The only thing that I want to taste right now is you." She squeezed his thigh gently. She had always been surprisingly spontaneous about everything.

They kissed again. It was gentle but passionate. For the second time, Jasen was not sure if he was dreaming or not. He took her by the hand and led her to her bedroom.

They stood together by the queen-sized poster bed, and she put her arms around his neck and kissed him again. He noticed that her lips were unusually soft and supple. She tasted as fresh as early morning dewdrops. Her face seemed as happy as he had ever seen it. He thought to himself that this sort of romantic mood only came true in books or movies. It couldn't be happening to him.

"Please don't wake me up if this is a dream!" his inner voice said.

He lifted her and laid her gently on the bed, but she quickly sat back up. The clock radio/CD player was on very low. She had put in a selection of romantic love themes. She raised her arms above her head, and he easily slipped her gown over her head and tossed it to the floor. The room was dark, but he could clearly see her nakedness. She coyly lay back on her pillow and spread her arms as if to say "I'm yours."

Jasen began to remove his clothes, first slowly, then in an almost mad frenzy. She seemed patient and amused by his clumsiness and haste.

An hour passed, but it seemed more like a minute to Jasen. Jade was as totally uninhibited and more than he had expected. Her complete enjoyment of every caress and touch was more than he deserved. Beautiful and passionate, she was the lover of every man's desire. But that night she belonged to Jasen. A fantasy had come true. No one would ever believe him. But then, no one could ever know the truth. Their sin must never be revealed.

They rolled onto their backs and stared at the ceiling. He held her hand and sighed.

"I have never been happier," he told her. "I've wanted to tell you for such a long time why I have been totally swept away by you. I have thought about the reasons so often and have wanted to tell you, but I never got the chance. I have also been afraid that if I told you, it would drive you away from me again. I've never really known where I stood with you. You really can be difficult to read, you know."

"Do you have any doubt now?" she asked as she turned her head and kissed him softly on the lips.

"I know how you feel tonight, Jade, but I also know how you don't want to hurt anyone else."

"Jasen, if this is truly what we both want, we must be prepared to deal with what comes next. If you pick up one end of a stick, you get what's on the other end too. An old Choctaw Indian saying, I think.

"I'm sure now, Jasen. I've realized over the past few weeks that I've been lonely long enough, and I know you're lonely too. And, yes, I really do love you and want you. More than I have ever wanted anything. We were destined to find each other. I really believe that. I'd be a fool to let you go. You are really a good man. Please try to forgive me for the way I've treated you. I've just been so afraid to admit it to myself. I think my son, James, would want me to do what I felt in my heart was the right thing for me. I think he would have liked you very much. I wish you had known him. He was such a terrific kid. I still miss him so—in a way only a mother could understand."

As he looked into her hypnotizing jade eyes, he saw a large tear flow down her soft white cheek. He had never seen her cry before. He reached across her and held her tightly. She must have trapped those feelings inside for a long time.

As they embraced, Jasen felt forever bound to her. His life was never going to be the same again.

Jasen was suddenly distracted by a distant beep coming from Jade's kitchen. He sat up.

"Did you hear something, Jade?"

"No. What is it?"

"I thought I heard a beep or something."

"Just the bells ringing in your head," she chuckled under her breath.

He listened for a few more moments but only heard the soft music coming from her CD player.

"I really thought I heard something. I'll be right back."

He moved cautiously away from her bed and walked into the den, forgetting he was sans clothes. He looked around and saw nothing and then walked into the kitchen. He flipped on the light switch, and in an instant his eyes focused on the large, imposing stuffed rooster on the kitchen table. He instinctively jumped back.

"Damn it!" he blurted out loudly. Every time he saw that stuffed bird he flinched. It looked so real. And he hated roosters, this one in particular. He could not imagine why Jade kept it, except that it had been her mother's. For an instant, however, he noted almost subconsciously that the rooster was not in his usual place on the center of the table. Had Jade or maybe someone else moved him? The thought passed quickly.

Convinced that all seemed well, he turned out the kitchen light and walked back to the bedroom. He lay back down beside Jade and held her close.

"Everything OK?" she asked.

"Guess I'm hearing things. Forgive me, Where were we?"

He began to study her wonderful body all over again. She truly was beautiful. He pulled her on top of him and then hugged her tightly.

In the next instant something caused Jasen to look toward her bedroom door. For a brief second he wasn't sure if he was seeing shadows or if his eyes were playing tricks on him. His brain registered what seemed to be a silhouette of something or someone. Suddenly his heart accelerated like a speeding train and pounded in his chest like a cacophony of kettledrums. He could not breathe. He wanted to believe that it was an illusion. His gut instincts told him otherwise. As he refocused in disbelief at the dark image, it suddenly lunged toward the bed. Jasen caught a glimpse of a raised hand with something in it.

Without thinking, he grabbed Jade even more tightly and did two complete body rolls. As they were about to go off the bed, he felt a sharp sting across the top of his right earlobe. They tumbled onto the floor between the bed and the wall, Jade on the bottom. The attacker had plunged a long knife into the pillow on the left side of the bed. Jasen reached for his ear and felt something wet. The knife's razor-sharp edge had dealt a glancing blow across the top of his ear, which was now bleeding. Most of his ear was still there, he quickly assessed.

At this point Jasen was reacting totally in survival mode. Fight or flight—he had no choice. He stood quickly, oblivious to his nakedness. It was now kill or be killed. There was no time to sort out what was really happening. Jade was behind him on the floor between the bed and the wall.

She was either hurt or too stunned to say anything. Whoever this crazed intruder was would have to get past Jasen to get to her.

The intruder seemed to be a large person, his face covered by what appeared to be a dark-colored ski mask. The room was quite dark and everything looked like shadows dancing in frantic and random directions. The attacker was pulling the knife from the pillow as Jasen literally vaulted toward him. He grabbed the attacker's right arm before the knife could be repositioned for another strike.

The attacker's momentum carried both of them careening backward toward the door. He made a feeble attempt to stab Jasen again, but Jasen's grip was like a vise. Locked in a life or death struggle, Jasen began to bend the attacker's wrist into a painful, contorted extension. It worked, and the knife fell to the floor. Jasen kicked the knife just to the edge of the bed almost by reflex.

They wrestled as Jasen held his opponent's arms and rendered them ineffective in mounting any counterattack. Their bodies rolled two 360s around the wall, and both slammed to the floor with a loud thud, the force of the fall leaving Jasen breathless. He lost his grip, and his adversary broke free, standing over him and letting out a guttural snarl.

Jasen looked up just in time to see him retrieve a small snub-nosed revolver from a front pocket. He pointed it dead-aim at Jasen's head and grinned like a ravenous jackal.

"I'm going to send you straight to hell, lover boy. And that slut over there is going to be right behind you!"

What the attacker did not know was that Jade had regained her senses and had retrieved the knife by the bed. Before anyone could take another breath, Jade charged the would-be killer. Driven by fragments and megabytes of memory from times long past, she plunged the knife without hesitation into the attacker's neck. At the same time, like a flashing lightning bolt, her temporal synapses took her to Eutaw, Alabama, and back into a deeply repressed nightmare.

The shadowy figure reached reflexively for the knife, now buried near vital structures. The revolver fell from his hand, and as life rushed out of the gaping hole in his exposed neck, he fell to the floor beside Jasen and went limp.

In less than two minutes, both Jasen and Jade had seen a lifetime flash in front of them.

Jasen sat up and looked at the body in disbelief. Jade slowly turned toward him.

"Jasen, are you all right?"

He didn't answer her.

"Jasen! Are you all right!?" She was nearly screaming.

He finally responded. "I'm OK, I'm OK. Are you hurt?"

"No, I'm fine. In shock, I think, and maybe a little sore from you rolling off the bed onto me. Who *is* that? That crazy animal was trying to kill us!"

Jasen stood and turned on the light. "Do you think?!" he said more in shocked reality than sarcasm.

He bent and put his ear to the chest of the now lifeless body. He thought he heard nothing. He felt the right side of the neck opposite the knife for a carotid pulse. Nothing detected.

"I can't feel a pulse. No breathing. Dead, I think. The knife seems to have found its mark. Jade, I think you've killed this maniac. What in God's name are we going to do?"

Flashes of her mother's demonic nemesis suddenly flickered madly through her confused mind. It was déjà vu all over again. Jade the Savior. Jade the Killer.

They both suddenly realized that they were standing totally naked in a room with a bloody body. Jade instinctively covered herself with her hands. She picked up her gown from the floor and quickly pulled it over her head. Jasen grabbed his trousers and sat down on the edge of her bed and stepped into them.

She finally dared to look down at the body. She stooped forward and pulled the ski mask up and over the head and finally saw his face.

Without warning Jade said, "I think I'm going to be sick." She ran to the bathroom, and the retching sound echoed loudly into the bedroom.

As Jasen stood there, he felt a gnawing feeling in his gut. He walked toward the bathroom and stopped in the door opening, leaning against the door frame as he stared at Jade hugging the commode. Even in her compromised moment, somehow he felt closer to her than ever before.

Suddenly Jade looked up at him and screamed, "Jasen! Behind you!"

In a split second, Jasen turned and raised his right arm to block the thrust of the knife aimed at his chest by the bleeding attacker he thought Jade had killed. He reacted on instinct. There was no time to think.

Jasen grabbed the arm holding the bloody knife and twisted it violently with all of his strength. He heard a loud snap and the resurrected assassin moaned loudly. The knife fell to the floor a second time. Jasen lunged at the ghost of the living dead man in a defensive rage and propelled their bodies backward. The killer's head slammed loudly, like a massive wrecking ball demolishing a wall, into the large, solid wooden bed post, and he slumped to the floor. For a second, his limbs convulsed and then he was lifeless again. The violent impact had snapped his cervical spine.

It was over. A demon had been unleashed on the lovers. Their lives would never be the same. The fury of the winter storm was raging outside.

CHAPTER THREE

Following Elephants

Greenwood, Mississippi
1955

She was the only child of Ethan and Rebecca LeFlore. Ethan claimed to be a very distant relative of the early-nineteenth-century legend Colonel Greenwood LeFlore, the Choctaw chief for whom the city was named. Jean LeFlore's stunning looks quickly became apparent as she grew up, especially to men. And she would always be attractive to men, all men...*always*. Her looks would become one of her demons.

In her hometown of Greenwood, Mississippi, it wasn't difficult to be noticed if you were the most perfect female that Mississippi schoolboys and good ole cotton-picking farmhands had ever imagined, much less seen. Yes, Jean was a real looker, her Indian heritage accentuating her natural beauty. Her auburn hair flowed down below her shoulders and seemed to glow in the sunlight. Her first child bore a striking resemblance to her. The birth certificate said Delta Jade Colton. Jean chose to call her Jade because her eyes were a deep jade green the likes of which she had never seen. Jade's father, Eddie Colton, thought it was corny.

Eddie left home before Jade was eight months old, leaving Jean at age seventeen to raise a child on the salary of a cotton exchange manager's bookkeeper and Girl Friday.

She had not finished high school because she had gotten pregnant by her first boyfriend. He had agreed to marry her, but both knew that it wouldn't work. He worked at a local foundry as a welder and was known for thinking only of his next conquest. He was nineteen and thought he was God's gift to women.

Jean had fallen for his fast talking "I love you more than I've ever loved anyone" crap, and the next thing she was missing was her period and an honest chance at a future. So she dropped out of high school and in an unexpected twist of luck landed the job with Jake Luther at Bigelow's Cotton Exchange located along Cotton Row, near the corner of Front and Howard Street.

Jean had a natural talent for numbers and basic math and had convinced Jake that she could easily keep up with all of the cotton inventory and buying and selling. Piece of cake, she had told him. She wasn't sure if he bought it or had hired her because of her looks. Big Jake, as he liked to be called, was only thirty-eight years old but looked much older to Jean. He was a massive man, tall, with broad shoulders and long, muscular arms. His size alone was intimidating, but his dark hair, sallow skin, square jaw, and a scarred right cheek suggested a rugged and dominating heavyweight boxer, perhaps in his younger days. She did not dare ask about his past life. He was strange and scary to Jean in every imaginable way, but she tried to ignore him when she could and just do her job.

The most perplexing thing about Jake that she never really understood was his "pet" rooster. He proudly displayed a huge, colorful barnyard rooster stuffed and mounted on a small piece of wooden fence rail right in the middle of his desk, staring intensely and directly at any visitor that came into his office. The rooster's gaze seemed to be saying, "I am the guardian of this space."

On her very first day, Jake caught her moving the rooster as she was cleaning and rearranging the papers on his desk, a small gesture at "neating" things up for her new boss. She almost jumped out of her skin when he yelled from the doorway.

"Put that damn rooster down! Don't ever let me see you touching it again. You got that? Put it down *now!*"

She immediately moved the rooster back to his spot and backed away from the desk, shaken by his angry shout.

"I was just organizing your desk for you. I'm sorry, Mr. Luther." After that outburst, Jean was never able to muster the courage to ask him what it was all about. Weird wasn't the right word. What was the big deal about a dumb stuffed rooster? She steered away from the bird after that.

After the rooster encounter, Jake realized from Jean's cowering reaction that he could have his way with her any time he desired. She was vulnerable in every way and he knew it. Plus, if she complained, she'd lose her job, and jobs weren't that easy to find for high school dropouts with a baby to raise. He wasn't that bad looking, but when he grinned, his yellow, tobacco-stained teeth dripped with the disgusting sludge of his Skoal smokeless. He wasn't worried about exercising his control over his employees, especially women, as corporately forbidden sexual harassment in the workplace hadn't even been invented yet.

Jean became a slave to "Creep-o," as she named him. She waited on his every whim, getting his coffee, walking the short two blocks to the Delta Bistro over on Main Street whenever he commanded her to get his lunch, making the bank deposits for him; whatever he asked, she did it. Once a month he made her walk all the way up to Carrollton Avenue and then east a few blocks to the Crystal Grill to get his favorites—fried green tomatoes and lemon icebox pie. The train depot was just across Carrollton from the Crystal Grill, and on many trips to get his lunch she daydreamed about taking her baby daughter Jade on the next train to just about anywhere to escape Greenwood and her evil boss.

She grew tired of cleaning his brown-stained coffee cup and cleaning up his filthy fingernail clippings from his desk. She had a baby to support and she couldn't lose her job. Before the end of her first week at the exchange, he made his first contact with her.

At first it was just an "accidental" leaning against her ample breasts, then a pat on her rear, and sometimes he would just come up behind her, part her long auburn hair, and sniff behind her ear.

"M-m-m-m, you smell g-o-o-o-o-d! Do you smell that way everywhere?" Sniffing her became a daily ritual with Creep-o.

She tried to ignore him, but it became more and more difficult. If she pulled away from him, he grabbed her arm and squeezed until it hurt. Once he squeezed hard enough to leave her black and blue. She wanted so badly to run or to fight back, but she couldn't. Maybe if she just kicked him in the...no, she couldn't...a one-way ticket to end up on the streets. She somehow sensed what he would eventually do to her.

Her fear of Big Jake grew. He was weird all right and very private about his comings and goings, and she often speculated about his strange telephone calls. He got frequent calls from a local judge, a big shot banker, and even John Thomas Rodgers, the LeFlore County sheriff. She knew he often met them in the alley behind Cotton Row in the hush-hush back room of the Cotton Club. She dared not talk to anyone about it, but her biggest shocker came several weeks into her job.

She had steered clear of the guardian freaky rooster but was putting away some invoices for Big Jake one morning before he came bursting through the door, huffing and demanding his coffee. She noticed that the bottom right desk drawer was not locked. Big Jake *always* kept it locked. She slowly opened the drawer even though she knew she shouldn't. Her eyes immediately fixed on a neatly folded piece of clothing. It was solid white and silky. But it wasn't the clothing that instantly froze her into a catatonic posture. It was the insignia sewn into the garment.

Jean had seen it many times before. Segregationists were very active and openly visible in Greenwood in 1955 after the history-making Supreme Court decision in Brown v. Board of Education. Robert B. Patterson had founded the White Citizen's Council locally to fight against racial integration. The civil rights era had arrived in full force in Greenwood and all around the South.

Jean hated the threats of violence from the activists. She struggled to understand both sides but just wanted to stay away from the circus-like goings-on around town.

So seeing the well-known KKK insignia on the white garment caused her to take in a huge gasp of air. It was a black-rimmed red circle with a white cross in the center of the circle. There was a small red blood drop in the center of the cross. In Greenwood, the Ku Klux Klan was quiet active and visible at rallies and in newspaper reports of alleged hate crimes, cross burnings, and racist transgressions. The Klansmen called their costumes their "glory suits."

Released from her catatonia, Jean quickly stepped backward, almost stumbling. Her heart suddenly sped up, then galloped like a spooked horse and pounded painfully against her chest wall. She was working for a Klansman! It was a terrifying revelation.

Her thoughts shifted briefly to the janitor, Willie. It began to make sense to Jean why Jake treated Willie Campbell with such disdain and loathing. She often felt so sorry for Willie and the hatred that seemed to never end—"Do this, boy. Do that, boy." Ethnic slurs, undeserving verbal abuse, and insults seemed to go on nonstop, especially when Jake had not had his daily quota of coffee and Skoal.

Jean had gotten to know Willie fairly well, befriending him right after she started her new job. She was careful to not let Jake or anyone else see her talking to Willie, as white women just didn't fraternize with coloreds. She naively did not understand why people in Greenwood were treated differently just because of the color of their skin.

Willie seemed like a nice man to Jean. He told her that his full name was William Jefferson Campbell, and that he and his wife, Thelma, had four sons—William Jr., Samuel, Joe, and Thomas. He lived just off South Main Street past Carrollton Avenue in a small one-room wood-frame house. It was the poorest area of Greenwood. They had no bathroom, just a "privy" behind the house.

He said that his parents had lived on one of the large cotton farms to the east of town toward the Carrollton community and not too far from the site of Chief Greenwood LeFlore's palatial plantation Malmaison, modeled after one of Napoleon and Josephine's four mansions. The mansion had burned to the ground back in 1942 and was never rebuilt. There was much talk about the cause of the fire, but despite unfounded rumors of who or what might have been responsible, the evidence suggested a faulty fireplace was to blame.

Willie told her that he had actually been on the LeFlore property when the house caught fire, but he and four other farmhands had no water or way to fight the fire. He told her that the mansion had been magnificent and was considered to be one of a kind in the South. He and his friends were able to save several pieces of custom-built furniture from the dining room, some silver serving pieces, and the dining room table centerpiece, the unusual rooster. Everything else was destroyed in the fire—rare tapestries, handcrafted solid mahogany furniture from France, chairs upholstered in the finest of crimson silk damask to match the ornate drapes, exquisite imported linens, and many other very valuable fixtures and furnishings that LeFlore had imported from some of the finest European markets and craftsmen.

Willie had not shared Jake Luther's secret with anyone until now. The rooster on his desk and Malmaison's rooster were one and the same. Suddenly Jean understood why Jake had almost attacked her when she touched the bird. Willie was not certain how it had fallen into Mr. Luther's hands, but he knew it was the same rare rooster that LeFlore had displayed in his dining room. Willie guessed that it had had great sentimental importance to the colonel. The family had maintained its prominence on the dining table for all those years since LeFlore's death in 1865. Willie always suspected that there was a lot more about that rooster than had ever been told. Now it belonged to Jake Luther. No one had ever questioned him about it, and Jean wondered if he would deny that it had come from Malmaison if he had to.

Willie's entire family had worked on LeFlore's fifteen thousand acres of cotton until machines began to take over just before World War II. Jean was intrigued when he told her that his great-great-granddaddy was one of the four hundred slaves owned by Colonel LeFlore after he earned his fortune and built his plantation empire. Willie said that his family often bragged about the colonel's humane treatment of his slaves. He said that the slaves called the plantation "The Big Sandy Place." It was said that LeFlore considered his slaves to be family and told them that any one of them was free to leave any time they desired. None took him up on the offer until after his death and the end of the Civil War. Jean knew that her father had been related to Greenwood LeFlore somehow and thought it ironic that she and Willie were connected. Coincidence? She listened with renewed interest as he continued.

When cotton started giving way to corn and soybeans, Willie said he moved to town and had been doing janitorial work since then. He said that he worked three jobs just to get by. Thelma was the maid for a nice, wealthy white family that lived near the Greenwood Country Club. Raising four boys was demanding on their meager income. The ubiquitous and cultural prejudices against blacks only made life for them more challenging. The recent KKK activity had them and other blacks around Greenwood constantly on guard and afraid.

Willie and Jean became secret friends, but she silently worried that she would be labeled as a sympathizer if their friendship was discovered. With a Klansman for a boss, she knew she had to be careful about appearances.

Jean's mother told her to call blacks "colored folk." It was the Deep South, after all. Jean saw racial prejudice everywhere. She wished that Southerners could get along regardless of race, as the Good Book taught her at church. She sometimes felt as if she shouldn't feel different about blacks than most other whites, but she just knew in her heart that people were just people. She wondered if the South would ever change.

Jean had bragged to Willie over and over about her baby daughter Jade and how precious she was. Jean's mother Rebecca babysat while Jean worked.

Jean was pleasantly surprised one Saturday evening just after sundown when an expected visitor knocked on her back door. It was Willie!

"My goodness, Willie, whatever brings you over here on East Claiborne?" Jean and Jade lived with Jean's parents in a modest but nice three-bedroom house just across the Yazoo River Bridge from downtown.

"Well, Ms. Colton, I just wanted to bring you some of those homegrown tomatoes that I keep telling you about. You have always treated me so kindly. Just want to return the favor."

"Don't just stand there! Come on in here." She welcomed him, but couldn't help worrying that someone might have seen him on her doorstep.

"Thank you, Miss Jean." He was more than polite. "And, well, you talk so much about little Jade. I just wanted to come by and see her for myself. I don't want to intrude."

"You are not intruding, Willie. I am honored that you came by. Please sit down here at the kitchen table and I'll fetch her."

She brought the only joy of her life into the kitchen and sat down beside Willie.

"Here, you can hold her," she insisted as she handed Jade to Willie.

His eyes opened wide and his smile showed his snow-white teeth in stark contrast to his deep ebony skin. "Why, Miss Jean. She's a spitting image of you. She's a beautiful baby!"

He smiled as the alert infant's curious gaze fixed on him. No black person had ever held her. She smiled back at him, not at all afraid. Neither realized it nor could have predicted it, but they would meet again years later.

***

And then the nightmares started. Barely one month after she started her job, Jean was in the storage closet behind Jake's office, bending over getting some typing paper out of a box on the floor. Suddenly there was a hand between her legs. She rose and tried to turn around, but there was no place to go. He pushed her against the wall and in a split second was groping her and trying to kiss her.

"Don't, Mr. Luther! Please don't! Please don't do this."

"Hush, missy, hush!" He reached back toward the door and pushed it closed with his hand.

"You know you want it. You've been begging for it ever since I hired you. Well, now you can have it. And listen to me, pretty lady, if you know where your bread is buttered, you'll stay quiet and enjoy it."

It was over quickly and he left her on the floor sobbing and devastated.

She hated him, but she hated herself more for letting him do this to her.

For the next six months Big Jake met her in the storage closet at least weekly. It was hell on earth for her. She often thought of quitting and even wondered if suicide would be better. She wanted to kill the creep too. She hated him for all of his evil assaults. She hated him too because she knew he was a racist who had probably committed unspeakable attacks against colored people or those who sympathized with them. She hated him more than she could share with anyone. She felt trapped and desperate. She thought about going to the authorities, but thought better of that idea since she knew that Jake and Sheriff John Thomas Rodgers seemed to be very close buddies.

It took more courage than a young single girl with a small baby was supposed to have to leave her hometown and every ounce of security that she once had, but leave she did. It was survival. It was an escape from the jaws of a monstrous beast. She silently worried that he might follow her or track her down someday, but she had to take that chance.

She chose Jackson, Mississippi, the capital and largest city, ninety-six miles south, as she had a distant cousin, Maxine, who lived in nearby Clinton. Maybe Maxine could help her. She packed three boxes and two worn suitcases of worldly possessions. She told her mother that she wanted to find a better life in Jackson. Rebecca LeFlore did not know the real reason for her daughter's abrupt departure from her roots. Jean was too frightened of Jake to tell even her mother the truth. She convinced her that she would be fine. Rebecca and Ethan could come down and visit any time. It was final. No need to argue.

Unexplainably, as if an unknown force was driving her, in her plans to leave she decided to pack one other thing.

She did not know why she did it, but something very deep in the recesses of her mind propelled her to go to the Cotton Exchange late on the night that she and Jade left. She had asked Willie to help her get into the building, which he reluctantly did. He understood why she was leaving but begged her to reconsider and maybe tell someone about Jake. She told him that her mind was made up. She also told him that she would miss him.

She walked without hesitation over to Jake's desk and tucked his forbidden Malmaison rooster gently into a very large shopping bag. She wanted to hurt him and thought this would be one way to get revenge. Plus, she was related to the great chief, so maybe the rooster really was hers. She was family, after all—well, if you stretched it, sort of. She told Willie that it was best if he did not know where she was going. He understood and wished he too could someday find a way to leave Greenwood.

She gave Willie a warm hug and then hurried out as he locked the door, and she drove south to Jackson in innocence, unable at that point to fathom the dangers and intrigue that would follow her, Jade, and the rooster for many years to come.

CHAPTER FOUR

Jackson and Damian

In Jackson, Maxine recommended a church to Jean that was known for helping wayward teenagers and single moms. It was late when they arrived, but the staff was more than kind and eventually found her a room to rent in the basement of a middle-aged couple's bungalow just west of downtown off Capitol Street. Her first job was at Woolworth's Five and Dime on Capitol Street in the center of downtown.

It wasn't easy, but Jean and Jade managed to somehow survive. Jean eventually got a respectable job at South Central Bell Telephone Company, in the early days before mergers and deregulation. Jade often wondered later how her mother had failed to become pregnant from all of the horrible encounters with Big Jake Luther that she eventually told her about. Maybe, she thought, God was being merciful, in a twisted sort of way. But where was the justice?

Exactly one year to the date after arriving in Jackson, Jean met and fell in love with Damian Scott Winters. She met him at the Krystal hamburger joint on Capitol Street across from the railroad station. Those were the days that were to become the beginning of Jade's earliest nightmares. Damian worked for the Illinois Central Railroad. He was a food manager on the City of New Orleans, a grand lady of the rails that made its daily sojourn from Chicago to New Orleans and then back again to Chicago. He was gone all week but had a week off every other month and was home every weekend. Jade was three and a half when her stepfather "entered" her life.

She barely remembered those early years, but what happened as she blossomed into a beautiful young girl forever stained her soul.

Compared to Eddie Colton, Jean thought Damian hung the moon. In fact, she enjoyed the weeks when he rode the Grand Lady as "her own time" but looked forward to the weekend, which she thought belonged just to them.

It would be two and a half years before she had an inkling of the real Mr. Winters. In later years, she always hated herself for not ever thinking that the impossible could happen to Jade. Demeaning, exploiting, and abusing an adult was sick enough, but invasion of your innocent child's privacy was simply a mother's worst nightmare. It had happened to her, but it was *never* going to happen to her child. Yet the nightmare was real and it cut like a razor-sharp saber through her heart. She remembered the day so clearly when the devil came calling.

"Momma," Jade said, so matter–of-factly. "Are all men like Damian?" Damian had not wanted to adopt Jade, and she always called him Damian. She was eating Cheerios from the box on a lazy Sunday morning while everyone slept in. Jade had been awake and up watching cartoons long before her momma and Damian. For a six year old, she was a pretty bright and independent child.

Jean had just walked into the den and was still stretching and yawning off the cobwebs when Jade launched her question. For a few seconds, Jean was puzzled. She glanced at the TV wondering if something on that satanic box had provoked such an inquiry. She didn't know where the conversation might lead, and she subconsciously suppressed any negative thoughts about Damian.

"Why, Jade, child, whatever do you mean? I suppose he is like most men. What are trying to say?"

"I mean, you know, down there, are all men like that, that big down there?" she asked in a way only an innocent child could.

Jean was shocked and numbed as she listened to Jade's almost matter-of-fact recounting of all the middle of the night "playtimes" with Damian. She did not want to believe what she heard. The encounters were obviously more hideous than a six-year-old could adequately describe. But it was clear enough to Jean what Damian had done. It was worse than despicable. It was sickening.

"That monster!" she muttered as she clenched her teeth and flushed with anger, contempt and a sinking feeling of utter and total violation. How could her husband be a *child molester*? What had she done to either encourage or discourage Damian to stoop to such depths of perverted and fiendish acts perpetrated on such a vulnerable and beautiful child? She blamed herself.

The demons of her past were unlocked. She had never felt such hatred. Creep-o Luther was one thing. She had rationalized that part of her life, but she had moved on. Now, to think that any human could be capable of such behavior! And she was married to him! It was every mother's worst nightmare come true. The urge to kill came over her again.

She sat back and held Jade close to her body. She began to cry. Jade began to cry too. She sensed that their lives would never be the same again.

The very next morning, Jean packed all that she could fit into her two worn brown leather suitcases and their '53 Chevrolet. Damian was riding the City of New Orleans and would not return for a week.

As they backed slowly down the driveway, Jean looked into the rearview mirror. She stared in disbelief at the massive figure she saw blocking her exit —it was Big Jake Luther!

He stood defiantly, snarling from a corner of his tight-lipped mouth, with his arms crossed, daring her to run him down. Her life was unraveling. She looked at Jade for a second and knew what she had to do.

CHAPTER FIVE
Taming Lions

Without hesitation, Jean slammed her foot down on the accelerator and raced the Chevy in full reverse. In a split second, the right side of the rear bumper caromed into him, and she caught a flash of his body catapulting into the privet hedge alongside the driveway. As hard as the impact was, she imagined that he was either dead or at least severely maimed.

She turned the Chevy sharply into the road and the tires squealed loudly as they left a trail of smoking, burning rubber. She jammed the shifter into first gear and sped off without looking back.

She glanced over at Jade whose hands were frozen on the door handle, her expression wide-eyed with confusion and horror.

"It's OK, sweetie. We'll be OK. Let go of the handle and sit back. Mommy will take care of you. Please don't worry." She needed to hold and console her, but it wasn't the time. They had to escape. She could not be sure if Jake was dead or alive or was following them.

Jade did not say anything. She began to cry softly. She was only six years old and was struggling to understand what had happened. She had no idea of what was to come, but she knew that her mother was in real danger. She was afraid that it was her fault. The innocence of her childhood was no more. She felt ashamed and confused.

Jean knew she was speeding, but she also did not know what had happened to Jake Luther back at 155 Magnolia Avenue. She was only focused on getting as far away as possible from her past. The thought of going directly to the police came and just as quickly disappeared. Irrational or not, she had to get away from Jackson, from Damian, from Jake Luther, from her demons. She guessed that Jake had come for his rooster. Something told her to just run. Get as far away as possible. Disappear. Run, Jean, run.

She turned out of the neighborhood onto Robinson Drive and headed toward East Pearl Street, which would take her to State Street, US Highway 51. She momentarily looked in the rearview mirror to see if they were being followed but could not see any sign of Big Jake's red Ford pickup truck—one very familiar to her from her Greenwood nightmares.

She finally merged onto US Highway 80 and motored east toward Meridian. She glanced occasionally at the speedometer. She tried to stay around the fifty mile per hour limit. Her only thoughts were of keeping Jade out of harm's way. She had no real idea of where they would stop.

The route along US 80 grew more and more boring as they passed grove after grove of loblolly pines separated occasionally by neatly plowed fields ready for the next plantings of cotton, soybeans, and corn. The small towns she passed through were a blur. Her mind was focused. Move on. Escape. Don't look back.

It was almost two hours later before Jade finally spoke. "Momma, I'm hungry and I need to go to the bathroom."

"OK, sweetie. Maybe in the next town. Can you wait a little while longer? Please?"

"I think so. Momma, are we gonna be OK? Where are we going?"

"Yes, Jade. We are going to be fine. I will find us a place to stop soon. We'll figure this out. Please don't worry."

She did not sound very convincing. Jade turned and looked back in the distance through the back window and then turned her head forward and stared down the road ahead. Her mouth was tight and dry. Her stomach growled angrily at her and she crossed her little legs to try and stop her urge to empty her bladder. She would hold on.

Jean drove on through Meridian and followed the highway signs that indicated a turn onto US 11. She wasn't sure but thought that that route would take her to Atlanta. She turned north onto the new route.

For some reason, she thought a big city would be a safer haven from danger. She could find a new job and perhaps "hide" from any pursuers in a large city. She worried about Big Jake "Creep-o" Luther, but then there was Damian. When he finally returned from his Illinois Central run, what would he think? She had cleaned out all of her meager possessions and had not left a note. What would he do? He really would have no way of knowing where she went or why. Hopefully. But she thought again about the dastardly things he had done to Jade. She worried that he would track her down. She didn't want to go there.

The fuel gauge was nearing "E" as Jean crossed the incorporated city limits of Eutaw, Alabama. US 11 became Main Street and then Tuscaloosa Street. She saw a "Pure" sign and gasoline pumps just two blocks past the town square, and she pulled up to a full-service pump. Jade looked up as an attendant came out from the building and around to the driver's side and asked, "Fill 'er up?"

Jean rolled down her window and nodded. "Yes, thanks."

"Momma, I need to go the bathroom *real* bad!" Jade said with emphasis.

"OK, sweetie. See that little diner across the street?" She pointed toward a wood-framed building with a large Coca-Cola sign hanging a little crooked above the entry. The letters to the right side of the door identified it as The City Diner.

"Uh-huh."

"As soon as we get some gas, we'll head over there and get some food and you can go."

It did not take long to fill the 12.5-gallon tank with regular. Jean was not happy to see the price was twenty-two cents a gallon. Almost three dollars to fill up! Everything was getting so high. But it did not matter. Moving on was all she could focus on for now.

She parked the old Chevy in the alleyway pretty close to the left side of the café and near what looked like a storage shed at the back of the building. They both got out and walked around to the front entry and opened the screen door that had a ragged, diagonal tear in the middle. The diner was empty except for an elderly couple seated at a small table on the right. They were sipping what looked like iced tea.

Jean approached the lunch counter where a thin, black-haired woman whose back was turned was writing on something and asked, "Where are your restrooms?"

The waitress turned her gum-chewing head and with her pencil pointed to a sign behind the counter. She did not speak and turned back to her writing.

After relieving their aching bladders, Jean and Jade finally got to sit down and enjoy their first bite of food since fleeing from Jackson and the horrors they both wanted to forget. Grilled cheese sandwiches had never tasted so good! Both of them slurped down an ice-cold Coca-Cola. For just a few minutes, Jean did not worry about constantly looking in the rearview mirror or over her shoulder to be sure no one was following them. She reflected to herself that it was very unlikely. For now, it was time to keep going and get as far away as she could before it got too late in the day. Atlanta was probably five or six hours away. She was a determined mother protecting her precious only child.

She asked for her bill, paid the waitress, and took Jade's hand as they walked back to their car. Jade let herself in the passenger's side as her mother walked to the driver's side. Jean looked briefly down the alley in front of them and caught a glimpse of a red truck. Before her brain could sound an alert, a hand clamped atop hers as she reached for the door handle. The grip was painful and powerful.

Simultaneously, an arm reached around her face and a hand covered her mouth tightly before she could react.

CHAPTER SIX

Surviving

"Don't try to scream or resist if you don't want something bad to happen to that girl of yours," the attacker growled. "Little girl, just stay where you are and keep quiet, or something bad will happen to your mother. Do you understand?"

Jade was frozen with fear. She could not move or respond.

"*Do* you understand?" he asked again.

Jade managed a feeble nod of her head and sat riveted to her seat. Her hands trembled. She did not understand what was happening or what to do.

The awful man grabbed Jean's hair from behind and jerked her head back. He turned her and pushed her in the direction of the storage shed behind the café. The door was ajar, and he opened it with his foot and pushed her in, closing the door behind him with his body and maintaining the tight grip across her mouth.

He told her that he was going to take his hand off her mouth and if she uttered any sound or tried to scream or run, he would kill her and her daughter. He asked her to nod if she understood. Quickly she complied with his command. Somehow, she was not totally surprised that her world had spun out of control around her.

He pushed her away, and she saw that he had pulled a knife from his belt. It looked very sharp and shiny as it reflected the light from the small overhead light bulb hanging from a braided electrical line.

"You made a huge mistake when you took my rooster. Took me a while to track you down, but now you are going to pay."

It was Creep-O himself, Big Jake Luther, and she knew he meant what he said. Obviously the collision with her car bumper that had sent him airborne earlier that day had not incapacitated him. His face revealed several deep, linear scratches covered in dried blood, probably courtesy of the privet hedge. His left eye was nearly swollen closed and he sported quite a shiner. It was her worst nightmare come true again.

He made her take off her white cotton underpants and lie down on the dirty floor of the shed. What choice did she have? She obeyed, knowing what would come next.

He switched the knife to his left hand as he began to unzip his pants with his right hand. He approached her with a crazed, penetrating stare, not noticing that the storage shed door was slowly opening. He knelt down and was about to have his way again as he had done so many times before back in Greenwood in the back room of the Cotton Exchange.

Suddenly, and seemingly without reason, he glanced over his shoulder but could not see clearly from his swollen left eye. He saw someone but could not tell who was moving quickly toward him. In a fraction of a second, she had raised her right arm and with strength seemingly impossible for a six-year-old girl, Jade thrust a pair of long-bladed scissors deep into the left side of his neck.

The unexpected counterattack caught him totally off guard. With a knife in one hand and his zipper in the other, he could not react. The sharp scissors had penetrated deep, and within a few seconds, his eyes rolled upward, and his hulk of muscle and massive bones went limp. The full weight of his body fell forward on top of Jean.

Both Jade and Jean reacted with a stunned and deafening silence. Jean tried to push the dead weight of Jake's large body off of her, and finally, after several tries and what seemed like an eternity, she somehow managed to roll out from under him.

"Jade, sweetie, what have you done? My God! What have you done!"

"Mommy, he was going to hurt you. I had to save you," Jade said calmly. It was so matter-of-fact.

Jean stood up and found her white cotton Fruit of the Looms and clumsily stepped into them. She turned and looked down at Jake. She could not tell if he was alive or dead. Her first thought was to pull the scissors from his neck. Slowly she extracted the weapon that had vindicated many encounters of savage assaults against her, and she wiped off the blood with the hem of her dark blue dress. Finally she felt some justice had been rendered.

"Come on, Jade. We have to get out of here, *now!*"

She took Jade by the hand and quickly exited the small shed, scanning the alley for any passersby. No one was there, and they ran to the Chevy and got in. Jean put the scissors back in her purse where Jade had found them. She put the key in the ignition and turned the starter. It made a grinding sound for what seemed like forever, and finally the car lurched forward a bit. The motor had started, but then it died again. Jean began to panic.

"Momma, hurry! We have to go." For a brief moment, Jade almost seemed to be the stronger of the two.

"The car won't start," Jean said with real fear as she twisted the key and tried again.

The steady grinding noise of the starter began to grow weaker and weaker, and Jean began to worry that the battery was being drained. Then suddenly the engine perked to life and began to hum.

"Finally!" she sighed with relief.

She put the car in first gear, let out on the clutch, and headed down the alley. Just as she was turning right out of the alley onto the street, she passed Jake's red pickup. They passed the truck slowly, and Jean suddenly slammed on the car's brakes. Jade was thrust forward but she quickly braced herself with her hands against the dashboard.

"Momma, why are you stopping? We have to go!" It wasn't fear anymore. It was a child's innocent determination and a sense of accomplishment in having set her mother free.

Jean put the Chevy in reverse and backed up until she was even with the red truck.

"Jade, look! The rooster is in Mr. Luther's truck. Get out and get it, *now!*"

Jade didn't move. She was confused and did not understand what could be so important about that stupid rooster.

"Jade, get out and reach in there and get that rooster. Hurry!"

She obeyed her mother and retrieved the stuffed rooster. It was heavier than she thought it would be and a little cumbersome, but she managed. She got back in the car.

"OK, Momma. What do I do with it?" She spoke so casually now.

"Put it on the back seat. Quickly, do it!"

Jade reached over the front seat and dropped the bird on the back seat.

Jean immediately put the old Chevy back in first gear and popped the clutch. The car lurched as they sped away, this time not leaving a trail of rubber behind. She turned right toward Tuscaloosa Street, and at the next stop sign she turned left and headed in the direction of Atlanta. *Run, Jean, run* was her only thought.

CHAPTER SEVEN

Run, Jean, Run

There wasn't time to really think about the intensity of the past few moments. Her attention was on her driving and getting as far away from Eutaw as possible. Jade sat silently. Occasionally Jean saw her turn and look over the front seat at the rooster lying on its side on the back seat. Jade did not ask her mother again why she had to get the rooster back. She guessed that Jean would tell her when the time was right.

It was nearly two and a half hours later when Jean saw the Bessemer, Alabama, city limits sign. After a few more miles, she saw a Birmingham sign. She had never been to Birmingham, and the traffic on US 11 was quite congested. She followed the traffic, stopping at red light after red light. She kept her eye out for signs pointing to Atlanta.

As she and Jade passed through the downtown area, high-rise office buildings with bank and insurance company names began to fade away in the rearview mirror. They crossed over the First Avenue viaduct bridge, and Jade's attention was drawn to the red, molten pig iron that was being processed to her right at the Sloss Furnaces and then to the mountain in the distance to the south.

Jade broke the long silence. "Mommy? What is that big statue way over there on that mountain? He's holding a red light or something."

Jean glanced in the direction that Jade was looking. "I think that's Vulcan. I read about him in a travel magazine once."

"Who's Vulcan?"

"I'm not sure, sweetie, but I think he may have been some type of Roman god, mythology, you know."

"Mythology?" Jade did not understand. It sounded too confusing. She was just glad that her mother was finally talking again, even if she could not discuss what had happened a few hours ago.

"Mommy?"

"What is it, Jade?"

"Is Mr. Luther that man you told me about that was so mean to you when we lived in Greenwood?"

"Yes, dear, but let's not talk about him anymore. He was a very, very mean person to your mommy. He got what he deserved. Maybe one day we can talk about him. Not now."

"Mommy?" Am I in trouble for what I did to Mr. Luther? What if someone tells? What if they find us? Why didn't we call the police? Will I have to go to jail?"

"Hush, hush, Jade. No one will find us. You were very brave back there. You saved Mommy. You are the bravest little girl I know. Thank you. Now sit back and don't talk about it anymore."

They came to a stop at a red light at Forty-First Street in the Woodlawn community just past Avondale Mills, and Jean saw a sign pointing to Highway 78 and Atlanta. She turned right, and after three blocks, the signs pointed left. She turned onto Crestwood Boulevard, US Highway

78 East. She felt a sense of relief that maybe they were getting a little closer to her chosen destination.

She had not turned on the car radio during the entire trip, but finally decided that music might help divert Jade's attention. She turned the dial and found AM 610. WSGN radio, said the DJ, just as the end of Brenda Lee's "I'm Sorry" was playing. The irony made her gasp. Two men were joking about the mayor's latest gaffes. One reminded the listeners that they were tuned to the *Layton and Charles Show*. Doug Layton and Tommy Charles were huge radio personalities in the Birmingham area.

Jean quickly decided that the conversation was silly and inappropriate for a six-year-old, so she turned the radio off. She glanced at her fuel gauge and saw that it was getting low again.

As she passed a Shoney's Big Boy restaurant, she looked to the right and saw an Esso gas station. Behind the station was a massive construction site with partially erected steel girders and construction equipment of all types—giant earth movers, cranes, large dump trucks, and piles of more steel girders waiting to be raised. A large sign said "Coming Soon – Eastwood Shopping Mall – a new concept in shopping." Jean barely noticed but did not care. She had to get farther away from the horror scene in Eutaw.

She pulled into the station and up to a pump. An attendant came out immediately to fill the tank. Jean and Jade got out and walked to the back of the station to the ladies room. When they returned, the tank was full and Jean paid the $1.65 to the attendant.

"Check the oil, ma'am?" he asked.

"No, thank you." Jean was ready to get back on the road.

They headed back onto Crestwood and toward Atlanta. The sign said 148 miles.

"Mommy?" Jade was getting tired and a little hungry. The grilled cheese sandwich was long gone. "Do you think we will be OK? Do you think Mr. Luther is dead?"

Jean looked over at her beautiful daughter and longed for the right answer. She smiled reassuringly and touched Jade softly on her face.

"We are strong, sweetie. We will be fine."

"Mommy," Jade said softly, "I love you."

An oversized tear trickled down Jean's right cheek. "I love you too, baby."

CHAPTER EIGHT

The Meeting

Lawrenceville, Georgia
February 1995

Predicting winter weather in Central Georgia could be a serious challenge for prognosticating meteorologists. February 1995 was an unusually mild month. And for Jasen, moving into a new home in the winter would have qualified him for temporary insanity. But luck was with him and his wife, Caitlyn, on that first weekend of the month as they completed the backbreaking ordeal in the balmiest of conditions that he had remembered in recent winters. Jasen and Caitlyn finally sat back on their sectional sofa and stretched their weary bones and muscles at 11:00 p.m. on that Sunday night.

"Why do we hate ourselves so much?" Jasen asked with a sigh.

"Don't complain to me," Caitlyn snapped. "This move was your idea. I can't believe I let you talk me into a garden home. Just look at this chaos! Boxes and furniture everywhere. Why did you ever think we could put all of our worldly possessions from a four-thousand-square-foot house into a two-thousand-square-foot garden home with no basement? You're totally wacko. You know that, don't you?"

"Well, you wanted to lower our mortgage payments. You saw what the new payments were going to be on that adjustable loan. We had few options. I thought you had agreed to this. You can't have it both ways. Sorry." Jasen was tired of arguing the same thing over and over.

But, he knew it wouldn't matter anyway. He had never enjoyed arguing with her. Best to keep quiet. Even if it had been her idea, it would still be his fault. Besides, she was frazzled from three days of exhausting packing, loading, unloading, and unpacking, not to mention cleaning the old house from top to bottom. Neat and clean. A trait they both shared. Anyone who had moved into a house they had vacated (four moves in the past six years) was probably pleasingly shocked to find an almost brand-new house. OCD? Anal retentive? Whatever. It was true, at least for Jasen. He had just moved in and had already hung all of the pictures on the walls.

But it was the next weekend in the new house that changed Jasen's life, although it would be weeks before he understood what had happened. Ethics professors are programmed that way. Sins of the heart were transgressions that they taught people how to avoid. They set standards for the professional community—above reproach. They should set the example for others.

The cul-de-sac in Windermere Gardens just off the Lawrenceville-Suwannee Highway was typical of many neighborhoods springing up in suburban communities. The residents were a mixed bag of retirees looking for affordability on a fixed budget, singles with a strong career focus looking for a nice but low-maintenance home, and empty nesters looking to downsize. There were a number of single women on the street. Jade Colton was the newest and by far the best looking—the men had all agreed on that.

The Prosperos had already met the Spiers in the house to their left. Jasen thought Walter was a nerdy engineer type with his above-the-ankles trousers and black horn-rimmed glasses. But he respected anybody who had a Labrador retriever as a pet. Sandy was quite imposing, but gentle for a big dog. Jasen took to her right away and they became good buddies. Jasen had always been fond of dogs.

Walter was a Vietnam veteran, and Jasen had already heard his war stories at least three times. Walter's wife, Nancy, mostly kept to herself, but Caitlyn Prospero was impressed with Nancy's collection of Department 56 Christmas villages. She had them displayed all around their house, and they drew many oohs and wows from their rare visitors. Nancy loved putting out the houses at Christmas, and she kept them out most of the winter. The balmy weather this year just seemed wrong for her wintry-looking villages.

The Spierses seemed like decent folk to Jasen, and he felt comfortable with them as neighbors. He wasn't so sure about the Chamberses, who lived directly across the street. Before their movers had left, Earl and Rose had come over and introduced themselves to the Prosperos.

Earl was a burly sort of guy who strutted in like a peacock in the palace garden or a domineering rooster in the barnyard. He wore a World War II veteran's baseball cap and a brown tweed wool sweater that was buttoned all the way up. Rose was very thin and was dressed in her bathrobe and house slippers at two in the afternoon. Caitlyn tried not to stare at her hair still in rollers. Rose wandered freely about their house without invitation and even opened their closets. She and Jasen later had a good laugh about them and he tagged them as "The Duke of Earl" and "Nosey Rosey."

Earl made it clear that they were the self-appointed neighborhood watch committee and that no one on the street had anything to be concerned about—they were home almost all of the time and nothing happened on Windermere Cove without them knowing. Jasen was not sure if he was comforted by that or not.

A week after the Prosperos moved in, winter finally returned. The winds screamed with an arctic-like viciousness, and the temperature dropped thirty degrees overnight. Jasen shivered as he sprinted out the door to the mailbox at the curb, and as he reached in to get the mail, his eye caught a glimpse of a figure coming out of the house next door. She had just moved in herself only two weeks before the Prosperos. He had heard that her name was Jade something or other. The Spierses had told him that she was a strange sort, lived alone, was divorced, and was driving the builder of her new garden house crazy with constant demands to address a punch list that would not end. Walter had gotten the scoop from Jade's Realtor. He made her sound like the Wicked Witch of the East, West, North, or all of those...

She was coming out to check her mail too. It was an introduction that would leave Jasen with more of an impression than he had imagined. He had his eyes closed to other women. He did not allow himself to think of them as anything other than another person. He had been taught to respect and tolerate others at face value and blocked all thoughts of anything except trying to be friendly or neighborly. A married man for eighteen years, he was a faithful husband. Don't think impure thoughts, he told himself. It had seemed to work for eighteen long years.

Jasen introduced himself and she did too. It was a brief encounter, and as far as he was concerned, she seemed at first glance like just another nice person. Her long, unbuttoned winter wool coat and her wool scarf prevented him from appreciating how truly beautiful she was. But he was instantly drawn to her strikingly gorgeous green eyes. It was only for a split second, but it seemed longer as their eyes locked. If any witnesses had been there, the instant connection would have been noticed.

The warmth and radiance of her auburn hair was mostly obscured by the scarf. Physically she was a head turner...nature had been kind to her in many ways. Her silky skin was unblemished and appeared as smooth as the calm waters of a predawn lake. Her smile was warm and infectious and her eyes were that mystical deep jade green. Her small pixie-like nose was flushed red from exposure to the bitter cold winter wind. Even in that brief encounter by the mailbox, Jasen sensed that something was very different about Jade Colton.

As she walked back to her house from the mailbox, she momentarily sensed a kindness and softness behind his pretense of aloofness and disinterest. Jasen did not have a clue that day that he had looked into the eyes, ever so fleetingly, of the person who would soon send him spiraling out of control and into a world he had never known before.

She was a survivor. Her beauty was striking, yes, but ironically, it made her vulnerable to would-be predators and others with all sorts of evil intentions. Her nightmares haunted her, and she longed for a relationship with someone who understood her spirit and her soul and would help her find forgiveness for her past. Her mother had taught her to tame the lions in her life. In the circus world, Jean had told her, you don't want to be the person that follows the elephants in the parade, scooping up their business. You want to be the lion tamer—courageous, afraid of nothing, always in control. She clung to her mother's words. Her past had strengthened her, and she was resolved to never give up on anything. The future would test her in many more ways.

It would be weeks later before Jasen learned her secrets and heard about the land mine-filled and danger-pocketed roads she had traveled that most people could never imagine, much less endure. She somehow knew that she would eventually tell him, she thought, but only when the time was right.

She turned to close her front door and ever so briefly saw the plantation shutters on the front window of the house across the street close quickly. Someone had been watching, she thought. What she did not notice was the black sedan parked on the street three houses down. A dim figure sat in the driver's seat also watching.

Jade locked her front door and walked to her kitchen. She opened the refrigerator door and pulled out a cold bottle of Corona Extra. The season had nothing to do with her love for beer. She sliced a lime and tucked a wedge in the mouth of the bottle. She looked at her mother's stuffed rooster on her kitchen table and tipped the bottle toward him, as if toasting him. Thirty years had passed, but she had not forgotten. She walked to her den and sat back in her recliner. Her old diary was on the adjacent end table. She took a gulp of beer and opened it.

CHAPTER NINE

The Diary

She had dog-eared a favorite page in her diary and now she turned to it.

"1961"

It had been only one hour since they left the lights and traffic of Birmingham. Jean knew that Jade was hungry even though she had not complained. She had dozed off just before they passed through Pell City.

The Anniston city limits sign brought hope of a diner or restaurant. Jean soon saw a Golden Rule Barbeque sign, and she pulled off of US 78 into the parking lot of the small but well-lit building.

Jade opened her eyes and sat up. "Where are we?"

"We're going to get a bite to eat. It's getting late and I know you're tired and hungry. Come on. Let's get out and stretch our legs, kiddo."

"Kiddo?" Jade pondered silently. "Momma never calls me that," she thought with a slight smile.

They walked into the BBQ establishment hand in hand and were soon refreshed and ready to finish their trip.

Then, as Jean reached her car door, a twentyish-looking stubbly bearded dude with a toothpick angled out of the right corner of his mouth dressed in faded jeans and dirt-covered cowboy boots approached her and Jade. He pulled the broken toothpick from between his yellowing teeth, stained from too much coffee or chewing tobacco or both. Jean thought for a second of Jake Luther's disgusting Skoal habit. The man pursed his lips and let out a loud wolf whistle.

"Well, lookie here! If you and that little missy there aren't the prettiest looking thangs I've ever seen. Could you give a fella a ride?"

Jean's immediate reaction was to step back. She was caught off guard and did not know what this guy was really up to.

She pulled Jade close to her and pushed her behind her. The stranger was grinning like a Cheshire cat and getting closer. Jean looked around, but no one else was in the parking lot. She thought about just getting back in the Chevy and taking off, but he was too close and she was not convinced that he was just trying to bum a ride.

"No, I don't think so," she said. "Look, mister. We're not locals and just want to get back on the road."

He did not stop and was now within a few feet of them. She kept her eyes on him as he scanned the parking lot nervously.

Jean was now on automatic. She only thought of protecting Jade. Then she remembered. She quickly reached into her purse and pulled out the long-bladed scissors that had been wiped clean of Jake Luther's blood earlier that day. She thrust the weapon toward the stranger.

"Stop right there! We don't want any trouble." She waved the scissors at him in a tight circular motion and positioned herself defensively with one foot a little forward of the other.

The stranger was totally unprepared for any resistance, much less from a female with a weapon and with moxie. He stopped in his tracks and began to back up a bit.

"Hey, hey, wait a minute!" he said as he reassessed the situation. "Hey, lady, I'm not looking for any trouble. Besides, what makes you think I'm afraid of a pair of lady's scissors?" He chuckled nervously.

"Let's put it this way, punk." Her teeth were clenched tightly and she tossed her head confidently. "This morning these scissors were buried up to here in another creep's neck." She pointed to the end of the blades. "So if you want a piece of me and my daughter, then go ahead and try me!" Jean was more than convincing.

He looked at the scissors and then looked back at her face, which was stamped with deadly seriousness. He turned without another word and ran like a whiney, whipped dog around the corner of the BBQ joint and disappeared.

"Punk," Jean muttered, disgusted.

Jade looked up at her mother with pride. "Let's go, Momma," she said, as if she was in charge now.

Jade took her mother's hand and they got in the car and drove off.

They arrived in the Atlanta area after 9:00 p.m. that eventful day. Jean located a Holiday Inn just past the downtown area in East Atlanta off I-85 and checked them in. She did not see any signs of being followed and felt more relaxed. But as she checked the latch on the door of room 306 for a third time and tucked Jade in the bed and finally lay down herself, she realized how extremely exhausted she really was. Sleep came quickly, and the next thing she was aware of was the light from the morning sun filtering through the sheer beige curtains covering the window of the room.

***

Jade sat back in her recliner and held the dairy up to her chest and took another gulp of her Corona. She had not read the old diary in a long time, and she was amazed at herself for remembering so much detail of her sixth year. She thought about her mother's Mississippi upbringing and how many demons had followed both of them for so long. She smiled thinking about how much she was like her mother. She missed her dearly. She suspected that Mississippi women were just born strong, especially if they were part Choctaw. She picked up her diary and opened it again...

CHAPTER TEN

Calvin

As Jade sat back and turned the next page of the badly faded brown leather diary, her doorbell chimed. She wondered who could be bothering her so late in the afternoon. For a fleeting moment as she walked to the front door she recalled her brief encounter with her new neighbor Jasen and a smile crossed her face, but just as quickly it left as she looked out the side door transom.

It was Calvin "Cal" Caliban, the peculiar home inspector who had taken an unwelcome interest in her and had volunteered to help her get her builder to finish his punch list of incomplete items. He was probably in his early fifties and had a coarse, weathered face. Even though his frame was large and as bulky as a bull, he seemed harmless enough, but she had learned through many experiences with men to stay on guard and be ready for the unexpected. Her mother had certainly reinforced that over and over.

Calvin had been recommended to Jade by her Realtor, and he had seemed to be thorough and bland enough when he first came to complete the check list for the inspection. But she began to feel more and more uncomfortable with his leering eyes and constant focus on her cleavage. She refrained from wearing revealing low-cut blouses or dresses around him after that, but his gaze always seemed to drift to her generous physical attributes.

He began coming by every two to three days after the first visit. She had made the mistake of telling him the problems she was having getting her builder to complete some unfinished work—missing doorstops, poor paint job in the den, crooked light fixture above the kitchen table, cracked toilet seat, broken doorknob in her bedroom, and a list of other minor annoyances. Calvin was much too eager to intercede with the builder. He told her that every woman needed a man she could count on.

If only you knew, she had thought to herself.

She opened the door and greeted him reluctantly but acted surprised. "Calvin! What are you doing here?"

"Hi, Ms. Colton. Please, it's just 'Cal.' Just in the neighborhood and wanted to check one more time on some of those issues you're having with Mr. Eastman, your builder. Can I come in? It's really cold out here."

She really did not want to invite him in but finally said, "Sure, come on in, Cal."

As they walked into the den, Jade was immediately aware of his piercing stare. She put her hand to her robe and pulled the lapels together. She quickly asked him if he wanted to sit down or if she could get him something to drink.

"Oh, no thanks. Just came by to see what Eastman has completed. He can be tough to deal with, you know, so if I can see what isn't finished, I can look him in the eye and get his butt in gear. You know, he's the kind of builder that they say only lies when he opens his mouth! Anyway, I'll just be a minute. Let me check the bedroom first."

Jade followed cautiously as he quickly headed for her bedroom. She could have told him what had or had not been done, but he insisted on checking for himself.

He next went to her kitchen to check the chandelier. The guardian rooster was centered on the table. He was an unusually large bird, about eighteen inches tall, mounted imposingly on a piece of split wooden fence rail. His buttercup comb was a deep red and had grown down to his beak before he died. The wattles matched the red of his comb, and his cape was a mix of blues and purplish black, silky feathers that mirrored his primary and saddle feathers. The taxidermist had realistically positioned his magnificent main tail feathers and sickles in an upright posture, a barnyard sign of "I'm the king around here." The auburn color of his hackle was brilliant and complemented his bluish feathers. He was by any comparison a very unusual and rare rooster.

Calvin leaned over a chair toward the rooster for a closer inspection.

"Please, Cal! Don't touch the rooster. He's an antique and might break."

"Antique? How can a rooster be an antique? Does he have a name or something? Where'd you get him?"

"His name is Willie," she answered in a subdued voice. "He belonged to my mother and really has a special meaning to me. Please, don't touch him, if you don't mind."

"Sure, sure, just looking. That's what we inspectors do—look at things! Hee-hee."

He was not funny, Jade thought to herself. She wanted him to leave. His attention changed to the light fixture.

"Damn electricians. They seem to always install these things crooked. And did you notice? It's not even centered over the table. Idiots! Say, Ms. Colton?"

She held her breath, waiting for his next question.

"I see that you met that handsome Mr. Prospero next door. Looked to me like you two kind of hit it off." His eyebrows rose a bit and he winked at her.

She looked at him curiously. "What do you mean, and how do you know that I met him? I didn't know anyone was watching. Were you spying on me, Cal?"

He stammered a bit, "No, no. I was just down the street checking with the Joneses at 716 about something and just happened to see you two at the mailbox, that's all."

"Is your vision that good, Cal? What exactly did you see?"

"Hey, don't get bent out of shape, Ms. Colton. I'm just real observant, you know. That's what I do..."

"Yes, I know," she interrupted him. "You *look* at things."

What Jade did not know was that he had been looking at them with binoculars. She had no idea that Calvin was stalking her and was aware of her every move.

"Yes, ma'am, that's what I do." He turned and walked out of the kitchen. "Well, I suppose I had better be headed out. Seem to have worn out my welcome here."

What made him think he was welcome? she said to herself.

She walked with him to the front door, opened it, and thanked him for dropping by and helping with Eastman. He turned and fixed his gaze on her slightly exposed cleavage, and she quickly covered herself.

"I'll be in touch," he said with a grin and winked again, almost devilishly, as he hurried into the cold, brisk breeze back to his black four-door sedan. She stood on the stoop shivering in the cold air until he backed out of her driveway. As he drove away, she noticed he was still looking her way. She stepped inside the threshold and turned and looked across the street just in time to see the Chamberses' shutters snap closed. Sure seemed to be a lot of "lookers" in this neighborhood. She shrugged and decided it was time to get back to her memories.

CHAPTER ELEVEN
Mississippi Comes to Georgia

1961

The morning that Jean and Jade left the Holiday Inn, Jean found a pay phone and called Juanita, her boss at Bell Telephone in Jackson. She tearfully told her about her wretched husband and what he had done to Jade. She told Juanita how she felt she had to escape and that they had ended up in northeast Atlanta with just five dollars and some change left. She did not tell her about Jake Luther. That was a secret she would die with.

She made Juanita promise that she would never tell anyone where they went, especially Damian if he happened to show up at the center where Jean had worked.

It looked as if her fortunes were changing though. Juanita knew someone at the Atlanta Bell Center and gave Jean a number to call. She found the local YWCA as Juanita recommended, and they stayed there that night. The next day she reported to the very large personnel building for Bell Telephone in downtown Atlanta and was hired on the spot because of Juanita's good word. More luck—the branch where she would work had a child care center, free to employees. Later that week, she found an affordable one-bedroom flat for rent. A year later, they moved to a small house that Jean rented in suburban northeast Atlanta. Jean and her daughter had started a new chapter in their lives—a long way from the Mississippi Delta.

***

Jade began to rapidly turn page after page of her diary until she came to her twelfth birthday page. It was still all too surreal to her. And it was almost comical to her now, but she still remembered the intensity of that day.

Her mother had invited six of Jade's sixth-grade girl classmates over for ice cream and birthday cake. The house was soon filled with echoes of giddiness, giggling, and silly talk about boys. They played records of many of the 1960s' teen idols—Frankie Avalon, Elvis, the Beatles, Frankie Valli, Paul Anka, Sonny and Cher, and many more. Jade loved playing "I've Got You Babe" because it was her mother's favorite song. It had been the top record of 1965, and it reminded both Jean and Jade of their special bond even though the song was about a guy and his girl. She loved the part that said, "There ain't no hill or mountain that we can't climb 'cause I've got you, babe." They had depended upon each other through many trials and tribulations.

The girls flipped through a small stack of *Teen* magazines and swooned and giggled over every cute guy on every page. It was a time of fresh awareness and happiness for Jade. She and Jean were finally settled, and life was sweet.

The girls were noisy and oblivious to the rest of the world as they played in the den, which was in the back of the house. Jean had slipped into the kitchen to start some green beans simmering on the stove top. Suppertime would be soon after the girls had been picked up by their parents. Jean was happy that Jade seemed to be really happy to have her friends over and to just be a typical twelve-year-old. She had worried that Jade had grown up way too fast. Sometimes she seemed more like an adult.

As the green beans began to steam a little, Jean heard the doorbell ring. She headed toward the front door, thinking that one of the parents was a little early to pick up their daughter. She opened the door without hesitation or without looking through the peephole. She froze when she saw him, and as her mouth gaped open, she dropped the glass bowl she was holding onto the floor. It shattered into pieces.

Damian Winters stood in her doorway with his right hand leaning on the door jamb. He had not changed much in the six years since she and Jade had suddenly packed up and moved away from him. He was wearing his black Illinois Central baseball cap and blue denim bibbed overalls over a dirty white T-shirt. A pack of Camels was tucked into the rolled right sleeve.

"Hi, sweetheart," he smirked and took one step across the threshold so that she could not close the door on him. "I think you broke that bowl there," he added, pointing to the broken shards on the floor.

"Damian! Why are you here? You are *not* welcome, and I want you to go back to Jackson or wherever you came from. Please, just leave. We have company and this is a bad time."

"Hey, I've missed you. We are still married, you know."

"Not as far as I'm concerned, you pig! You child molester! Now, just get back in your car and leave!"

"How about just letting me in for a minute to see Jade? Maybe I can apologize to her. I sure do miss you girls!"

"Just go!" Jean insisted. She tried to close the door.

Suddenly he pushed against the door and surged into the entry hall, grabbing her left arm at the wrist. He closed the door behind him.

Jean demanded, "Let go of me and get the hell out of my house, *now*! I'll call the police and then you can explain how you molested my daughter and now have assaulted me in my own home." She tried to extract her arm but his grip was unrelenting.

"Come on, darling, this is just a friendly argument between husband and wife, that's all. How about a little kiss for your husband?" He pushed her back against the wall and pinned her so that she could not escape. He tried to kiss her, and she turned her face away in disgust. This was a side of Damian that she had never seen before.

Instinctively and with lightning speed, her right leg flexed at the knee, and with an upward thrust, she found her target in his groin. He bent forward and moaned in pain. Jean knew this would not stop him, and indeed he gripped her even tighter.

The assault on his manhood also triggered something unexpected, and he clasped her around the throat before she could scream or react. He began to choke her, his face reddening with anger, his teeth clenched tightly.

As his large hand wrapped around her delicate windpipe, she began to feel light-headed and the room began to darken around her. She tried to kick and free herself, wishing that she was stronger, but she was growing more and more defenseless by the second. As her sight began to fade to black and her lungs burned for lack of air she knew her life was being choked from her and she was becoming limp. Damian was becoming a murderer.

Without warning, Damian felt an enormous impact against the back of his head. Dazed, he relinquished his grip around Jean's neck and arm and slumped to the floor unconscious.

Jade stood behind him, both hands still gripping the handle of the large iron skillet Jean had left on the stove top in preparation for supper. Jade had grown concerned when her mom did not return to the den to check on her and the other girls. She had heard the struggle as she approached the hallway and reacted from experience. Flashes of Jake Luther had triggered her protective instinct.

Hurrying into the kitchen, she had grabbed the skillet and with unbelievable strength had stopped the brutal and nearly lethal attack on her mother.

"Jade." Jean's voice was weak as she felt the blood rushing back to her brain. She staggered a step and then lurched forward, stepping over Damian to hug Jade tightly.

"Thank you…again." Jade had been her savoir for a second time.

By this time the other girls had heard all the commotion and were standing in two rows of three in the opening between the kitchen and the hallway. They were wide-eyed and slack-jawed with shock. Mary Susan Thomas was the first to speak.

"What in the world is going on in here? Who is that man? What happened?"

Broken shards of glass, an unconscious man on the floor, and a hallway full of bewildered twelve-year-old girls and one adult woman—it was an interesting sight, thought Jade.

"He is a pervert and a very evil man who hurt Jade a long time ago," Jean explained.

"What's a pervert?" Nancy Bell, the youngest of the girls, asked.

"Just a bad person, dear. Get your parents to explain it to you sometime…something all of you girls need to understand about some bad men out there in the real world. Mary Susan, go call the police and explain to them that we have an intruder and they need to get over here as fast as possible. OK?"

"Yes, ma'am." She went back to the den and dialed the operator and asked to be connected to the police department.

Jean and Jade looked at each other, and each knew that memories of six years ago behind that small café in Eutaw, Alabama, were circling in the other's mind. Brain synapses began to fire and a plan was born.

"Girls," Jean directed, "we need to 'prepare' Mr. Winters here for the police. I'm going to need your help. Jade, go in the kitchen and get me that jar of honey out of the pantry."

Jade looked puzzled but was beginning to see that her mom had something deserving and maybe a little devious in store for Damian. She headed into the kitchen and returned with the honey.

"You other girls, come over here and help me get Mr. Winters out of the house. Grab his arms and legs and we'll drag him out the door."

They hesitated briefly then grinned at each other and grabbed a limb and headed out the door. Between Jean and the girls, the task wasn't too daunting, and they dragged him out of the door, down the steps, and into the yard. His head bumped with a cracking thud down each of the three steps. He was out cold and even the hard thumps to his head did not rouse him.

Jean directed the girls to keep pulling him into the yard. They stopped in the grass just beside a large fire ant hill. Jean took the jar of honey from Jade and began to pour it over Damian's face and arms. She looked up at Jade and smiled devilishly at her, then unbuttoned Damian's denim bib overalls and poured the remainder of the gooey honey over his abdomen. Then she asked the girls to help one more time as they rolled him right on top of the ant mound, face first.

They all jumped back as the huge ant colony was suddenly awakened by this intruder, and thousands and thousands of small red fire ants immediately covered Damian's body. It was obvious that the ants were following the sticky streams of honey.

As the ants' burning stings unleashed their toxic poisons, Damian finally began to stir. Suddenly he opened his eyes, acutely aware of the excruciating pain in his face, arms, and groin. He sat up, screaming and slapping the massive army of ants. Then he stood, twirling round and round in circles, slapping and screaming just as an Atlanta Police Department black-and-white cruiser pulled up to the curb and two uniformed policemen charged up the walk. Jean, Jade, and the girls were all gathered on the front porch giggling and pointing at Damian.

"This man forced his way into my house and tried to choke me," said Jean with a very straight face. "He ran when my daughter flashed a kitchen knife at him. It seems he tripped and fell right on top of that ant hill. Serves him right."

She glanced at Jade and the other girls. They all smiled with satisfaction.

***

Jade sat back as she finished reading the account of that crazy day at her twelfth birthday party. She could not help but laugh out loud and feel vindicated all over again. She briefly thought about the frequent nighttime encounters with Damian. She was only six years old, but the memories were still intense. She quickly dismissed the images of those nasty bedtime visits from Damian. He got what he deserved, she reasoned. It was justice.

She laid her diary down, remembering how the police had handcuffed Damian and taken him away. She wasn't real sure how believable her mother's story had been about the series of events that day, but the police seemed to be more interested in getting the sticky, ant-covered intruder into their cruiser without getting bitten themselves and taking him off to jail. They told Jean that she would have to come to the station later to file a report and charges.

It was getting late and Jade was beginning to get sleepy. She pushed back in her recliner, closed her eyes, and wondered how things would have been if she had not been home when Damian came calling that day in Atlanta. Although she did not really care, she wondered what had happened to Damian.

CHAPTER TWELVE
The Chamberses

E arl and Rose Chambers were pleasant enough to Jade, but she never really developed any kind of fondness for them. As a single woman, she found little comfort in neighborhood watchdogs who seemed to spy on her every move. At first it annoyed her. But Jade eventually became determined to give the Chamberses more than they ever bargained for. She never understood if Earl was simply a dirty old man revisiting his adolescence or if he by nature just did not trust anyone. As a veteran of World War II, he seemed to like his self-appointed role as colonel-in-charge of Windermere Cove. Jade learned later that he had been in army intelligence, a term that she thought sounded more like an oxymoron than a true description of his role in the army. But being in the spy business certainly explained a lot of his clandestine behavior.

Two weeks after moving in at her 708 address, she glanced out her front window on a dreary and drizzly Saturday morning and saw Earl and Rose walking across the street in her direction.

"Oh my gosh," she whispered to herself. "I hope they're not coming to see me!"

Wrong. Her doorbell chimed and she greeted them graciously, hoping they didn't sense her slight air of dread.

"How to do, Ms. Colton." Earl spoke first. "We're your neighbors across the street at 709. Earl Chambers the name. Retired US Army Colonel Earl Martin Chambers, and this here is my wife, Rose Marie. Rose, say hello to Ms. Colton."

Rose forced a half smile and pushed right past Jade, walking directly into her neatly organized kitchen, which was off to the left of the entrance hallway.

"Glad to have you in the neighborhood, Ms. Colton," Rose called over her shoulder, but she did not sound that sincere. She did not seem to even notice the brilliant orange and purplish rooster perched in the middle of Jade's kitchen table with his piercing stare aimed at those entering his domain.

"We have to be sure that your house is secure so I'm just going to check and see if your house looks safe. Single ladies can't be too careful these days, you know. Can't trust anybody. But no worry. The colonel and I are always around, so if anything happens, you know, like a break-in—things like that—we'll know. We're like that insurance company, you know, you're in good hands with...the Chamberses."

Jade was speechless as she tried to follow Rose, who was walking quickly, going from window to window, checking the back and side garage doors, and then checking out her closets.

The colonel was following behind recording details in a small spiral notebook with a stub of a green pencil that had no eraser—probably one he had gotten at a golf course for his scorecard.

Jade felt as if her home had been invaded, but she couldn't seem to muster the courage to challenge the odd couple's behavior. Finally she managed a modest response to the uninvited but apparently well-intended pair. They were probably in their seventies, so Jade tried to be respectful of their ages and sound polite and appreciative.

"Well, Earl and Rose, thanks so much for coming and checking on me, but I assure you I am very independent and my house is as safe as any. Plus, I've signed up with the Sentinel Alarm folks and the house is well-monitored. It was really nice meeting you. Let me show you out. I'm sure we will have more opportunities to chat."

"Well, now that you mention it, Ms. Colton," offered Rose, "you just plan on coming over to our house tomorrow afternoon at three, and I'll fix you some nice hot spiced tea."

"Oh no, no thank you, Rose. I wouldn't want to bother you" (unlike the way they had just bothered her, she thought).

"Won't take no for an answer. Be there or I'll send Earl after you."

As she and Earl headed out the door, she turned and muttered over her shoulder, "Oh yes. If I were you, I'd trash that horrendously ugly rooster on your kitchen table. Bad omen. Trouble with a capital T. Trust me."

They strolled back across the street to 709 and disappeared behind their door and closed plantation shutters.

***

The next morning Jade searched for any excuse she could dream up to avoid the invitation to visit the Chamberses. She felt eerily uncomfortable around them even after just that brief encounter yesterday. But she correctly surmised that Earl would stick to Rose's threat of coming to get her if she did not show up. The brisk winter wind had subsided as she walked up to their door and rang the bell.

She saw Rose peep from behind the small curtain on the side door transom and heard several locks clicking open. Rose greeted her and let her into the gloomy entry hall.

"Well hello, Ms. Colton. So glad you could make it. Come on in and take your coat off."

"Please, Rose, call me Jade. You make me sound so, uh, so 'mature' calling me Ms. Colton." Saying "old" did not sound politically correct. Offending the Chamberses in any way was probably not a good idea, she thought.

As Jade maneuvered her way past Rose, she saw Rose step across the front door threshold and look up and down the street. Jade could not imagine what that was all about. Rose closed the front door and immediately reset the deadbolt latch, chain lock, and the keyed door-knob lock. Jaded noticed a stepladder in the hallway leaning against the wall.

"Can't be too careful, you know. The colonel and I believe in security."

The Chamberses were growing more interesting by the minute. Jade tried to hold back any hint of amusement.

Rose took her navy three-quarter-length wool coat, hung it on the pine hall tree, and directed Jade into the modest family room to the right of the entry hall.

Jade couldn't help but notice the décor was straight out of the sixties. The sofa, tables, and chairs were tacky French provincial, and a console stereo record player hugged the side wall. A few family pictures were displayed on a round end table, and a very large family Bible was centered on an oval pecan-colored coffee table that matched the end table. A large rectangular mirror was centered above the sofa with silver tinsel draped across the top in swags. Jade guessed that it was left over from Christmas or maybe Rose kept it there all the time. Weird. Above the stereo was a familiar picture of a Southern belle in a long yellow formal dress seated at a black grand piano that was centered in the large sitting room of a stylish Southern plantation home. Jade had seen that picture before—her mother had one that she had bought from a door-to-door salesman when Jade was much younger.

As Jade seated herself on the sofa, she noticed that a small telescope on a tripod metal stand was pushed into the corner of the room near a front window. These two characters were probably not just stargazers, she guessed.

Earl walked into the family room. He was still decked out in his veteran's baseball cap and brown tweed wool sweater. A very handsome pipe protruded from the lower right pocket of his sweater, and thankfully, Jade thought, he did not light up while she was there. She hated pipes and cigars. Damian's bad cigarette smoking habit had been bad enough. She did not miss that at all.

"Ms. Colton," he said. "So nice of you to come over. Rose and I like to get to know our neighbors as soon as possible. We hope you are getting settled over there."

"Rose, don't just stand there. Fetch the spiced tea that you promised Ms. Colton."

"Jade, please, just Jade, Mr. Chambers." Jade hated the formality.

"Oh, OK, fine…Jade. But it is 'Colonel' Chambers, if you don't mind."

"Oh, yes, sorry…Colonel Chambers."

Rose returned within a minute with a tray containing a small teapot and three small cups. The style was very Victorian and quite attractive for serving pieces but a little too "frou-frou" for Jade's taste. Jade and the colonel had not spoken while waiting for Rose. He had studied her face and impeccable skin tone with an unblinking stare and glanced down several times at her very ample chest with a glare and an ever so slight twitch of his mouth that made her uncomfortable. It was a tense minute for her.

As Rose served the tea, Jade broke the tension. "You two have a lovely home. Reminds me of my mother and growing up in Atlanta."

"Oh, are you from Atlanta?" Earl inquired.

"Well, no, not actually. I was born in Greenwood, Mississippi. Momma and I moved to Jackson when I was still a toddler, and eventually we moved to Atlanta. Momma named me 'Delta Jade' because she was very proud of our roots in the Mississippi Delta. Of course, you know where the Jade comes from," she said, pointing to her eyes. "Georgia was our adopted state, and all my friends are from Georgia. To tell you the truth, I have never been back to Greenwood to see where I was born. Someday I will go back. I always loved Momma calling me her Delta Jade."

"Where is your mother now, Jade?" Rose couldn't help but pry.

"She's not with us anymore." Jade lowered her head and her voice softened.

"Oh, I see." Rose sensed her sadness and looked at Earl.

"What about brothers and sisters?" Earl kept up the probing.

"None. Just me and Momma, until…"

"Until…?" Rose pushed for more.

"I'd rather not talk about it right now. Thanks for asking."

"Well, you have not mentioned your father at all. Where's he?" Rose was not letting up.

"I was raised by a single mother. I never knew my father. He was from Greenwood too, but I was too young to remember when we moved to Jackson."

"Interesting," quipped Earl.

"So we heard that you work for South Central Bell; what do you do there?"

"I'm the branch director at the Lawrenceville office. Very good job."

"Oh, I see." Rose couldn't miss the opportunity. "So that makes you a big shot, sort of."

"Well," Jade responded, "I guess you could say that, but I don't really think of myself that way. I worked my way up in the company, and good fortune was with me."

"Don't be so modest, Jade." Earl was a little intrigued. "Tell me, how did a female like you get to be a director over such a large operation? I would have thought that would be a man's role."

"Earl! " Rose interjected, coming to Jade's defense. "You're beginning to sound like a sexist pig. Watch yourself. Jade may get the wrong impression of her neighbors. Besides, Ms. Colton impresses me as a very smart lady. Someone else at the Bell must feel the same way."

Jade was beginning to get enough of Earl Chambers. "A female like you." What the hell did he mean by that? She almost bit her tongue to keep from jumping down that rabbit hole.

Earl continued curiously and unapologetically, "Is there a Mr. Colton?" He had already heard that she was divorced.

"I've been a single woman now for eight years, and when I divorced, I wanted to go back to my maiden name, Colton, and almost decided not to because of my son, James. Too many bad memories with my ex, but I legally divorced him, so I'm a Colton again. I love my privacy and freedom." She spoke with emphasis and stared into his eyes to make her point.

Earl grinned as he put his cup down after taking another sip. "Well, yes, I am sure you do. You mentioned a son, James, I think you said. Where is he?"

Jade was suddenly done with the third degree. She *did* protect her privacy, and the Chamberses had learned more than she cared to share. She put her cup down and stood up.

"I think I had better get back across the street and get some housework done. Thanks so much for the invite and your hospitality. I really need to be going."

"No need to rush off, Jade. We don't get much company, and we love learning about our neighbors. Helps us understand the comings and goings." Earl spoke with a military-like command.

No, Jade thought indignantly, it satisfies your weird compulsion to poke your noses into everyone's business.

Rose walked with her to the hallway, retrieved her coat, and opened the front door. "Jade, we loved getting to know you and hope you'll come back soon."

As she was exiting, Jade noticed a shotgun standing in the corner behind the front door. Looks like the colonel is prepared for anything, she concluded. What a twosome.

As she walked back to 708, a smile came to her face and she wondered if she could one day outwit her new "protectors" and neighbors at 709 Windermere Cove. Nosey busybodies. What good could come of that?

CHAPTER THIRTEEN

The Prosperos

Caitlyn and Jasen Prospero were just as "nonmysterious" as Jade Colton was mysterious, private, and unintentionally seductive to most men who could not help but stare at her natural beauty. Jasen and Caitlyn had met at a pep rally at the beginning of their junior year at Gwinnett County HS. Both were new to the area. From a casual conversation that began more out of politeness because they were standing next to each other, Jasen asked Caitlyn out on a first date to a movie. Jasen never saw it as love at first sight, but he loved her pixie-like smile. As an added bonus, she turned out to be a terrific kisser! Caitlyn had reciprocated, telling him that he had plush, soft, and very kissable lips that were well-shaped plus enticing and addicting. They began to date steadily and eventually became engaged and then married all too young before Jasen finished college. A baby came a year later.

Their marriage was to follow an all-too-common sequence of events for the youth of the late '60s and early '70's—marrying your high school sweetheart, starting a family while still very young, finding a way to borrow money to complete your education, finding the right job, getting trapped in the rat race to succeed, discovering that young love is very difficult to sustain, feeling trapped in a relationship because of kids or too many financial commitments, hanging on hoping things will get better, drifting apart, feeling alone and isolated, and eventually splitting up. Divorce City, USA—the outcome of over half of all marriages by the late 1990s.

Jasen Michael Prospero was the third of four children of Margaret and Mikolas Prospero, an unassuming couple enjoying the American dream in suburban Atlanta, Georgia. His mother preferred the Greek spelling of his name Jasen. His three sisters were all very attractive, and Jasen enjoyed the respect they gave him as the only male sibling. Mikolas Prospero's family had immigrated to the United States at Ellis Island in 1905 from the small Greek isle of Santorini.

Margaret and Mikolas had met in the City of Brotherly Love just at the end of World War II, in June 1945. Mikolas had not served in the military due to his hearing loss that gave him a 4F disqualification. As the son of very proud Greek immigrants, he had been eager to join the army and fight for America. It wasn't in the cards, and he settled for learning the food business from an acquaintance who owned an Italian restaurant. He and Margaret had learned much about Greek cooking from the Prospero clan of in-laws, cousins, and many Greek friends. They discovered that their combined talents were a natural fit for opening a Greek restaurant in Philadelphia.

Their first business venture was tagged as Theos, after Mikolas's grandfather in Santorini, Greece. It was an incredible success, as Philadelphians had developed quite a diversified taste for European cuisines. The Prosperos had a large support group of relatives in the Philly area, so finding help to keep the restaurant a hot item was not a problem for Mikolas and Margaret. Even as Margaret got pregnant every other year for the next eight years, she amazingly juggled motherhood and restaurant cooking seamlessly. Her favorite dishes that she had learned to make from Mikolas's mother were fasolada soup, moussaka, souvlakis, and pastitsio. Mikolas bragged to everyone that she made really superb baklava. Those were sweet times for the Prosperos.

Jasen was born in 1952, and it was later that year that lady luck turned her back on the family. Ethnicity-themed restaurants had sprung up all over Philadelphia. The competition for the Greek food business was choking Theos, and profits hit all-time lows. Mikolas looked at the Deep South and concluded that the time was ripe to try a new location. Jasen was only two years old when the Prosperos and their four children moved to the Atlanta, Georgia, area.

It proved to be a wise decision. Atlanta had very few good Greek restaurants, especially in the northeast suburb of Buckhead Park. The new venture was christened Taverna Mikos, and if location mattered, the Prosperos had hit the jackpot! It proved to be more successful than Mikolas had ever imagined. Margaret had turned most of the cooking over to a newly hired Greek chef who continued to use her proven recipes and added many more to the menu. His biggest success was the incredibly delicious lightly battered then fried lobster, not exactly an old Greek dish, but wildly popular with Atlanta patrons. Sweet times returned.

Jasen's earliest memories were of the large family gatherings in the private dining room in the back of Taverna Mikos. He loved the Greek food, but as he grew up he developed many other interests and never had a desire to work in the family business. Margaret Prospero was a devoutly religious mother who raised her four children to, at a minimum, always follow the Golden Rule. Jasen was very close to his mother, and he was fortunate to inherit her strength, endurance, and kind heart, but, alas, not her cooking talents! Tolerance of others was his strongest suit. He learned the value of patience and forgiveness. He matured into a well-balanced and stable adult with lofty dreams of a bright future. His parents' success was a constant inspiration and motivated him to excel at everything he did. He wanted to make them proud.

Jasen had met Caitlyn in high school and they married during fall break of his senior year at the University of Georgia in Athens. They lived just off campus in a one-bedroom garage apartment. The demands of education—studying nonstop, late nights cramming for exams, research time in the campus library, theme papers to write, etc.—were physically and emotionally challenging for a newlywed husband. Caitlyn had wanted to postpone the wedding until Jasen graduated, but he insisted, arguing that after undergraduate school he would enroll in graduate school and maybe even pursue his doctorate in history and philosophy. If they waited until he had finished school, it would be years.

So the young couple managed to find their way on Caitlyn's insurance company secretary's modest salary. Jasen's partial scholarship helped with college expenses. When Jasen graduated summa cum laude, he won a scholarship to graduate school, working as a graduate assistant teaching American history to naive and eager Georgia Bulldog freshmen.

It seemed to Jasen like a fair but challenging assignment for an ethics course. "Moral Dilemmas in American History" was the theme assigned by his professor. The students were allowed to choose their specific subject from a short list. Jasen had always been intrigued by the plight of American Indians who were forced onto reservations scattered across the nation but often far removed from ancestral lands. When he saw the "Trail Of Tears" story of the Mississippi Choctaws, he was hooked on his choice. It was a moving experience that he never forgot as he researched the tribe of Native Americans led by the respected but controversial Chief Greenwood LeFlore. He had never realized the persuasive influence that LeFlore had commanded that had led to the displacement of thousands and thousands of America's aboriginal native settlers.

He found himself transported back in time to the Dancing Rabbit Creek ceremonial events and trying to fathom the conflicting emotions that LeFlore must have experienced. His thesis on LeFlore's moral dilemma earned him an A-plus, as he laid out a compelling argument that corroborated LeFlore's ultimate decision to agree to his tribe's relocation. It would be almost twenty years before Jasen's first graduate research project came full circle and catapulted his life into a dimension he could have never imagined. He could not have predicted the irony of life's twists and turns and that he would eventually fall madly in love with a descendant of Greenwood LeFlore.

***

Caitlyn Whittaker was the middle child of three sisters. Her parents, Bob and Sela Whittaker, were typical middle-classers struggling to follow their dream. Mr. Whittaker had found happiness in the HVAC business after high school and had eventually started his own company in Alpharetta. Mrs. Whittaker taught third graders at a Fulton County school. Caitlyn's sisters were goal-oriented overachievers, but she somehow never seemed able to muster the same ambition or energy to set the world ablaze. She had thoughts of majoring in accounting at UGA, but an early marriage and a baby one year later took care of that idea. She worked at various secretarial roles to help pay the bills as Jasen pursued his vision. It went unsaid, but she secretly resented her husband for his success at her expense, in her mind anyway.

One year to the day after their marriage, Ariel Nicole Prospero arrived. Caitlyn was not thrilled that their first child was a girl—perhaps a reflection of an all-girl sibling background. She had set her mind on a son. It would become a bitter disappointment that would drive a wedge between mother and daughter.

The grandparents "oohhed" and "aahhed," and everyone except Caitlyn was happy with their beautiful new granddaughter. Jasen was a proud father and bonded instantly with his new daughter. Their close relationship would be tested by Caitlyn's jealousy of Ariel's obvious emotional attachment to her father. It was a stormy mother-daughter push/shove childhood that set the stage for a defiant and rebellious adolescence. The "I hate you," "I'm leaving," "Dad loves me more than you," and assorted temper tantrums became the norm. It was a trying and tumultuous time for the young Prosperos.

Caitlyn found refuge from the rigors of raising an only child teenage daughter in the commercial insurance world. She worked her way up to an adjuster position and eventually a division manager's role. Ariel spent less time with her mother and more time with Jasen, who had introduced her to golf when she was only eight. She found that she had a natural ability for the game and joined the school team in high school.

The Prosperos' marriage hit rock bottom near Ariel's last year in high school. Both Jasen and Caitlyn inwardly knew that the flame from their early years had been snuffed out long ago. They were just going through the motions.

Neither knew why. Hoping things would get better? Maybe when Ariel moved out they could "find" each other again? Marriage counseling? Caitlyn rejected the thought. No one was happy. Dinnertime was often highlighted by hurtful digs and insults. The tension was acrid and ate away at egos and nerves.

Three months before she graduated from high school, Ariel announced that she had made up her mind about college. She had accepted a golf scholarship at Mississippi State University in Starkville. She and her best friend, Teenie, had arranged to be roommates. For Ariel, leaving for college could not come soon enough. She was sick and tired of her mother's verbal bashing of her dad. The happy times of her early childhood had vanished. She often wondered why her parents had stayed together. She blamed herself. In a way, she hated to leave her dad. But she somehow knew that he would be OK. He had taught her about self-confidence, trusting yourself, and never giving up on your dreams. Of course, it was all about her golfing ambition, but she knew he meant it about her life overall. She loved her dad very much. At times she felt sorry for her mom and her self-invoked pity. But, hey! Wasn't life all about choices? You could choose to be happy or choose to stay miserable—she would tell her mom before she left.

Jasen, Caitlyn, and Ariel moved into their Windermere Cove garden home in the winter of 1994. Life for Jasen was moving headlong into a six-degrees-of-separation fairy tale, toward the pasts of two strangers colliding in a climatic discovery of a century-and-a half-old mystery. For Jasen, it was time to make a choice.

CHAPTER FOURTEEN

James and James Jr.

Atlanta 1973

After Damian's unexpected visit to their rented house in the suburbs of Atlanta, Jean and Jade had settled into happy times together. Damian was taken care of eventually through the legal process, and in time they moved on, their strength and their mother-daughter bond growing and becoming hardwired into their very fiber. The nightmares of Greenwood for Jean and Jackson, Mississippi, for both of them faded further and further into the past. Survival was their modus operandi, and the courage of a lion was their grandest attribute. Jean often wondered if her father had been right about their Choctaw DNA. Jade had learned from her mother that nothing was impossible and that a strong and determined woman could do anything she wanted.

Jade blossomed into a beautiful teenager who began to attract the interest of many adolescent guys with raging hormones and pimply faces. Jean knew about the challenges and choices that her daughter's beauty and attractiveness would bring. It was inevitable. She had had first-hand experience in Greenwood. She had a favorite admonition about men in general that she constantly shared with Jade:

"Remember, Jade, an erect penis does not have a conscience."

Jade laughed to herself every time she remembered her mother's warning.

Every guy she went out with seemed to be the same. The gaga-eyed boys lined up to get a date with her. Jade was the best-looking girl at their school, hands down. They all said how much they loved her, but she knew what they really meant.

Her mother had told Jade about her father, Eddie Colton, who had used almost the exact come-on line. Being cheated out of a normal childhood and the horrible experiences with Damian had hardened Jade and prevented her developing any meaningful and loving relationship with her suitors.

James Lee Mitchell probably came closest, she thought, to understanding her and treating her as more than a scoring opportunity. They met the summer between her junior and senior year of high school. She had gone to Panama City Beach with some girlfriends. He was "different"... quieter, kinder, and more romantic than the others. He really seemed to care about her as a person rather than just for her looks. She regrettably overlooked his tendency to overindulge in his love for beer, shrugging it off as just what young males liked to do.

They wrote to each other for the next six months. Their young relationship grew. Jade began to feel that all men were not jerks as her mother had suggested; at least James wasn't, she thought.

They married the summer after she graduated from high school. James was a jock, tall and muscular and rather handsome, Jade thought. He had played high school baseball in his hometown of Lacrosse, Georgia. After graduation, he took a job as a baseball trainer's assistant at West Georgia State Junior College in Carrollton. He should have been a student and on the team, but an early marriage had ruined that chance. Moving there from Atlanta was a big change for Jade, but she could endure and overcome anything. She had survived Jake Luther and Damian Winters and all those wild, hormone-pumped dates with roving eyes and roaming hands. Fear was not in her vocabulary. She had clung to one of her mother's favorite quips: "Strong women scare weak men." Jade was a strong woman.

James Lee Mitchell Jr. was born eleven months later. Jade remembered the day as one of overwhelming joy and the most painful experience of her life. It was almost the end of her life.

The baby was breech. The doctor had left the labor room to find James and explain to him that Jade needed to have a cesarean section. But the baby wasn't going to wait. Before he could return, Jade had other plans, and James Jr. was born. The nurse had miraculously delivered the baby in spite of his breech presentation, and for a brief but tense moment everything seemed fine.

Then Jade began to bleed, and bleed, and bleed. Externally, she had a fourth-degree laceration. Internally, a major artery had ruptured. The nurse screamed for someone to get the doctor, but Jade was already going into shock. The bleeding became more and more profuse. Jade was losing the battle and was at God's mercy. Her senses faded into sheer blackness and silence, a blissful tranquility. Then she suddenly saw an incredibly brilliant white light far in the distance. She imagined she was dead and heaven was ahead. A calm, peaceful serenity surrounded her. She seemed to be floating or hovering above her physical body. She was not afraid.

In reality the delivery room was in utter chaos as nurses and staff scrambled in all directions and shouted for additional help. They were losing a life and had no solution.

It was only pure, dumb luck that saved her. Another obstetrician was passing through the labor and delivery area and heard the frantic pleas for assistance. He rushed in to help, and the bleeding was finally controlled. Mother and baby survived. Jade was back.

Jade liked to brag to others that she was a "natural" at motherhood. She enjoyed the contact and bonding of breast-feeding. She felt it was the best choice for a baby. She and James Jr. became very close. She was always there when her son needed her. James Sr. was not around much. He preferred to hang out with the other Georgia State coaches and baseball players. They frequented all of the local honky-tonks after ball practice. He was always too busy to do things with little James. Jade became both momma and daddy to James Jr.

Eventually James began to accuse Jade of flirting and cheating on him. His claims were totally unfounded, but he was convinced. He was insanely jealous of any other man looking her way, yet he was rarely there when she needed him. She even imagined that he suspected that James Jr. was not his own. Jade knew better.

The marriage grew distant. James gradually became less and less intimate with her; he was always too juiced to make love to her. When he did come home, he usually crashed on the sofa drunk or went straight to bed. Alcohol had conquered him. Jade wanted to confront him with his addiction, but she feared his retribution, especially considering his alcohol-induced temper. Living with an alcoholic was daily torture for Jade.

Jade longed for real intimacy, but it seldom came. Their emotional connection had vanished. She was caught in a nightmarish marriage with hope of a decent future dimming. James Jr. was her life now. She knew what she had to do.

Jade and James Jr. moved out the day after his fifth birthday. James had missed the party. As he often did, he was out with his drinking buddies. Bad enough that he had begun to criticize everything she did or said. The verbal abuse had taken its toll. She silently dared him to try and strike her. It would have been the last thing he ever did. And she even accepted the fact that he thought pregnancy had ruined her looks and her body. The marriage was not meant to be. James did not deserve a woman with such incredible strength and caring, she thought. And he did not want to be a father or a husband. James needed help that Jade could not provide.

She left not knowing where the next crossroads would lead, but it had to be an improvement. She was building an impenetrable wall of emotional fortitude that would constantly convince her that most men really were monsters. It seemed as if her life was filled with them. It was a wall that would challenge anyone who tried to get close to her, and it was destined to cause many heartaches.

Jade and James Jr. settled on Lawrenceville, northeast of Atlanta, because Jean knew someone at Bell Telephone there, and without much effort she got Jade a job. She was an assistant to the technical support manager. It wasn't exciting, but it paid the bills. For the next twelve years, she and James Jr. lived in a small one-and-a-half-story house on the edge of Lawrenceville.

Jade was bright, a hard worker, and she impressed her boss. She gradually moved up the ladder and eventually was promoted to a manager just after James graduated from Gwinnett County High School. Ultimately the director role was offered to her, and life was good. She seemed to have established a good future with the now deregulated BellSouth Corporation.

James's problems almost surely began in early childhood. His father had never really bonded with him in the true sense of a strong, proud father/son relationship. Jade had constantly worried that the absence of a real father figure would doom James to a life of confused sexual orientation. Amazingly, James developed a strong masculine sexuality...maybe too strong, Jade often thought.

He became an avid hunter, joined a hunting club, and was always gone with his hunting friends during deer and turkey season. His outdoorsman buddies were his age, and they became even closer drinking pals. James could put away two six-packs of beer while hardly taking a breath. Jade saw the "James Sr." in him, and she hated it. She could not help herself with her constant nagging about his friends, his drinking, his neglect of his school work, his reminding her of her ex. It was a nonstop barrage of maternal overprotection and overreaction. It drove James further and further from his mother.

When James brought his friends over to visit, they couldn't help but stare at and admire Jade. James told her once that the only reason they were his friends was because they loved to come over and check her out. Typical teenage boys, she thought. She took it as a compliment. She sometimes forgot that her outfits were a little too revealing for oversexed boys. They loved every minute of it.

The guardian rooster that ruled over her kitchen became the brunt of many jabs, jokes, and sick retorts from James's friends. It maddened James when one buddy accused him of being a chicken killer.

"Is that stuffed bird the most ferocious thing you've bagged?" needled one friend.

It infuriated James. He knew that the rooster meant something weirdly special to his mom. He always defended her against sick jokes about Willie even though Jade had never told him the secrets of Willie's mystery-shrouded past. No need to know, she had determined. He never really probed her about the rooster. And he never once picked it up or touched it.

James began to feel more and more isolated and depressed. Jade knew that he blamed her for not having a father around. It had been her idea to leave James Sr. James Jr.'s resentment grew out of control. Jade had no idea of the events to come.

It was a Saturday night in October. James was out with his misguided band of drinking buddies. They had cruised around the red dirt roads of Georgia away from town and had soaked up brew for hours. James was driving his small white Nissan pickup truck that Jade had bought him for his sixteenth birthday. Jade constantly worried that James's drinking and driving would eventually bring trouble to their lives. It was just one more thing to nag him about.

Jade had drifted off to sleep, giving up on James getting home at any reasonable hour of the night. She always told him that nothing good ever happened after midnight, so try to get home at least by 12:30. He never listened to her maternal advice and common sense. What do adults know anyway? I know what I'm doing, he had said defiantly many times.

She was aroused by the sound of his truck pulling into their driveway, heard the door slam, and then the front door opening. She met him in the hallway just as he was turning to go upstairs to his room.

"James," she said sleepily, "why can't you ever get home at a sensible hour? Do you realize that it's three o'clock in the morning?"

She was more awake now.

"I'm sick and tired of having to constantly wonder and worry whether or not you are all right out there. If you would get rid of those alcoholic drunks you call friends, maybe we could get along better. Where have you been?"

James had stopped at the foot of the wooden staircase as she admonished him, the same as she had done a hundred times before. He let her release some pent-up maternal steam, and when she had finished, he looked away without a word and hurried up the stairs, his cowboy boots clopping loudly on each step. He slammed the door to his room behind him, and Jade heard the lock click.

She stood at the foot of the staircase and sighed, then muttered a vulgarity under her breath. She checked the lock on the front door, turned, and went back to her bedroom. Exhausted and emotionally spent, she collapsed on her bed and tried to get back to sleep.

Sleep was elusive as she tossed and turned and hated herself for her verbal berating of James. She knew that he was sick and tired of her harassing him. Raising a teenage son alone was too difficult, she thought. The kid needs a father.

Eventually she drifted off into a light sleep—just as a loud blast reverberated through the house.

"My God! What was that?" she said out loud.

She listened for another sound. Nothing. Then a horrible, agonizing, sinking feeling consumed her. She leaped from her bed and bounded up the stairs two steps at a time to James's room.

The door to his room was locked. She shook the doorknob and screamed, "James! Are you OK? Open the door! James!"

She pounded violently on the door, thinking she might have to break it down.

She heard nothing. In a panic, she could not think how she could open the locked door. She ran back down the stairs to the kitchen, fumbled through several drawers, and found a screwdriver. In a few seconds, she was up the stairs and outside his door. Clumsily she tried to jimmy the door open. It would not give. She poked the screwdriver in the keyhole and violently twisted and prodded at the lock. She was frantic with fear. Her hands were trembling almost uncontrollably. Her strength was evaporating. She was becoming a helpless noodle, unable to get to her son.

Just as she was about to give up, the door popped open.

The room was dark, the blinds closed. She held her breath and turned on the light switch. She stared in disbelief.

James's cowboy boots were neatly placed by his bedside, and his cowboy hat was perfectly centered on the pillows on his bed. An eight-by-ten framed picture of his dad was positioned just next to his hat.

He lay prone on the carpet at the foot of the bed, motionless. An enlarging puddle of dark maroon blood was oozing from his head. James's short-handled shotgun lay next to his body. One side of his head had been blown away by the blast.

Jade dropped to her knees and cried out, "No-o-o-o-o-o-o! James, what have you done? What have you done? Oh God, no-o-o-o-o!"

She rolled him over and tried to cradle him tightly against her. She cried loudly and without control. The wrenching pain in her heart was more than she could stand.

She sat and held him for what seemed like hours as she sobbed and begged him to forgive her. She tried to explain what had happened with his dad. She needed him to understand.

Blood soaked her pale blue gown, but she was no longer aware of anything except a life of monsters and nightmares, and she could not understand why she had deserved any of this. Surely God must hate her, she concluded. Would the punishment never end? Where was her justice?

Part Two

CHAPTER FIFTEEN

Jasen and Jade

1994

It was an early spring in Georgia, and eager, impatient gardeners were already out in their yards on Windermere Cove preparing flower beds, scalping the dead tops off of their bermuda and zoysia lawns, and mulching their beds and gardens. Jasen loved the opportunity to get his hands dirty and the relaxing mood that yard tasks gave him. It was also an escape from the intense friction and stress brought on by the Prosperos' recent move into their new home and his wife's ill temperament. Caitlyn was depressed, moody, and painfully grating on Jasen's last nerve. He was usually extremely tolerant of pressure, his wife's personality quirks, insults, verbal battering, and life's daily challenges. He was an unselfish sort, but he was now being driven by emotions foreign to him.

Jasen was on his knees by a flower bed holding a planting trowel in his gloved hands when he suddenly felt a tap on his shoulder. Startled, he nearly fell forward but balanced himself and pushed himself back.

"Hi, neighbor," he heard a soft female voice behind him. He turned his head and saw Jade standing behind him. She was dressed in tight-fitting jeans and a white blouse with the top three buttons unfastened. "Wow!" was all he could think. He felt awkward.

"Oh, I'm sorry. I didn't mean to sneak up on you. It's Jasen, right?" Jade asked, even though she had remembered.

He stood and turned toward her. "Yes. Jasen. How are you, Jade? I hope you're getting settled in over there. Guess we haven't bumped into each other since we chatted at the mailbox. Big change in temperature since then! So what can I do for you?" He was feeling more composed but could not help quickly surveying her beautiful presentation, even in her casual jeans. She smiled back at him, sensing that he liked what he saw.

"Well, I hate to ask or to impose, but I really, really need some muscle power over there," she said, pointing to her house. "I have a few projects that I started. Are you for hire?" she asked coyly.

"I'd love to help. Hey, what are neighbors for? Not sure you can afford my hourly rate, though, ha, ha!" he chuckled. He did not sense that a stronger force was reeling him in. "Let me brush the dirt off and I'll be right over."

"Great! Thanks so much," Jade said as she turned to walk back to her garage door. "Just ring the front bell."

He opened his front door and called to Caitlyn. "Honey, I'll just be next door. Jade, our next door neighbor, asked me to help her with some handiwork. Back in a few." He did not wait for a response and headed to Jade's with an eager spring to his step. He rang the bell as instructed.

"Thanks, Jasen, come on in." She stood to the side as he glided past her and turned around near her den.

"What have I gotten myself into?" he asked with a smile.

"Well, for starters, I need some help with that large clock over there," she said, pointing to a large cuckoo clock that was propped against the back wall of her den. "It was my mother's clock—she loved cuckoos.

It's pretty heavy, solid mahogany, so I can't lift it and get an idea of how high to hang it. It doesn't work, by the way. Know anything about fixing clocks?"

"No, I'm not a clock guy. Sorry. But hanging it—no problem. Do you have hangers and a hammer?" Jasen asked.

Jade was prepared. "Right there on the sofa table." She pointed behind him.

Jasen grabbed the necessary items and walked to the clock. He took note of her taste in furniture and decor. Quite traditional, but warm and inviting. Earth tones with a crimson-red accent. Cheerful, he thought approvingly. She seemed to be well-organized and neat. He did not see unpacked boxes stacked around. She seemed to have settled into her house pretty well, he thought to himself.

He asked her to come over and hold one end of the clock while he mentally and then physically made note of the approximate spot to hang it. She stood next to him and their bodies suddenly touched. He turned and looked down at her. She did not withdraw and instead smiled warmly. Eyes locked on eyes. He couldn't help but glance briefly at her partially unbuttoned blouse, teasing but not revealing. It should have been an awkward moment, but they were both at ease. Their smiles matched.

He found just the right spot and height for the beautiful, handcrafted mahogany clock, and in no time he had it secured on a picture hanger that could support one hundred pounds. He estimated the clock weighed less than twenty pounds.

"Doesn't it bother you to hang a broken clock?" he questioned.

"No. It's more about the sentimental thing, you know." She looked down, sadness in her voice.

"Yes." Jasen understood. "So, if I may ask, your mom is no longer alive?"

Jade answered softly, "I lost Momma eight years ago. Caught me really off guard. A very tragic accident, the sheriff said. Mom and I were very close. I'm told that I am her 'twin.' We really did look a lot alike. And thought alike. Mom was a very strong lady. We both had more than our share of hard times." She looked up at Jasen. He was focused on her face and looked sincerely interested.

"Oh, I'm sorry. I know I'm boring you."

"No, no, not at all. You were the only child?"

"Yes." She was surprised to find that she was enjoying their frank exchange.

"Losing parents is difficult no matter what the age or circumstances. Thankfully my parents are still with us. Not living with us, you know what I mean."

"Yes," she said. "I know what you mean."

"Well, not trying to pry. What's the next task?" Jasen was enjoying his visit although he knew he shouldn't be. He tried to get back to business.

"Follow me," Jade said, leading him into the kitchen. "I have some plates I need hung on the wall near that front window. Just one above the other is fine."

He noticed it as soon as he stepped into the kitchen. He stopped and stared at the large rooster standing on her table like a Buckingham Palace guard protecting royal treasures. The colors reminded him of the NBC peacock. He knew it was not alive but was totally amazed at its life-like features. Ceramic roosters in kitchens were common, he thought, but this was an actual rooster that had been intricately preserved and mounted by a master of his trade. He had never seen such a realistic specimen outside of true outdoorsmen's trophy rooms. The only word he could conjure was "weird."

"Weird, I mean egads," he said as he fixed on the rooster. "I don't believe I've ever seen such a, uh, well, such an unusual rooster. Is there a story behind this guy?"

"Relax, Jasen. Willie is my silent pet. Harmless, of course, *and* housebroken! No, seriously, he belonged to Momma and I guess, well, I guess I inherited him. Can't say that I'm a big damn deal rooster fan, but there's more to Willie than meets the eye, so to speak. Maybe one day I can share the whole story with you."

Very interesting lady, mulled Jasen to himself. Beautiful. Friendly. Needy. Dead rooster for a pet. What more could a man ask for! His mind was turning triple somersaults.

They moved on to more tasks. More pictures to hang. Heavy boxes to lift onto closet shelves. A Christmas tree to store in the attic through a pull-down ladder. A bookcase in a box that had to be assembled. Eighty-two pieces! Hmmm. Jasen was now making the ultimate sacrifice; he waffled a little. But she *was* beautiful. And nice. Plus, she had offered him a cold Corona Extra with a lime. How could he say no?

The time seemed to fly. He learned a lot that morning about his new neighbor Delta Jade Colton.

When she told him about her birthplace in Greenwood, Mississippi, how she got her name, and her possible remote kinship to the great Choctaw chief Greenwood LeFlore, his heart seemed to stop beating for a moment. It was too uncanny and wildly coincidental. He had not forgotten his graduate school thesis on the moral dilemma that LeFlore had faced in 1830, and he was still proud of his passionate defense of LeFlore's influence over his tribe.

He told Jade the details of the Choctaws that he had learned through his research. Jade and her mother had never talked much about her heritage or bloodline with the Choctaws or her alleged relationship to LeFlore other than her grandfather's claim. It was ancient history to her, and she had always thought that it didn't have anything to do with anything. But then she momentarily thought of her mother's friend Willie Campbell, who had helped Jean steal the rooster from Jake Luther. Didn't her mother tell her about some possible connection of the rooster and LeFlore's Malmaison? The memory was foggy, but she couldn't tell Jasen about Jake's pursuit of her and Jean and what happened in Eutaw. No, not yet. Maybe never. Try to forget, she thought.

Nevertheless, Jasen was an engaging storyteller, and she was fascinated with his recall and level of detail about Choctaw history. Jasen wanted to learn more about Jade and her mother, Jean. But it would have to wait for another day. He had to get home.

Jasen met Caitlyn in their kitchen after spending two hours helping Jade. "Where have you been? I thought you were digging in flower beds, 'connecting' with nature." She sounded a little pissed.

"Well, yes, I was," he stammered a bit. "I mean I was, but Jade next door asked me to help her hang some pictures and move some heavy boxes and stuff. Guess I got a little distracted from the yard. So what's for lunch?"

"You figure it out," she snapped and turned and walked away.

"Hmmmm," he thought silently. "Wonder what that was all about?" He opened the fridge and scanned each shelf for something to eat. He couldn't help but smile to himself thinking of the way the morning had gone. No big deal. Just helping a neighbor in need. Probably won't see her again, he guessed. In his heart, he hoped he was wrong. He couldn't get her off his mind.

Jade did not disappoint. Over the next weeks and months, she frequently asked Jasen for more "use of his muscle power" and advice on gardening and landscaping ideas. She recognized his talents with leveraging the natural and simple beauty of flowers and garden delights. It was a means to an end in Jade's mind. They bonded as their relationship seemed to be controlled by a mysterious force. Jade felt it. Jasen denied it. He admired her courage and independence as she shared unimaginable stories from her past. He fought his urge to get closer to her. Infatuation? Yes, for sure. Love thy neighbor? His emotions oscillated and he battled his fantasies and his marital commitment. He dismissed Jade's intentions as simple loneliness, a decent person just seeking a platonic friendship. Privately he was tormented with thoughts that continually tried to attack his moral filters that were now leaking like a worn-out wooden sieve.

It was late one early fall evening, just past 10:00 p.m. Jasen was stretched out on the sofa in the sun-room at the back of the house watching the ten o'clock action news. Caitlyn was in the master bath soaking in the Jacuzzi, her daily ritual for thirty minutes from 10:00 to 10:30 p.m., a religious time of recharging and undisturbed solitude for Caitlyn. It was her private time, and she attacked anyone who intruded on her nightly bath. Jasen had learned the hard way years ago. He kept his distance.

Jasen was half-dozing, half-watching boring news stories on the TV when he thought he heard a tapping against the window behind the sofa. At first, it did not register as anything. Then louder—tap, tap, tap! He opened his eyes wide and sat up, more startled than curious. He turned his head to inspect the total darkness outside his sun-room. He could not believe what he saw next. He rubbed his eyes and tried to focus. It was Jade! And there she stood smiling and waving at him. He shook any cobwebs of sleepiness from his spinning head. He looked again. She was still there, and to his shock, she was totally nude! His mouth dropped open and he gulped for air. He spun around on the sofa and stood up. He looked out the window—she was gone. Nothing, no one was there.

He pushed closer to the window and peered into the darkness. Nothing. He stared into the night for several minutes, his mind reeling and rewinding what he had seen or thought he had seen. Was he hallucinating? Dreaming? Did he really see a naked Jade in his backyard? His rational mind said no. His fantasies were out of control. He went to his front door and looked out the side window transom. Nothing unusual. All was quiet. Then, as he glanced across the street, he saw the shutters at the Chambers house quickly close. He wondered if Earl had been watching and may have seen Jade. No. No. He was imagining things. He sat back down in the sun-room and stared blankly at the TV.

Fifteen minutes later he went to the bedroom, disrobed, and climbed into bed before Caitlyn had concluded her nightly bubbly soaking. He closed his eyes and saw the naked image of Jade that kept playing over and over again on the inside of his eyelids like a slide show. Sleep finally overpowered his irrational thoughts. He drifted into another world.

It was Saturday morning again and Jasen headed over to Jade's to get the keys to the white Nissan pickup truck parked in her garage. He had asked her about the truck that morning in late March when he had hung the cuckoo clock. He had noticed it in the garage when he took some empty boxes out there to be discarded. She told him about her son, James Jr. It was his truck, her gift to him on his sixteenth birthday. She told him that James had died, and as she wiped away a tear she said that she kept the truck because it was James's. She could not sell it. She did not explain his passing and Jasen did not probe. He assumed it was something either very tragic or a severe illness or something.

Jade had asked Jasen to come over on Saturdays and drive the truck around the block a time or two, just to keep the battery charged. She said she just couldn't handle it emotionally. Seemed like an innocent enough request, so Jasen willingly obliged her. He even "borrowed" the truck a few times to haul garden supplies. The small truck had been well maintained and had less than ten thousand miles on the odometer. James Jr. had been an avid hunter and made numerous off-road trips but had never damaged the paint job. Jade proudly told Jasen how responsible James had been with his truck. It was obvious she missed him dearly.

The James Jr. emotional ballet that she had perfected became strikingly apparent to Jasen when he had passed by the spare bedroom upstairs while storing the Christmas tree in the attic. James Jr. had never lived in this house on Windermere Cove, he knew that. He stopped in the doorway to the bedroom and saw a very handsome tan Stetson cowboy hat positioned exactly between the two pillows. Beside the Stetson on the right pillow was a framed eight-by-ten picture of a young man, obviously James Jr. On the carpeted floor, just to the right side of the perfectly made-up bed covered by a wrinkle-free camouflage comforter, were two expensive-looking cowboy boots neatly arranged together in precise alignment and appearing ready to be stepped into by the bed's occupant upon arising for the day. Jasen never asked her about that apparent tribute but could only imagine the despair she must have felt when she lost her son. He thought the whole "shrine" idea was unusual if not a sign of serious unresolved grief, but it was none of his business to judge.

As they shared more and more time together, the bond grew tighter and tighter. Jasen had never met such a remarkable woman with so many nightmarish stories about courage and survival. He was stunned at the stories of her stepfather, Damian, and his perverted abuse of her. The details of Jade and Jean's frantic escape from the clutches of Big Jake Luther and Jade's brave attack on Jake was something right out of a best-selling thriller novel. The fire ant revenge concocted by Jean and a group of twelve-year-old girls against Damian was a hoot of a tale. Jade's near death experience during childbirth, the sadness of her loss of Jean, then her son—he was overwhelmed with all the bad things that had happened to such a good person. He was in awe of her strength, her resolve, and her strong sense of independence.

In turn she had found in Jasen a kind man with a good heart who seemed to have no selfish motives or lecherous attraction for her physical attributes. In fact, she sometimes marveled at his ability to deflect her flirtatious gestures, teasing, and often downright in-your-face invitations to kiss her. In part, it was why she was falling for him. The trust factor was unlike anything she had known.

They talked a lot about Calvin Caliban and his apparent stalking. Jade told Jasen that she suspected he was spying on her. He seemed to constantly be in the neighborhood. She told him that Calvin had begun to ask a lot of questions about Willie, her rooster. She said that he almost always picked him up and inspected him head to toe every time when he visited. The inspector—"hey, that's what we do, we inspect things"—Calvin. She felt he was obsessed with it for some reason. For a fleeting moment she wondered then just as quickly dismissed the notion that somehow there might be a connection between Jake Luther and Calvin. It was farfetched. It had been over thirty years. Just a creepy guy. She and Jasen began to lay a plan for Calvin. And as far as spying, the Chamberses were probably not missing anything either. The colonel needed a dose of his own "army intelligence"!

Thanksgiving came and went, and soon Windermere Cove began to come alive with Christmas wreaths on windows, bright red ribbons on mailboxes at the street, twinkling lights on evergreen arborvitae trees and sometimes lining the leafless limbs of small deciduous trees, and windows filled with Christmas trees bursting with bright white and sometimes multicolored lights and ornaments. The residents of Windermere Cove really got into the deck the halls mentality. The quaint neighborhood was magical, charming, and festive.

Jasen continued to get mixed signals from Jade. Weeks would go by and he would not even see her coming and going. He secretly fantasized about a new life with Jade. He did not know how to confront Caitlyn. He tried to convince himself that nothing good could come of leaving his wife for his next door neighbor. Duh! He felt a little stupid. Life must go on. It was all about choices. He had made his years ago. The love was no longer there. He was silently tormented. Deal with it. Move on. Besides, Jade was probably happy with her independence. He needed to shake his infatuation and get on with his life.

It was 10:00 p.m. and Jasen was making his nightly rounds to unplug the Christmas lights adorning the trees that bordered his house and Jade's. As he bent down to unplug the extension cord, he heard a familiar voice.

"Hey! Jasen," Jade called out in almost a whisper. She was standing in the open doorway of her side garage door.

He turned toward the voice, not sure what he would see. She was leaning against the door frame, smiling "her" smile, and with her right index finger motioned for him to come over to her. She was barefooted, dressed in a loose tank top and blue jeans. Even in the cool night's darkness she possessed a radiance of simple, natural beauty.

He walked over to her and spoke. "What in the world are you doing?" Jasen, looking down, suddenly became aware that he was in his socks and walking across a soaking wet lawn.

"What the heck," he shrugged to himself.

She took him by the arm and gently pulled him into her garage. They stopped in front of the Nissan truck.

"Haven't seen you for a while, Jade," he said with a sad puppy dog face, but then he beamed with a wide grin. "It's good to see you."

They stared into each other's eyes for what seemed like minutes. Neither spoke. Then she pulled him to her, taking charge of the moment, and her face reached for his lips. It was a quick and feather-soft kiss on his lips, cooled by the November night air. Then, like a single frame in a romantic movie, it was over.

"You had better get back next door, sweetie." She pushed away from him. "I just wanted to see those soft brown eyes of yours again. We'll talk soon."

She took his hand again and guided him out the side door, then shut and locked it behind him. The garage light went off, and as Jasen looked back at the garage, he scanned the area to see what truck had hit him. It was a stunned moment, and he turned and walked to his house looking down at his soggy socks.

"Which Jade was that?" he asked himself, or was he hallucinating again? He thought about the naked vision again. He had never asked her about that. He still thought he had imagined it. Caitlyn was soaking in her Jacuzzi, and he sat down in the den, not sure if he was excited or perhaps going crazy. He had to sort out his life. He had to make sense of what might be next. He had to make a choice. But alas, tomorrow is another day! He retreated to his bed. Come, sweet sleep, come. He closed his weary eyes and drifted into his fantasy.

CHAPTER SIXTEEN

Jean

Atlanta, Georgia
1967

After Jade's twelfth birthday and her mother's near death experience at the choking clutches of Damian Winters, mother and daughter formed an unbreakable alliance. Damian was a wolf in the proverbial sheep's clothing and Jean and Jade had prevailed, just as they had in Eutaw, Alabama. They have never heard any reports about Jake Luther's death, and fortunately no one had followed them or traced their whereabouts until Damian resurfaced.

Jean had driven down to the local police precinct just off Peachtree and filed assault charges against Damian, who was spending time in the hospital under police guard as he recovered from those nasty fire ant stings. She was told that he had spent a day in intensive care.

"Really a strange but fortuitous thing," Jean had told the police sergeant taking down her story. "I guess he was so freaked out when my daughter defended me and saved me from a sure death that as he ran like a whipped, cowardly dog down the front walk, he stumbled and fell right into that ant hill. My, my. Such a shame. But maybe it was just long overdue justice. Mr. Winters is a very sick and twisted man, Sergeant, make no mistake." She shared for the first time with anyone what she had told her friend Juanita about the disturbing sexual assaults on her daughter. It was difficult for her to relive.

"So why didn't you report that to the authorities in Jackson, Mississippi, Ms. Winters?" the policeman pressed, assuming this should have been a no-brainer.

"I don't know, Sergeant. That was six years ago. I had already fled from my home in Greenwood from a monster—my despicable, vicious boss. The things he did to me are unspeakable. You are not a woman. I don't think you can understand. I just wanted to protect Jade. In Jackson, all I could think about was getting as far away from my horrible husband as I could. I had to save my daughter from that animal." She could not tell him about nearly running down Jake with her car and then his attacking her and Jade's courageous defense of her, especially if she had killed him, and about the stolen rooster and the KKK and about her other demons. Best not to open that can of slimy worms.

"Just take care of Damian," she urged him. "I don't want to ever see him in my life again."

The Georgia judicial process was slow, bureaucratic, and frustrating but eventually punished Damian Winters with eight to ten years at the medium-security United States Penitentiary in Atlanta. He was eligible for parole after three years. Jean thought the punishment did not fit the crime, but was comforted to know that Damian would be permanently recorded as a sexual offender. She filed for an official divorce before his trial and took back her maiden name, LeFlore. Jade had been a brave and credible supporter of her mother throughout the pretrial and trial. She was allowed to testify about Damian's abuse, and Jean marveled at her composure and courage as she recounted detail after detail. It was a gut-wrenching experience for Jean. Jade was mature beyond her twelve years. It was a Thelma and Louise time of cementing their bond and their determination to overcome all odds.

Six years later Jade graduated from Gwinnett County High School and told Jean that she and James Mitchell were getting married. She was just eighteen. Jean knew that they had maintained a very romantic correspondence but was not convinced that either of them had grasped the true concept of unconditional, unselfish love. Jean also did not know about James's drinking habits. She tried to compare her past mistakes as a two-time loser when it came to picking men to Jade's choices. Eddie was only interested in her body. As for Damian, it turned out he was only interested in Jade.

Now her only child seemed to be following in her footsteps. Another potentially bad choice along life's unpredictable journey. The odds were stacked against her, Jean concluded, knowing that 70 to 80 percent of men tended to be jerks. Was Jade picking a winner or another loser? How could you be sure? And Jade was much too young in years but much, much older in experiences. But she knew that Jade would be a survivor, not matter how the marriage turned out. Her remote Mississippi Choctaw lineage was her strength. She had grown up taming lions.

Jean had resolved to never remarry, after her disasters with Eddie and Damian. For the next ten years, she devoted her life to "being there" for Jade. She agonized over Jade's challenges with her young and misfit husband, James. The split-up was not unexpected. Babysitting James Jr. became an important and cherished piece of her otherwise boring life. She had several lady friends from work at Bell South, and they all played bunko together twice a month.

There were days when she thought about her horrible moments with Big Jake Luther. She could not shake her nagging curiosity about his fate back in Eutaw. Her heart seemed to palpitate every time she saw a red pickup truck. Was he dead? What if he had survived Jade's heroic attack? Would he continue to track her?

She had held on to the mysterious rooster and named him Willie in honor of her friend from the Cotton Exchange in Greenwood. What was so special about him? Was that the reason Jake had tracked her to Jackson? Would his pursuit be relentless? If he was still alive, then her life was still in danger. A lot of time had gone by. Nothing bad had happened, and Jean tried to reassure herself that it was only her imagination haunting her, trying to triumph over her. Jake was dead. She was safe. Jade was safe. Live your days in peace, Jean, she consoled herself. But, what about the rooster? She had to know his secret.

It had been five years since Jade and James Jr. had left James Sr. Jade and her son were finding that life was a struggle for a single mother raising a stubborn but gentle-hearted son, but with Jean's help they had settled into a modest lifestyle and were getting by without a husband or father. Jean was proud of her daughter's perseverance and independent strength. Jade was a constant reminder of her own victories over fiends, devils, and injustices.

It was approaching dusk on a crisp November evening. Jean had lived alone for over twenty-five years and had fallen into a predictable behavior of following her same route home from work, stopping off at the local supermarket near her small house in northeast Atlanta, and settling into another lonely meal and evening in front of the television before retiring to bed by 10:00 p.m

As she left the congested parking lot of the supermarket after picking up a still-warm rotisserie chicken for a quick supper, Jean almost unconsciously registered the image of a very large fire engine-red four-door pickup truck that pulled out of a parking space and quickly accelerated to catch up to within five car lengths of her Chevy Malibu. For a fleeting second, visions of Jake Luther's red truck flooded her memory banks. Just as quickly, she shrugged and dismissed any connection. Jake had an old truck. This was a new shiny red pickup, and a much larger one. And besides, she knew he was dead. She glanced in the rearview mirror and saw the truck closing the gap. She silently laughed at her momentary paranoia.

The last few miles between the supermarket and Jean's home demanded keen attention to the curves and bends in the winding road and deliberate slowing before the final S-curve that hugged the top edge of a steep ravine. As she approached the final leg of her route home, she noticed that the truck was following closer than she liked.

The fool! His lights were on high beam and beginning to annoy her. Jean slowed and started to act a little passive-aggressive, hoping to return the unwelcomed annoyance.

Then, thoughts of road rage maniacs and their unfortunate victims began to circle her logical and rational analysis of what was happening. She picked up her speed and waved her right hand back and forth across the rearview mirror, hoping to alert the rude driver behind her of the bright beams. The truck continued to follow closely and was now within a few feet of her rear bumper. Jean considered slamming on her brakes but thought better of it.

As they approached the first snake-like curve of the now dark and unpopulated stretch of the county road, Jean was caught off guard as the truck slammed into the rear bumper of her Malibu. She had a vise-like grip on the steering wheel but was propelled forward and her head nearly hit the front windshield. In a contrecoup reaction, her head reversed directions and hyperextended above the back of the driver's seat. The split second forward-then-backward jerking of her head sent stabbing pains down both sides of her neck and she reflexively grabbed the back of her neck with her left hand, her right hand still gripping the steering wheel. The pain sent electrifying, needle-sharp impulses down both of her arms all the way to her fingertips.

The Chevy lurched ahead and began to swerve to the left. Jean reacted just in time to avert what surely would have been a fatal head-on collision with an approaching car and corrected the direction, steering back to her side of the narrow road. Her instincts were now on surviving. It was obviously a deliberate assault by the pursuing red truck.

As the next curve filled the headlight-illuminated roadway, the red truck sped up and again slammed into her from behind. Jean had braced herself this time and had better control of the wheel. Her head did not flop as much and she was able to keep her car on the right side of the road. But panic began to slowly drain the color from Jean's face, and in the rearview mirror she caught a glance of her ashen face and dilated pupils as she tried to guess the truck's next move. She felt totally defenseless.

Stop? No, too risky. Try to outrun the truck? The tricky, dangerous curves ruled that out. Her mind raced with thoughts of who could be trying to injure or kill her. She did not have enemies, she thought.

As the two dueling vehicles sped toward the final and most treacherous S-curve, Jean tried to focus on speed control and staying just ahead of the truck in hopes of avoiding a third assault. The unknown driver had backed off a few car lengths, and Jean felt a tinge of relief. But then, as she entered the curve that followed the rim of the ravine, the red pickup suddenly accelerated and caught the tail end of the Malibu with the full force of its intimidating bulldozer-like size.

Jean was not prepared, and her car spun out of control and headed directly toward the wooden railing guarding the ravine. The large truck's momentum was too great and pushed the much lighter Chevy unmercifully into the railing. Jean was powerless to stop the car as it crashed through the railing in a wood-shattering and tire-squealing nightmare and dove off the narrow rim into the waiting jaws of the ravine. The Malibu was still spinning and had turned on its head as, moments later, it caromed into the rock-strewn, brushy bottom of the pit.

In the dark silence of the early Georgia night, the crash echoed loudly against the jagged, rocky sides of the narrow ravine, and a cloud of dust and broken brush limbs and scattering rocks mushroomed upward into the night sky. Five seconds later, the crumpled Chevy burst into flames at the rear near the gas tank, followed by an exploding array of metal, glass, and tires that flew in all directions as the car and its driver were consumed in the fiery catastrophe.

The red truck had stopped just in time at the edge of the rim, and the driver was just getting out as Jean's car burst into flames and exploded. He stood and looked down at the chaos, devilishly satisfied and grinning slightly with a snarling, turned-up lip. He calmly walked back to his truck, turned the key, and backed up into the road. No other cars passed by as he reversed directions and drove off to consider his next mission.

***

Jade and James were just settling down in their den after an unmemorable supper of leftover spaghetti, salad, and warmed-up French bread. The phone rang and Jade answered, weary and frazzled from a long day at the branch office. It was the Fulton County Sheriff's Office.

They said there had been an unfortunate accident on County Road 30. It looked as if Jean had lost control of her car on the dark road and gone over the side railing into a ravine. No other cars were involved, they said. Nothing anyone could have done. She likely died on impact. They were so sorry to have to report the tragedy. She could come down to the county coroner's office the next day to take care of legalities. That was it.

Jade was frozen in disbelief. What? No, there must be some mistake. She had just spoken to Jean before she left work. Surely a case of mistaken identity. Jade was in shock. She dropped the phone and turned to look at James, who was staring at her curiously. He saw the pallor and her gaping mouth.

"Mom!" He knew it was not good news. "Who was that? What's going on? Is it Grandma? Mom, say something!"

She walked over to James, who was now standing by the sofa. She didn't speak as she reached for him and with both arms surrounded him in a tight, loving embrace.

***

The wake was solemn and lightly attended, mostly by Jean's and Jade's friends from their offices. The LeFlores had driven over from Greenwood enveloped by an aura of fatigue and extreme grief. They had not seen their daughter often due to the long distance, but Rebecca had written to her regularly. Retired, they had settled into a boring existence in their small house on East Claiborne Street. They had never really gotten close to Jade or James Jr. Jade had always felt an emotional distance, but that day she shared their aching sadness. Jade's mother had been her closest friend, bonded tightly by their shared demons. Her grief gnawed at her soul. The pain was penetrating.

As the days after she had laid her mother to rest began to pass, Jade's grief turned to anger and suspicion. They had been pursued all of their lives. What if Jean's accident was really not an accident? Had her past caught up with her at last? It was a nagging worry that Jade could not shake. Jake. Damian. Who knows if there were others? Were unknown forces circling, stalking, like a deadly coiled serpent ready to strike again? The thought began to haunt Jade night and day.

She pressed the sheriff's office for more details about her mother's death but was reassured repeatedly that it was just an unfortunate accident on a dangerous, curved county road. Probably her mother had been speeding, they said. Jade knew better. Jean was a cautious driver who obeyed speed limits, traffic lights, stop signs, whatever. It just did not make sense. The sheriff said that the car was totaled and burned to a shell. There was just nothing to suggest more than an accident. Case closed.

Jean had left a simple will. She had little in material worth and only very modest savings. She gave instructions to use the money for James's education. Besides her meager household items, she asked that Jade keep her beloved unique cuckoo clock and Willie, her mysterious rooster, safe. Her friend Willie Campbell in Greenwood had shared myths with her of the Malmaison rooster's magical abilities. The LeFlore family was aware of their chieftain ancestor's attachment to the rooster as a good luck charm of sorts but never quite understood the colonel's fondness for it.

Jean had told Jade that that was not why she stole it from Big Jake. It was more for revenge. But, like many before her and unknown to her, she had often questioned the good versus evil side of Willie the rooster. Something deep within her subconscious had compelled her to keep Willie safe. Now the rooster was Jade's. She was now the guardian of the guardian. She wanted to trash it or burn it. It had not brought good fortune to Jean, and she saw nothing good about it. It made no sense, but it was Jean's last and most adamant request. Willie the rooster moved in with Jade and James Jr.

CHAPTER SEVENTEEN
Ariel Prospero

Caitlyn and Jasen Prospero were young but loving and responsible expectant parents-to-be. Ariel Nicole was born exactly one year after their early marriage. She was a beautiful child with features more like her father's Grecian heritage than Caitlyn's DNA line. Jasen had bonded with her the very first time he held her after her precipitous but otherwise uneventful delivery. It was a devoted father-daughter connection that would last.

Caitlyn had wanted a boy and struggled to accept the dark-haired baby girl who looked a lot more like her father than Caitlyn wanted to admit. But Caitlyn was a devoted and capable mother and did her best to disguise her disappointment. Still, outsiders sensed the disconnect. The unemotional body language spoke for itself.

Ariel grew up a "daddy's girl," no doubt about it.

By school age, Ariel's resilient persona was taking shape, and the power struggles with her mother became all too frequent. Ariel had already shown a very competitive side, especially when it came to sports and to her mismatched parents. "Strong willed" would become a well-earned descriptor and badge of honor, as her self-confidence expanded into an assertive and strongly opinionated adolescence. Like an eager, idealistic, and overenthusiastic young politician, she seemed to have an uncanny sense of engineering conformity to her ideas. She was mature beyond her chronological years.

Standing by her convictions and principles was a bad thing and a good thing for Ariel. Her friends called her rigid and stubborn. Adults called her interesting, intellectual, and ambitious. Her trust in her ideas eventually led to leadership roles in high school. Jasen called her a "born leader." He considered himself the proudest of proud fathers. To Caitlyn, Ariel was almost an adversary, competing for affection from Jasen. It wasn't healthy for a mother to resent her child, but it happened. And Ariel knew it.

By high school, Ariel's natural beauty and love for always being a true "girly girl" prompted her to enter beauty pageants. Talented and good-looking with her shiny, dark brown hair and gentle brown eyes, and brimming with self-confidence, she was a no-brainer winner whenever she competed. She was elected head cheerleader and always had to be the best of the best.

Her father introduced her to golf at age eight. Jasen was totally amazed at her natural, graceful swing. Her perfect rhythm of coiling and uncoiling her arms, hips, and legs gave her exceptional distance for a young girl. By age fourteen, Ariel had exceeded her father's medium-level golfing skills. It didn't matter. He beamed with satisfaction and pride in his baby girl.

Academically, Ariel was proud of her perfect 4.0 GPA, but golf would become her favorite venue to assert her competitiveness. She joined the high school golf team as a freshman and eventually was offered golf scholarships at five different universities. She chose Mississippi State University in Starkville. Her best friend, Teenie Marshall, was going there, and they both loved State's bulldog tradition, the charming campus, and the winning legacy of the State lady golfers.

Halfway through Ariel's senior year in high school, the Prosperos moved into the garden home on Windermere Cove. Ariel spent most of her time studying, practicing golf, cheerleading, and fostering her friendship with Teenie. Both were excellent golfers, on the cheerleading squad, good students, and interested in the same guy—Joel Burdine, the school's star quarterback. They shared the common thread of competitiveness but still managed to remain best of friends. It was a unique loyalty and friendship.

Ariel had not paid much attention to their new neighbor Jade Colton, but she had curiously observed her father's behavior and the ever-so-slight sparkle in his eyes at the mention of her name. Ariel was extremely intuitive and had made a mental note of the subtle hostility from her mother directed toward the attractive single lady next door. Caitlyn thought she had hidden her impressions well, but Ariel was becoming a master of reading body language. Eyes did not lie.

Jade had learned a lot about Ariel during casual chats mixed with Jasen's increasing visits to help Jade with handyman jobs and assorted excuses that Jade used to explore her evolving interest in the handsome and vulnerable Jasen. Jade wanted to know more about Jasen's intriguing golfing prodigy and young beauty queen daughter.

It was late spring and nearing high school graduation for Ariel. She and Jade both drove into the Cove late one afternoon at about the same time. Jade was headed to her mailbox when Ariel pulled up to the curb and parked her dark green Honda Accord just ahead of Jade's mailbox.

"Well hello, neighbor," said Jade as Ariel opened the driver's door.

"Oh, hi," Ariel responded, a little surprised that Jade was being so friendly. Usually they just waved when they saw each other.

"I guess it's about time for your graduation, Ariel, right?" Jade already knew. Jasen was excited and had shared all of Ariel's plans with Jade.

"Yes, ma'am," Ariel said. She knew her manners and was socially polished. "We graduate in two weeks, and I am *so* ready to go to college."

"I can identify with that, wanting to move out from under your parents' thumbs, be on your own, all the things young folks look forward to sooner or later." Jade had felt that way only a little. She had been so close to Jean. Leaving was more about falling in love with James, not so much about being determined to leave the parental nest. Regardless, she knew a little about Ariel's conflicts with Caitlyn. She knew Ariel was not particularly anxious to leave her dad. But it was time to do her own thing.

Keeping the conversation alive, but knowing the answer already, Jade continued, "So where will you be going to school?"

Ariel was more relaxed and a little puzzled at Jade's friendliness. "Mississippi State. I accepted a golf scholarship. My best friend Teenie and I are going to be roommates. I can't wait to finally be on my own at school. Of course I'll be home for holidays and semester breaks."

"Sounds like you have a plan, Ariel," Jade said. "I wish you and I had gotten to know each other a little better."

She didn't really know why, but Jade had developed a distant admiration for Ariel because of Jasen's shared details of the daughter who truly lit up his heart with love and pride. She just had a strange yearning to learn more about her.

"Ariel." The wheels in Jade's brain were spinning. "I'd like to have you over for dinner one night soon to celebrate your graduation and upcoming college adventure. What do you think about that? I love cooking for others, and it's quite boring always cooking for one. What do you say?"

Ariel was caught a little off guard. Her head gyrated slightly as she digested the unexpected invitation.

"Well, thank you, Jade. That's very kind of you." Ariel could not think of any excuses to reject the request. It seemed odd to her in light of their minimal encounters in the past.

"Sure. Why not? I'd love to come over for dinner. Do you have a day in mind?" Ariel had committed. No turning back.

"How about Friday week at seven? Does that work for you?" Jade seemed pleased with Ariel's acceptance.

"OK. It's a date." Ariel smiled and chuckled a bit. She turned and walked toward her house, glanced back over her shoulder, and waved. "See ya, Ms. Colton. Thanks." Out of the corner of her eye, she noticed the shutters closing across the street at the Chamberses'.

***

It was a cloudy and rainy Friday evening as Ariel headed next door for her special dinner with Jade Colton. Her dad had quizzed her quite a bit about the invitation. Silently he had tried to imagine the reason for Jade's warming up to his daughter. But he secretly loved the idea. Jade had fascinated him from the beginning. If his daughter befriended her, well, he thought, maybe he could get closer to her too. He tried to bury that thought.

Caitlyn had pooh-poohed the very idea of some crazy neighbor wanting to cook her daughter a graduation dinner. "Doesn't make any sense to me," she had snipped at Jasen's acceptance of the idea.

"Lighten up, Caitlyn," Jasen had shot back at her. "She's a nice person and just wants to be a good neighbor. Give the woman a break. Relax."

"So what makes you think she's a nice person? Caitlyn was bristling now. "She sure seems to be taking advantage of you with all of those 'help me with this, help me with that' requests. Can't you see that she is after more than your handyman skills? Don't be so naive, Jasen. I don't trust her."

Jasen was amused at Caitlyn's jealously. "Your imagination is on overdrive. I am sure Ariel and Jade will hit it off. I think it was a very kind gesture. Leave it be."

He turned and walked back to the sun-room and sat down in his recliner with his newspaper and his glass of merlot.

***

Jade was expecting her, and Ariel was prompt, her watch right on 7:00 p.m. She was just a little anxious as she was greeted at the front door.

"Ariel, come on in. I'm so happy you kept our 'date,'" Jade said, directing Ariel to her den with a motion of her hand.

"Thanks, Ms. Colton," Ariel said as she scanned the interior of the pleasantly decorated home. It felt welcoming, warm, and airy with very ample lighting. Ariel glanced into the kitchen as she passed the connector and briefly focused on the kitchen table centerpiece, Willie. Interesting, she thought.

"It's Jade. Please call me Jade."

"Oh, sorry, OK…Jade." The informality made Ariel feel more relaxed.

As she sat down on the den sofa, Ariel suddenly realized how beautiful Jade was. Maybe it was her attire or her hair. Her outfit, a crimson peplum jacket over a swingy short skirt, was quite stylish but seemed odd for a casual dinner for two females. Her below-the-shoulders auburn hair was stunning. Whatever it was, Jade would stand out in any crowd, she reasoned. Ariel's point of reference was her mother, whom she had never seen radiate like Jade. She wondered what her dad might think of Jade's appearance that night. Any man, she figured, would be guilty of staring if he saw her. But she had never thought of her dad as a guy with roving eyes. Dad, a lady chaser? No way.

"Just make yourself at home, Ariel," Jade said, playing the perfect hostess as she walked to her kitchen. "Can I get you something to drink? Iced tea? Water? Do you drink wine?"

"No, no. Nothing for me. I'll wait on dinner." Ariel was still studying the neat and orderly furnishings. "Jade, can I help you in the kitchen? I'm actually a pretty good cook," Ariel called out.

"No, no. Got it all under control. Thanks anyway," Jade responded, but just as quickly she realized that she did not. "Damn it," she muttered under her breath. She had forgotten to stop on the way home and get the salad dressing.

Untying the apron that covered her chic outfit, she walked back into the den and looked over at Ariel who was thumbing through a copy of *Southern Living* that had been left on the glass-topped coffee table.

"I can't believe it, Ariel. I have concocted a delicious Greek salad that you will absolutely love, but I forgot to stop by the supermarket and get the salad dressing. Can't have the salad without the correct dressing." Jade felt a little foolish for her forgetfulness.

"I am going to run down the Suwannee Highway to Food Way. Won't take fifteen minutes. I'm so sorry. Please forgive me. Just make yourself comfortable. But oh, I have a casserole in the oven. The timer is set so if it goes off, please be a dear and take it out. Is that OK?"

"Sure, Jade, no problem. I'll hold the fort down for you!" Corny, but Ariel was more than capable.

"OK. Great! I'll be back in a jiffy. Please help yourself to something to drink if you like." Jade grabbed her purse and keys and headed out the front door to her silver Maxima parked in her driveway.

Ariel suddenly realized that she was alone in a strange house. The anxiety was brief and she turned back to her magazine as she settled back into the left end of the soft three-cushioned sofa. Why was she looking at *Southern Living*? Boring. Didn't Jade have any *Golf Today* or *SI* or something?

She inspected the lower shelf of the end table. A few more decorating and home and garden magazines. Nothing about golf or sports. Then her gaze was drawn to a small faded leather-backed book. Curiosity won the "don't be nosey" battle, and she picked up the book and opened it. It was Jade's diary.

"What are you doing, Ariel?" her conscience demanded.

She had opened the diary to a dog-eared page. At the top of the page she read, "My 12th Birthday." Ariel read quickly, knowing that Jade would not be gone that long. She wondered to herself if what she was reading was true. It was bizarre. Jade's mother being attacked, Jade whacking the guy over the head with an iron skillet, knocking him out stone cold, giggling girls dragging the guy outside and rolling him into a fire ant hill. What in the world? This couldn't be true. Wow! This was good stuff.

She flipped the pages and briefly scanned other entries. An attack by some maniac guy in Alabama. Stabbing with scissors. Pages about a rooster. She glanced toward the kitchen. *That* rooster?? she asked herself silently. Very, very weird stuff here.

Who was this lady who called herself Jade Colton? Ariel began to feel a little uneasy, and at the same time guilt crept over her. She put the diary back exactly where she had found it. Her hands trembled ever so slightly. She got up and walked to the kitchen to check on the casserole. Ten minutes had passed. Only five minutes left on the timer. Jade would return soon.

She was startled when she heard the doorbell chime. Was Jade back already? She hadn't heard a car drive up or a door slam. Why would Jade ring the doorbell? She momentarily froze. Then the chime sounded again. She hesitated but decided she had to see who was there. Maybe Jade had forgotten her key.

She took a deep breath and walked to the front door and opened it.

CHAPTER EIGHTEEN
Stranger at the Door

Ariel tried to look cool and collected as she stood at the front door facing a stranger. She briefly wondered if she had acted wisely by opening the door. He was an older man, maybe in his late fifties or sixties, and was sporting a baseball cap with an IC RR logo, whatever that was. He wore faded blue jeans with ragged holes near one knee and a black T-shirt. She noticed that his tacky leather work boots were dirty with dried red mud along the edges of the soles. His wide brown belt was fastened by a shiny buckle adorned with a raised image of a train locomotive.

Ariel wasn't very experienced at guessing ages or practicing caution. To her, every adult looked older and suspicious. She grimaced noticeably at his scarred, pockmarked face. "Creepy," she thought, trying not to show her disgust. This guy looked as if he fell on a hornet's nest or something.

"Yes, may I help you?" She wanted to look in control.

"Oh, hi. Yes. I mean, well... is this where Jade Colton lives? Are you her daughter?"

Ariel wasn't sure how she should respond. Where was Jade? She looked up the street hoping to see Jade's Maxima rounding the corner. Nothing. She peered over the stranger's shoulders and saw the living room lights on at the Chambers house across the street. The front shutters were open. If the colonel was up to his usual snooping, she really hoped he was in his spy mode and focused on Jade's house tonight, just in case. Something just did not feel right to Ariel. Who was this creep and what did he want with Jade?

"No, no. I'm her next door neighbor. We were just about to have dinner and she had to run down to the grocery store. I'm expecting her back any minute now. How can I help?" she asked, immediately realizing that she had shared more than she should have. Hopefully he assumed others were inside.

"Well, just tell her that an old friend of hers and her mother from Mississippi came by. Can you do that? Sorry to bother you. Much obliged."

Ariel was feeling safer now that the stranger was turning to leave. She realized suddenly that she had not gotten his name. "Oh, excuse me, mister. What was your name?"

He stopped after a few steps, turned around, and took one step back toward her.

"That's not important. She'll know. Say, miss. Not trying to pry, but is Jade married? I haven't seen her in a long time. Been, ah...been away for a while. I heard that her mother passed a few years back. Sad to hear that," he said, but with a slight grin on his ugly, cratered face. Ariel did not get the impression of any real remorse or sincerity.

"Well, maybe you need to ask Jade. I'm just the neighbor." Ariel had said enough.

"Oh, OK. Thanks anyway. I'll come back later. Thanks again. G'night." He turned and walked down the driveway to the curb. Ariel watched as he stepped up into an extended cab four-door pickup truck.

"Man," Ariel said softly to herself. "That is one *red* truck!"

She hurried to close the door and watched out the side window transom as the truck circled in the cul-de-sac and headed out of Windermere Gardens. She breathed a little easier and walked into the kitchen. The oven timer was beeping so she found a potholder and took out the casserole that filled a deep crimson Pyrex dish and set it on the cooktop.

Ariel was beginning to feel that Jade should have been back by now. Where was she? It wasn't that far to the Food Way. Come on, Jade, before that nut case comes back.

Ariel had only caught a glimpse of the table centerpiece when she first came in. Now she walked over to the table and got a closer look.

"Very interesting," she mulled aloud. "A real stuffed and mounted rooster! Never heard of anyone doing that before. Must be a story connected to this bird."

Ariel couldn't even fathom a good reason for preserving and mounting a barnyard rooster. But then, he *was* a beautiful specimen. Like nothing she had ever seen—not that she had been to too many farms in her life. She was quite impressed with his strangely brilliant colors. Porcelain roosters that she had seen in kitchen shops were nowhere near this colorful. She debated with herself about asking Jade to explain the rooster's story.

Maybe she would. Maybe after she got to know her better. For now, leave the nosiness to the Chamberses.

"Uh-oh," she said, thumping her temple with her fingers. She had forgotten about reading the diary. Who's being nosey? She stopped staring at Willie and headed back to the den.

She sat down on the end cushion of the sofa and looked again under the end table where she had replaced the diary. She wished she had time to read some more. Surely that stuff could not be factual, she rationalized to herself. No way.

She heard a car door slam out front, and she stood nervously and began to wring her hands. Hopefully it was Jade. She was unaware that she was holding her breath.

The sound of a key turning in the lock was followed by the front door sweeping open.

"I'm back!" Jade announced as she closed and locked the door behind her.
Breathing again, Ariel bounded into the entry foyer and greeted Jade, who was headed into the kitchen with her Food Way sack.

"Guess it took a little longer than you thought it would, huh?" Ariel spoke with relief in voice.

"Yes, sorry, Ariel. I hope you didn't get worried. Check-out lines were long. The express line was closed. You can't get good help anymore, you know." Jade had already gotten the salad from the refrigerator and was reaching for the dinner plates.

"Are you hungry? I'm starved! Come on and let's get everything on the table. My favorite Greek salad, sesame chicken casserole, freshly snapped green beans, and Sister Schubert dinner rolls. How's that sound? Oh, and chocolate lava cake for dessert. Hope you like it."

"Sounds scrumptious. I'm starved too."

Ariel assisted with the rest of the table setup, and they both sat down and enjoyed a simple but tasty dinner together. Ariel could feel a genuine sincerity from her neighbor and loved the conversation, which was mostly about Ariel and her future plans. She somehow felt a connection and silently wished that she and Jade had met long before that night.

As Jade was serving the warmed-up lava cake, Ariel decided to tell her about the unexpected stranger in the red truck.

"Jade. I almost forgot (she hadn't) to tell you. While you were gone to get the dressing, someone rang the door bell and I stupidly opened the door without knowing who was there."

Jade looked up curiously. "Oh? Who was it?"

"Well, I'm not sure."

"Not sure? What do you mean?" Jade asked, a little more curious now.

"He didn't give me a name. Just said to tell you that he was an old friend of yours and your mom. Said he was a Mississippi friend." Ariel looked up to see Jade suddenly freeze with the cake server suspended in her right hand.

"A Mississippi friend?" The pupils of Jade's sea-green eyes were suddenly pinpoint. She sat down at the table and put the knife down.

"What did this guy look like, Ariel?"

Ariel thought she detected the faint scent of fear as Jade's warm and happy aura was replaced with a serious mask.

"Well, to be honest with you, he was a really ugly dude, a little tall, but he had these deep-pitted scars all over his face and on his arms. Either this guy had smallpox or the worst case of acne I've ever seen."

"What else?" Jade knew already who had come calling, but she was in denial.

Ariel had excellent recall. "Well, he was wearing a baseball cap with IC RR on it and a gaudy belt buckle with a train design on it."

Jade had more information than she needed. She had not seen him since her twelfth birthday party, but she could never forget Damian Winters and the horror he had brought to her and Jean's lives. Why was he here? She knew he had been in prison. Jean had told her all those years ago that Damian was out of their lives for good. What was happening? The wonderful evening of celebrating with Ariel had turned to black memories.

She tried to disguise her anxiety but couldn't. Watching her, Ariel realized she did not want to push any further. She could sense that Jade had correctly guessed the stranger's identity. Whoever the man was, it sure didn't look as if Jade would be happy to see him. Ariel struggled to change the subject.

"Dinner was wonderful, Jade. Thank you so much for this great idea. I truly enjoyed getting to know you. Dad told me that you were really a nice person, and he's right!"

"Well, the pleasure has been all mine, Ariel. I'm sorry if the stranger caused you any problem. I think he's just someone Mom knew a long time ago. Did he say if he was coming back?"

"I think he said that he would come back later. For your sake, I hope he doesn't. Really creepy looking. You don't think he's dangerous, do you, Jade?"

"No, no. Why would you think that, Ariel?"

"No reason. Just intuition, I guess. Hey, if he does come back, call my dad. He's a good protector, has a big gun, and looks pretty muscular from all his working out. Dad could handle that wimpy scar face," Ariel said, actually meaning every bit of it.

"You know, Ariel. I believe you. Your dad is quite a guy. We've become good friends. I wouldn't hesitate to ask for his help. I'll keep that in mind. But actually I'm pretty tough myself. Been down a few bumpy roads and slain a few giants over the years, sort of." Jade was feeling a surge of confidence.

"Yes. I know." It slipped out before she could retract it.

Jade looked up at Ariel. "What do you mean?"

Ariel stammered a bit and said, "I mean, yes, I can only imagine."

"Yeah. Sure. But you might be surprised to know the real Jade!" She laughed aloud, but the laugh was more serious than humorous. "Wait here," she added. "I've got something I want you to have." She headed to her bedroom.

Ariel wasn't sure what Jade might be fetching but sat back in eager anticipation.

Jade returned carrying something in her right hand. She stood a few feet from Ariel and unfolded a white T-shirt that she draped loosely across her chest. Ariel was immediately drawn to the red letters written on the front of the cotton shirt.

STRONG WOMEN

SCARE

WEAK MEN

"Ariel, I think this is perfect for you. You impress me as a very strong young lady with ambition, courage, and resolve. I want you to have this, and I hope you will wear it sometimes." Jade was gifting Ariel with one of her most treasured keepsakes from her mother.

"Let me tell you the story behind this shirt. Sure, it's just a T-shirt, but it stands for something special." Jade sat down at the kitchen table beside Ariel.

Jade continued, "Not sure if I told you, but I was born in Greenwood, Mississippi. My grandfather claimed to be a very distant relative of the last eastern Choctaw Indian chief, Greenwood LeFlore. My birth city is named after LeFlore. Anyway, before I was born, my grandfather took my mom over to Philadelphia, Mississippi, to visit the Neshoba County fair one summer. Mom was impressed because it was right in the middle of the Choctaw Indian Reservation. She saw a lot of Choctaws and remembered how beautiful the women were. Must have been an interesting trip.

"She told me about seeing this teenage boy with sandy, wavy hair perform on a stage set up in a tent. She thought he was trying to be another Elvis with all of his gyrations and fancy piano playing and jumping around. She said he was just sixteen. You probably don't know him—it was Jerry Lee Lewis, before he became well known. I never cared for his 'Great Balls of Fire' kind of rock 'n' roll, but Mom thought he was a hoot that day at the fair."

Ariel had leaned forward as Jade continued, fixated on the story.

"Sorry. Back to the T-shirt. Mom saw an Indian vendor at the fair selling these shirts, and she talked Granddad into buying her one. The Choctaw woman who sold it to her said that the saying on the shirt represented the essence of the Choctaw Nation. Strong Choctaw women basically controlled the Choctaws' destiny for hundreds of years, at least until most of them were forced by the government to relocate to Oklahoma. You may have read about the sad 'Trail of Tears.'

"The irony is that Mom's distant, distant relative, LeFlore, supposedly sold out the Choctaws to the federal government over a century and a half ago. She said that folklore around Greenwood stirred the notion that LeFlore died with extreme remorse about what he had done.

"I remember all of this because Mom had researched it many years ago, and she entertained me and my girlfriends with Choctaw tales at my twelfth birthday party. That was one day that I won't forget," Jade said, smiling at Ariel and nodding her head with emphasis.

Ariel dropped her gaze and kept her understanding of what Jade was talking about to herself. So, it *was* true, she thought.

"Well, that's the story behind the story, Ariel. You will do this shirt proud. It's yours!" Jade was pleased with her decision.

"Thank you so much, Jade. This will always be special to me too. Thank you." She embraced Jade with a polite but warm hug.

Ariel headed home replaying in her mind her visit with Jade and sorting all of the unusual and mysterious twists that the evening had taken. There was more to Jade Colton than met the eye. But she would not have traded the evening for anything. She would tell her dad all about it.

CHAPTER NINETEEN
Damian and the Colonel

It was a week after the college celebration dinner with Ariel, and Jade had treated herself to an evening out with two of her female co-workers. They had decided on dinner at Dominick's Italian Restaurant downtown and a movie afterward at Colonial Square. The chick flick *Before Sunrise* won out over the adventure/thriller/spy/tough guy stuff like *Golden Eye*, *Die Hard with a Vengeance*, *Heat*, and *Braveheart*.

Jade convinced her friends that a good love story was exactly what they needed that night. It was just as advertised, and Jade found herself privately comparing the two strangers in the movie who met by chance on a train to her relationship with her neighbor Jasen. In both the fantasy of the movie and in her own life, she was consumed by the powerful meeting of hearts and minds. She cried a few tears when the movie's lovers' brief romance had to end and wondered what fate lay ahead for her. It was just after midnight when the three finished their after-movie hot tea and left the Starbuck's in Colonial Square. She said good-bye to her friends and pointed her Maxima toward home in Windermere Gardens.

On Windermere Cove, a dark figure stepped silently around the corner and walked across the street toward 708, Jade's house. The street light in the cul-de-sac was burned out, and the street was quite dark on that moonless night save for the lights that illuminated two front porches five houses down the Cove, at the opposite end. He scanned the adjacent houses and was pleased that no one seemed to be burning late night oil.

The house directly across the street was dark, but he did not notice the front shutters that were still open.

He was dressed in black from head to toe and wore a ski mask showing only his evil-intent eyes. He saw that the house was dark and no porch light had been left on. He knew that Jade did not have pets and was not concerned about his stealthy approach being announced by a guard dog. The villainous figure first sliced her phone line on the side of the house and then went to the rear of the house and made a small cut through the patio screen door with his razor-sharp box cutter. He reached in to release the flimsy hooked lock—not intended to keep out serious intruders for sure. He knew Jade was not home. Undetected stalking was an advantage and a skill, and he had mastered it.

Damian Winters had learned much of his house invasion talents in prison while engineering and plotting his revenge to help speed the long days of incarceration. He was surprised at what he had learned from the real experts who were his inmates for so many years. His hate had become a pathological obsession that was finally coming full circle. The utter humiliation of women, yes, even children, defeating him—it was never going to happen again! He had labeled both Jean and Jade as irritating bluestocking females, but he would prevail. They weren't as smart as they thought.

His confidence and the anticipation of his impending victory surged as he easily picked the back door lock, let himself in, and went directly to the master alarm keypad to disarm the system. He had learned from a master burglar that speed was critical, and in thirty seconds he had bypassed the disarming code and silenced the steady beeping that had begun counting down to alert the monitoring company of a breach. He smiled at his precision and timing. Everything was falling into place.

He quickly scouted the interior of Jade's orderly home and removed his mask as he searched for the breaker panel box. Usually it was located in the master bedroom closet or in the laundry room. He found it in the closet behind her dresses and opened it with his gloved hand. He tripped the master switch, which shut off all power to the house.

Good, he thought. He was in complete control now as the total darkness would give him the advantage. He walked back to the front of the house, keeping his penlight pointed to the floor to avoid detection from anyone outside who might be coming by, but that was unlikely at such a late hour. He walked into her kitchen and shone the light on an object on her table.

"Well, would you look at that!" he uttered in a low, squeaky voice. "That stupid rooster just won't go away." He had tried to get Jean to junk it when they lived in Jackson. He hated it. Never understood her attachment to it. Now here it was decorating her daughter's table.

"They're both crazy bitches, I mean, they *were* both crazy bitches!" He smirked at the fear he imagined on Jean's face as she cascaded into the ravine. He was still cocky over the beauty of how he had orchestrated the crash and gotten away with murder. To him, it was well-deserved revenge. Tonight would be much easier, he assured himself.

He walked into Jade's den and rehearsed in his mind his next steps as he sat down and leaned back in the overstuffed chair out of the line of sight of Jade when she came into the room.

The house was eerily quiet. All power was off, so not even the usual hum of a refrigerator motor was audible. No clocks ticking. He tilted the tiny light beam up toward the back den wall and saw a large cuckoo clock. It had the wrong time, but he quickly saw that the pendulum was not swinging. He pushed up his sleeve and focused the light on his cheap wristwatch—12:20 a.m. He knew the movie had ended over an hour ago, and he was ready for Jade.

He panned the miniature light around the room and saw magazines and a little book under one of the end tables. He leaned over and retrieved the brown leather book and opened it. Obviously a diary judging by the dated entries, he surmised. He flipped to a flagged section and read the heading. "My 12th Birthday." He started reading and almost at once recognized Jade's recounting of his visit in Atlanta and the events that had nearly cost him his life.

He stood and cursed, "Damn her!!" then slammed the book closed and hurled it violently across the room where it smashed into a picture on the wall, shattering the glass.

He sat back down in the large chair and began to huff and puff. His scarred face had stiffened and was a fiery red. In a cartoon world, the black smoke of anger would have been pouring out of both ears. He was going to get his revenge.

Less than five minutes later he heard her car pull up in her driveway. He didn't hear a door slam immediately and wondered why she had not come right in. But then he heard the car door slam, and in less than ten seconds he heard the key being inserted into her front door lock. The door opened and he could hear the light switch in the foyer being flipped. Up, then rapidly down, and up and down. Click. Click, click, click. No lights. It was show time!

Damian sat silently in the dark den and waited for Jade to enter.

He heard drawers being opened then closed in the kitchen. Obviously a search for a flashlight or matches or anything to squelch the darkness. Then footsteps and a shadowy silhouette appeared in the arched opening to the den. He couldn't make out any detail in the pitch-black room, but he could hear heavy breathing. He decided the next move was his.

"Well, darling. Come on in. I've been expecting you."

Before he could stand or flick his tiny light on and shine it at her shocked face, a very bright beacon-like light flooded his vision, blinding him, and he could not see the shadow anymore.

A deep, masculine voice growled back at him, "Wrong, buddy. I am not your darling and you *definitely* were not expecting *me!*"

Colonel Earl Chambers had put on his army-issue night vision goggles before entering Jade's front door, and as he entered the den he could clearly see the otherwise invisible intruder. He removed his goggles but kept his military hand beacon focused directly at the startled home invader's face. In his right hand he held his prized factory-engraved Colt .45, a second generation "New Frontier" model that was trained on Damian's chest.

"Stand up and show me your hands," commanded the colonel. "And they better be empty or I won't be able to control my twitching trigger finger."

Damian, cocky and acting dumber than dirt, was slow to obey and reached deliberately to pull his .38 caliber snub nose revolver from behind his belt. Earl did not hesitate. A blast from his single-action Colt Peacemaker exploded in a thunderous echo and ripped into the big chair's armrest. The colonel had purposely fired a warning shot, missing Damian but sending a convincing message.

Damian took his hand off his gun and raised his arms. He knew it was advantage Earl and shrugged his shoulders in contempt and defiance, snarling and drooling like a cornered jackal. "Who are you and where is Jade?"

"Name's not important. Let's just say that I may be your worst nightmare come true, at least for tonight anyway." Earl needed to move the confrontation to a better light.

"First, slowly, very slowly, take that gun out of your belt and place it on the coffee table. If you even look like you want to use it, I'll blast your ugly head right off your body. Trust me. I will."

Damian reluctantly complied and looked at Earl, trying to plot a countermove.

"Now keep your arms up and cup your hands behind your head. Slowly walk toward me and toward the front door. If you're thinking of reaching for that gun, think again. Move! Now!" Earl confidently ordered.

Damian inched his way across the den, the bright beacon reflecting plenty of light to lead him toward the front door. Earl dropped in behind him, keeping enough space between the two to hopefully make a sudden move by Damian unlikely.

"And as far as Jade, she's already called the Lawrenceville PD. They may already be out there. Keep moving, buddy boy. Sorry to ruin your night. Ha!" The colonel was fully in charge.

Jade was standing near the front of her Maxima as Damian exited her house with Earl Chambers a few steps behind, his .45 still cocked and ready if Damian was stupid enough to try anything. Damian kept his hands cupped behind his head as he glared at Jade with a look that could kill. Jade returned the glare, relieved to see that the colonel was OK and seemingly in control.

Damian looked back at Earl just as the elderly colonel was stepping off the front stoop to navigate the last two steps. Unexpectedly, Earl stumbled forward and fell to the walkway. He fell on one knee and felt a loud crack and jarring, searing pain as patellar bone collided with concrete. The Colt and the light flew from his hands as he tried to soften his fall with his hands.

Damian was prepared for his chance, and as he saw Earl tumble, he quickly reached into his jacket pocket for his box cutter. Taking two steps toward Jade, he grabbed her arm and twisted it behind her back. He was now behind her with the razor-sharp blade at her throat.

Stunned, Earl looked up to see that Damian had gained the advantage and that the sudden turn of the tense events of the night had left him defenseless. Jade, too, had been caught totally off guard.

"OK, Mister Whoever-You-Are." Damian was cocky and maxed out on adrenalin. "It looks like I'm going to ruin *your* night instead of the other way around. You just sit back and don't try to get up. I also suggest you take that fancy gun and throw it over in the yard. Do it! Unless you want to see this little lady's throat slit and her blood spewing everywhere! Throw it!"

The wheels were turning in Earl's head, but he didn't have an answer to the box cutter that was pressed against Jade's throat. He did as instructed, gingerly flipping the .45 into the grass.

"Look, fella," Earl tried to reason with him. "You won't get away with this. Put down the cutter and just leave before the cops get here. Nobody has to get hurt. What do you say?" The colonel was trying to use his best negotiation skills. But Damian wasn't buying it.

"Shut up, old man! I came here with one goal. This beautiful woman has to die, and she knows why. She and her mother made the last twenty-five years of my life a living hell. Her mother had an 'unfortunate' fatal accident, and now it's her turn. It looks like you'll have to be collateral damage. Too bad you stuck your nose into this personal matter. Should have minded your own business."

Jade could feel the sharp razor blade cutting slightly into the tender skin of her neck. Damian's imprisonment had turned him into a dangerous psychopath and she knew that he would do what he said. Her twelfth birthday memories had become her newest nightmare. She could not believe what was happening. She was frozen glacier stiff in fear and paralysis and could see no escape. And now the colonel was likely going to die too.

Damian held the box cutter tightly against Jade's throat and began to push her toward Earl. A trickle of blood running down her neck was visible below the cutter's edge.

"Move!" he demanded as he pushed her.

He slowly maneuvered her over to where Earl had thrown his Colt .45 in the grass. Still holding the box cutter against Jade's larynx, he reminded her that with one false move, he would slit her throat. He kneeled beside the revolver, and as he carefully watched the elderly Earl, he picked it up and in a lightning-fast move shoved Jade forcefully in Earl's direction.

Jade, grabbing her neck and fearing he had slashed her, stumbled slightly as she stopped near the colonel. She looked down at the blood on her hand.

With the revolver aimed at them, Damian ordered Jade to kneel beside Earl. Damian was now the prepared and determined executioner. He stood and looked at their terrified faces, the lambs before the slaughter.

"I had something in mind that was slower and more painful for you, Jade. Guess a bullet in your brain will have to do. Sorry, darling. And, oh, thanks for your 'play time' with me back in Jackson." He cocked the .45 and aimed it directly between her eyes. He grinned, showing his yellowing teeth and the ugly gap between his decayed central incisors. "You can beg for mercy if you—"

Suddenly an explosive cracking interrupted him. His head jerked violently to his left and the lights immediately went out in his head. He toppled to the ground, knocked completely unconscious, the Colt falling from his hand. The full force of the bulky head of a 460-cc oversized Callaway Great Big Bertha golf driver had found its target against his right temple. Behind him, Jade and Earl heard the golf club's owner shout, "*Fore!*"

It was Ariel!

Jade and Earl were safe.

At that instant, Jade saw the flashing blue lights of a police cruiser speeding around the corner and jerking to a quick stop in front of her house. Two officers flew out of the doors, hands touching their unsnapped but still holstered service revolvers, and charged up to the scene.

"Glad to see you boys," Earl quipped as he rose to his feet, acting as if the cavalry had just saved the surrounded wagon train. "From what Ms. Colton here told me, the guy on the ground may have been stalking her. I saw him break into her house tonight. I knew she was gone—I, ahem, I keep up with what's going on in my neighborhood. Anyway, when she returned home, I intercepted her before she stumbled into an ambush. I don't know all of the details, but I think Ms. Colton knows this perp. Right, Jade?"

"Yes. I do. He's an ex-con, a sexual predator, and was married to my mom a long time ago. He needs to go back to jail. He's extremely dangerous. He came here to kill me. My neighbor here, Colonel Chambers, had him corralled, but he got the jump on us."

As one of the officers handcuffed the still-unconscious Damian, the other officer made some quick notes of the night's events. He was amazed at the details of Earl's confrontation in Jade's dark den, the box cutter held to Jade's throat, and the heroic climax delivered by young Ariel. A lot of details to unravel. He told them that they would all have to come down to headquarters the next day to file formal complaints and give statements. Both officers worked together to pick Damian up by his arms and feet and maneuver him into their cruiser.

Jade walked over to Ariel who was now grinning and leaning proudly on her golf club as the police car circled the cul-de-sac and then exited the Cove. She looked at Earl and they both suddenly realized that Ariel had saved them from a sure death at the hands of Damian. She gave Ariel a giant hug and stepped back from her as she noticed Ariel's white T-shirt. The red letters were easy to read even in the dark—"Strong Women Scare Weak Men."

"Well, I am suddenly extremely grateful for my neighbors! You two are unbelievable! I don't know what to say." Jade was happy but exhausted. "Thank you, both of you."

For all of the complaining about the colonel's snooping, she had no regrets now that he was a sincere guardian and protector of Windermere Gardens. All she could think of was what if Earl had not been up at midnight and spied on the dark, shadowy intruder? She did not want to go there. And Ariel? Where did she come from, seemingly out of nowhere?

Ariel explained that she had heard the gunshot as she was not asleep yet and her upstairs bedroom was on Jade's side. Her parents' bedroom was on the opposite side of the house and they had not awakened. Ariel said that from her bedroom window she had seen the tense events unfolding and decided to help. All she had as a weapon was her golf club and a mean, mean swing! It had worked to perfection.

As Ariel headed back to her house, Jade asked her to not tell her dad about the night's events until she could talk to him.

"No problem. Good night, you two," Ariel said as she smiled and disappeared into her house.

"Colonel, what can I say?" Jade walked up to him and put her arms around him in a warm and heartfelt embrace. He patted her on the back like a grandfather might do with his grandchild.

"I told you that I would watch out for you, remember? The colonel always keeps his word. Now come on. Let's get those lights of yours back on."

They walked into her house with the bright army beacon light showing them the way.

"Say, Jade. It's been a pretty rough night. How would you like to stay over with me and Rose tonight? Until your nerves settle down."

Jade looked at him with a childlike smile and softly said, "I'd like that. Thanks."

CHAPTER TWENTY

Jade and Calvin

Damian, Jade's nightmare that refused to end, was charged, arraigned, tried, and convicted for his newest crimes of breaking and entering, aggravated assault with a deadly weapon, and attempted premeditated murder. There was not enough evidence to try him for Jean's death. He was "rewarded" with another fifteen to twenty years in the federal prison in Atlanta, and Jade began to feel a little safer. The day after the bizarre events, she shared her near miss encounter with Jasen and revealed Ariel's role in preventing a horrifying crime.

To Jasen, it was like something out of a murder mystery novel, too terrifying to be real. Caitlyn would never believe that Ariel had actually prevented a double murder and had shown the courage of a lioness protecting her cubs. Jasen decided not to tell her for now. She was already much too suspicious and jealous of their neighbor Jade. He and Ariel would keep it to themselves. He privately beamed with pride at his brave daughter's actions.

Jade told him that Damian had indirectly implied that he had been responsible for Jean's accident on County Road 30 near Atlanta eight years ago. Now she wished that she could prove it. Damian needed to be confined for the rest of his life. Thank God for Earl Chambers and for Ariel and her golf swing!

In a strange and ironic twist of her imagined versus real pursuers, it was beginning to look as if Jake Luther was indeed dead and would not be returning from his Eutaw grave to extract his own revenge and reclaim the rooster that Jean had stolen. Jade felt less motivated to part with Willie knowing Jean would not be happy if she disregarded her mother's wishes even if the Greenwood connection to Chief LeFlore's rooster now seemed lost in the very, very distant past.

Jade had not seen Calvin Caliban for several months. She had resolved her house construction issues with the builder, Eastman, and was relieved that Calvin had no "excuse" for visiting or, she thought, stalking her. With Damian back in his orange jumpsuit, Jade felt renewed and speculated on the course change that her life seemed to have taken. She settled into her recliner on a rainy Friday night, alone with her diary and a cold bottle of Corona Extra with a slice of lime squeezed into the neck of the bottle.

After her harrowing childhood, a failed marriage, and the loss of James Jr. and then her mother, Jade found a new sense of courage and connection in her friendship with Ariel and her father, Jasen. Men in her life had tormented her, exploited her, abused her, and generally drained her dust dry down to the bone marrow of any interest in new relationships with men. Her presumed and self-judged punishment for her "crimes" was not deserved. She was guilty only of surviving. Prevailing. Having faith in herself. Persevering. Protecting lives—her own and Jean's. Having a strong mind and a good heart. Conquering the demons in her life. She *was* strong. Mississippi Delta, Mississippi Choctaw woman strong. Now she had reached a new crossroad on her undulating and unpredictable life's journey, an uncharted fork in the road, and she would have to choose again.

Her mind fixed on her neighbor. Jasen Prospero was different. He was more than a friend. She had sensed his vulnerability and had tugged at defining their relationship. She was in denial over her flirtatious come-ons and battled to rein in her true feelings. He had something intangible but very real to Jade. He was genuine. He was attractive. He was kind. He was very intelligent. He was sincere. He was trusting. He was reliable, and he understood her as no one else ever had. He had not judged her. He had accepted her as is and admired her endurance. He was special. But…he was *not* hers. He was a married man. She could not be a home wrecker. He was forbidden.

Jade closed her eyes, leaned back in her recliner, and drifted off to a faraway place, free from monsters and haunting memories, and held his hand as they lay in the white sand under a cloudless pastel-blue sky and a warm tropical sun, refreshed by a gentle ocean breeze.

Ding dong! The doorbell chimes were loud as they burst the fantasy bubble in her head, and she quickly sat up in her recliner, realizing that she was no longer with Jasen and her dream. The bell chimed again as she sat her Corona down and headed to her foyer. To her dismay, she saw Calvin Caliban with his nose pressed against the side transom peering in at her.

"What is *he* doing here?" she said with dread.

He saw her coming and waved like a kid, grinning like the classic Cheshire cat. She opened the door not knowing what to expect next.

As he took a step into her foyer before Jade could invite him in, Calvin spoke before she could.

"Evening, Ms. Colton. Bet you're surprised to see me after all this time."

"If you only knew," Jade mumbled under her breath. "Well, good evening, Calvin, I mean Cal," Jade responded, trying bravely to hide her disapproval. "What brings you out on this rainy night?"

"Well, I realized just two days ago that I had never circled back over here to verify the outcome of all of your building issues. I bugged that idiot

Eastman day and night to fix everything for you. I guess when I didn't hear from you, I just assumed that all was well. But, hey, a good home inspector, well…"

"Yes, I know. You inspect things." Jade was weary of his corny lines. "I assure you, Cal, everything was repaired to my satisfaction. I appreciate your concern, though. Was there anything else?" She noticed that his wet shoes had tracked dirt across her hardwood floor and she opened the door wider hoping he would take the hint and leave.

"OK, yes, actually there is something else." He took a few more steps past her and stopped at the kitchen entrance. "It's about that pet of yours, that rooster there on your table," he said, pointing to Willie. "Willie, I believe that's what you named him, if I recall."

"Yes, good memory," Jade responded, wondering where this conversation was going. She recalled her sharing with Jasen the strange obsession that Cal seemed to have about Willie.

"So, Jade, I forgot if I ever asked you where you obtained the bird?"

"I told you that it belonged to my mother, so I just kept it after she died. I don't know where she got it," she lied. "What is this about, Cal? Why are you so interested in Willie? You always stare at him and seem mesmerized by him. What's the big deal?"

Jade was growing more and more suspicious by the second that Cal Caliban might not be who he really claimed to be. Was he some kind of picaro, a master of deception, disguising his real intentions? Something foul was happening related to her fowl, and Jade felt the hair on her arms tingle with electricity and bristle to attention.

Cal walked over to Willie and leaned to pick him up.

"Stop!" Jade almost shouted at him. "I told you before that he's a rare and delicate antique. Please, if you don't mind, put him down, gently."

He disregarded her request and cradled the bird in both arms.

"Relax, Jade. I won't drop him." He proceeded to inspect the bird as if he was looking for something. He looked back up at Jade and asked, "What will you take for him? I think he is fantastic! What do you think? Name your price."

"Cal, he's not for sale. Please, put him back. I think it's time for you to go. I really have a lot to do, if you don't mind." Jade was getting edgy and needed the visit to end.

He looked at her with a smirk and then sighed. "Are you positive? I can make you a very attractive offer. Come on, I really would like to buy him."

Jade walked over to him, took Willie from his hands, and placed him back on her table. Cal didn't resist as he watched her strangely protective behavior. It was telling him all he needed to know.

"Well, can't say I didn't try. Look, if you change your mind, you have my number. I sure don't get your attachment to that thing. OK, well, I guess I'll be going. Good night, Jade."

He turned and headed to the front door. Jade followed and put her hand on the door handle as Cal smiled at her and took a step over the threshold then stopped. Instantly she sensed that he was not done.

He dropped his smile and his face suddenly tightened into a determined seriousness. He bolted past her and charged back into the kitchen, snatched Willie off the table, and turned and ran past Jade and out the front door.

Jade stood frozen, not having guessed at his intentions. Her mouth gaped open as he ran past her, Willie clutched in his arms, down her porch, a thief on the run.

Then, just as he turned to head down the driveway, his black getaway sedan in sight, he suddenly collided with an unexpected object.

Jasen Prospero, who had serendipitously headed over to Jade's to ask a favor, saw the fleeing Caliban bound from Jade's porch carrying Jade's rooster. He reacted on instinct and quickly intercepted him, using his muscular frame as a barrier. Caliban bounced off the taller man like a basketball off a backboard. He was caught completely off guard and stumbled a little but then regained his footing. He looked up at Jasen and weighed his next move.

"Hold it right there, Mr. Caliban. What's the rush? Isn't that Ms. Colton's rooster you're carrying there?" Jasen's well-conditioned physique was convincingly intimidating to the smaller Caliban. He knew that Jasen held the upper hand if a fistfight were to explode.

By now Jade had followed Cal cautiously out the door, not sure if he had intended only to steal Willie or if he had a weapon that he would turn on her if she pursued him. She was pleasantly surprised to see Cal confronted by Jasen. "Talk about dumb luck," she said to herself.

Cal looked at Jade standing on her front stoop and then back at Jasen, who now stood defiantly with his hands on his hips. Outnumbered, he hurled the rooster at Jasen and leaped past him while Jasen was distracted, luckily catching the bird in midair and keeping it from crashing onto the concrete driveway and being damaged. Caliban climbed quickly into his black sedan, and with tires squealing, he sped off into the darkness, sans Willie.

Jasen looked at Jade. She was smiling in her special way, pleased at the sight of her latest rescuer.

"What was that all about?" Jasen asked, but guessing that he already knew the answer.

"Just like we talked about, Jasen. Caliban is a nut case. A man with a rooster fetish? Something to do with the past? Who knows? I know this: I have about had it with that damn rooster. What can be so important about a stuffed chicken? I think I've been permanently cursed by that thing. Why did Mom insist I keep him? I hope that's the last we see of Cal. He tucked tail and ran like a scalded cat. Thanks for showing up just in time. I think I need to put you, Ariel, and Earl on my permanent payroll as bodyguards!"

"Jade, I think you're overly paranoid about Caliban. He's just an extreme eccentric or the cleverest picaro I've ever encountered. He won't be back. Just don't open the door if he ever does show up again."

"I hope you're right. Come on in. I think I need a beer! How about you?" Jade led the way inside, feeling the need to unravel mysteries and look for answers to their secret desires.

CHAPTER TWENTY-ONE
The Winter Storm Reprieve

A lifetime of nightmares had rushed from Jade's head as she looked with horror at Jasen standing over the dead body now slumped by the foot of her bed. They stared at each other realizing that some powerful and evil force had invaded their world of secrets and hopes for a new beginning. She walked toward him and fell silently into his arms, weeping openly. That night they had conquered an unknown enemy and she had again cheated death. It was all so surreal.

Jasen held her gently and whispered that everything would be OK. He wasn't convincing himself but knew he must find a way.

He knelt down beside the attacker and was now positive that he was dead. Jade turned on the lamp on the bedside table.

"Who do you think he is?" Jade barely managed in a shaky voice made painfully scratchy from the stomach acid regurgitated from her retching.

Jasen rolled the large man on his side and reached into his back pocket for a billfold. There was none. He checked the other pockets. Nothing except for what looked like a car key. Jasen took the key and put it in his own trouser pocket.

Jade took a long look at the face, now ghostly pale and drained of any life.

"It's been a long, long time, Jasen, but I can see a strong resemblance to Jake Luther. But, it's *not* Jake."

"You mean *the* Jake Luther from the Alabama ordeal you told me about? That's been over thirty years. His son or some other kin maybe?" Jasen was more than curious.

"Somehow, Jade, I think this attack may be about that damn rooster and Jake Luther. I don't think this has anything to do with that idiot Caliban. But just like Caliban, I think that is what this guy was after. And I think it's more than just about stealing a pet stuffed rooster. There's something very value and very sinister about that bird. Something that would cause people to kill. We have to figure this out."

She didn't say it, but Jasen knew her thoughts. The rooster was her curse. She was on a collision course with death if she did not get rid of Willie.

"Let's get out of this room." He took her hand and they stepped over the body and escaped from the freakish scene into the den.

She sat on the sofa and tucked her feet under her and held one of the sofa pillows tightly to her chest with both arms. "Jasen," she said, "We have to call the police. It's the right thing to do. We can't just pretend that this didn't happen. There's a dead man in my bedroom, for God's sake! What are we going to do!?"

They stared at each other with that "eyes glazed over" look. They were still in shock over the attack and the body in the bedroom.

Jasen glanced toward the window then back at Jade. He took a deep breath and re-focused. "For one thing, we would have to explain why a total stranger broke in and tried to kill us. That would mean trying to make the rooster mystery believable. Heck, *we* don't even understand it. Sure, the stabbing was self-defense. I think we could convince anyone of that. But, how do we explain this bizarre story to Caitlyn or Ariel?

How do I explain being in your bedroom in the middle of the night and being attacked by a stranger with a knife? Jade, I have to keep our affair a secret. We can't call the police. We have to find another way."

Jade wrestled with her thoughts trying to make the nightmare go away. Jasen was looking for a solution, and Jade could not counter his argument.

He walked over to the side window and stared out at the snow coming down. The ground was beginning to be blanketed a beautiful white.

He gazed next door at an empty lot where construction materials were stacked near the front of the property. A partially snow-covered clear polyethylene tarp was wrapped around the supplies. During the past week workers had already prepared the foundation of the new home under construction. Plumbing stubs were in place and six to eight inches of gray construction gravel had been poured to form the base of the foundation. The next step would be for cement trucks to come and pour an eight-inch-thick concrete slab on top of the gravel. They built these homes on slabs. No crawl space. But they would have to wait now until the snow melted and temperatures thawed before pouring the cement.

Then suddenly a light came on in his head.

"Jade!" he blurted out. "I've got an idea."

"What are you thinking, Jasen?" She had that special twinkle in her eye and she smiled in her special way. "You've figured it out, haven't you?"

"It may sound like something straight out of Alfred Hitchcock, but I've got a plan. Trust me on this, Jade. Get me an old sheet, a shower curtain, or something to wrap him in. I'll be right back. I need some warmer clothes and things from my house."

"You're leaving me here alone with a dead body in my bedroom? I don't think so!"

"Jade, I'll be right back. Come on, everything will be OK." He knew she was strong enough. Her past was testimony by itself.

Jasen put on the rest of his clothes, threw on his jacket, and left out her back door. He fleetingly thought about the snooping and spying from the Chamberses across the street. But the hour was late. They couldn't be up.

The snow was coming down silently but briskly. The flakes were large but had not accumulated more than an inch so far. The heaviest snow was due later in the night. Thank goodness, he thought. It would make the work ahead easier.

He was back in five minutes with a warmer coat, a hat and gloves, and a shovel.

She had changed into sweats while he was gone and had put on her running shoes. She had assumed that Jasen would need her help. She was right, as usual.

"Jasen, I'm still not comfortable with not calling the police. Are you absolutely sure about this? It scares the hell out of me."

"Trust me, Jade. This will work. No one will ever know what happened tonight but me and you. It will be like this never happened. Please, trust me."

"I'm trying. I'm trying, Jasen." She had learned from years of adversity to not trust anyone. She wanted badly to believe and trust him.

"You're going to bury him under that foundation gravel next door, aren't you? Interesting plan, except…Well, what do we do with his car? You know he didn't walk here. You found his car key, right?"

"I've thought about that too. He probably parked on another street or at the park around the corner. I know the perfect spot to take his car, but we'll have to wait until the streets are passable in a few days. Put on your coat and gloves and come help me get him to his permanent resting place. I don't know who he is, but it seems that your past is beginning to catch up with you again, Jade. We can't leave any trace that this guy found you. He probably has friends or someone who will miss him."

In what seemed like a rehearsed synchronized event, they rolled the body onto the old shower curtain that Jade had retrieved from her bathroom closet. He was a very big man—probably 230 pounds or more. And dead weight is not that easy to lift. They struggled somewhat, mostly dragging him to the back door and onto the back patio. Jade was really pretty strong, and Jasen was glad that she seemed to be more focused and more than determined.

They managed by lifting, dragging, and pulling to get him to the lot next door. Jasen decided to dig the grave in the area that would be the master bedroom of the new house. The owner-to-be of the house had been reported by the colonel to be another unnatural blond divorcee.

How appropriate, Jasen told Jade, to put this monster under the foundation of the house of a divorcee who reportedly had sworn off of any more men in her life. Scuttlebutt got around quickly in a Colonel Chambers neighborhood. And this lady would never know that every night when she slept there would be a man buried right under her.

Jasen quipped, "Is this just too ghoulish or what? It gives me chills to think about it. I think maybe *I'm* a bad person. But I couldn't think of any other way. I'm sure this will work. This will be our secret alone."

He was able to shovel the gravel away with minimal effort. The dirt under it was a different story. The ground was nearly frozen from the cold weather over the past two weeks. The pace of his digging slowed considerably, but he knew that he must dig deep enough to cover the body completely then replace the gravel so no one would suspect anything.

He had managed a grave about two feet deep after two hours of unbelievably difficult work. The temperature was below freezing, but he was actually perspiring. His earlobes and feet were incredibly cold and numb. In spite of his gloves, he felt blisters on both hands.

Jade had stayed with him the entire time. He knew she must be freezing, but she never complained. She even offered to help dig. Jasen refused. She more or less stood guard, hoping that no one would see them. The pile of construction materials screened them somewhat from the front of the lot, and the back of the lot bordered on a wooded area. Besides, it was late and snowing. No one would be out in this miserable weather.

Finally Jasen rolled the corpse into the painfully carved out grave. He covered the plastic-wrapped bulk with hard, half-frozen dirt and carefully replaced the gray gravel—at least eight inches of it. Jasen stepped back to assure himself that the area matched the rest of the house's foundation preparation. He had had a brief but passing thought of burying the rooster with the would-be killer but had dismissed the notion. He knew the dead man had probably been sent to steal back the rooster. He had to discover the rooster's secret. Somehow, before someone else did.

After the snow melted and the temperatures improved, the cement truck would come and cover the well-hidden burial site with an eight-inch-thick layer of concrete. The fate of their unknown attacker would be permanently sealed from the world. Jasen covered the area with snow.

It was really beginning to come down now. Several inches had stacked up around them as gathering white mounds of wet, wind-driven snow. They looked at one another. Jasen smiled through frozen lips and gave her a tight, reassuring hug.

"It'll be OK now," he said.

"I know." She had found her protector, her rescuer.

They slowly trudged through the deepening blanket of snow, breathing heavily with each step, and slipped, hopefully unseen, back into the inviting haven of her den. They took off their coats, and as Jasen sat on the floor in front of the fireplace, Jade went to the kitchen and poured two glasses of white wine. Jasen was trying to get the fire going again when she came back into the room and sat down beside him and put her arm around him.

Silently she calmed herself. Safe at last, for now, she said to herself.

They sat by the fire without speaking for what seemed like an eternity. Jasen embraced her and held her hands tightly. They were getting warmer now. The events of the night had bonded their souls.

Jasen still felt confident that they could move beyond the nightmare. In his own mind he had found serenity and happiness. He no longer felt alone. He had found a soul mate.

There were many things to be worked out before Caitlyn returned from her trip. He thought briefly of his plans, but the shock of the night had not yet worn off. Tomorrow was another day.

He glanced through the den window into the darkness. The fury of the Dixie winter storm had arrived. But inside his heart Jasen was at peace. He looked down at Jade. She had fallen asleep. He thought of her childhood abuse, her harrowing escape from Jake Luther, her brave revenge against Damian, the feeble attack from Calvin, her extreme grief and sadness after Jean's passing, her failed marriage, and her son's tragic ending. Her future had to be better. He would make it better. It was now his mission, his raison d'être.

CHAPTER TWENTY-TWO

The Rooster's Secret

Six months later...

Jasen looked out the window of the Delta MD-88 as it circled slowly waiting on clearance to land at Atlanta's Hartsfield International Airport. He was coming home from a business trip. His mind was still spinning from the unexpected turn of events that had resulted from his new and unexpected situation as an unmarried person...after so many years of marriage to someone who never really seemed to know or understand him but daily voiced her suspicions about his strange behavior and blamed him for anything and everything that went wrong, even suggesting that somehow he was responsible for bad weather. She had seemed unusually jealous of other women, especially their neighbor Jade. He had not been prepared for what happened next. It had totally blindsided him.

He had four days to rehearse the story he had reconciled in his mind for Caitlyn when she returned from the insurance company convention. The snowstorm had dumped almost twelve inches across two-thirds of the state, so traveling was difficult at best. Caitlyn stayed in Mobile an extra day until the airlines were back on a more normal schedule. As was common after southern snows, the weather began to warm two days later and the snow melted faster than expected. Travel on city streets improved quickly.

Jasen and Jade had decided that they could tell absolutely no one about their near death experience or about the nameless and now buried stranger who had attacked them. Jade and Ariel's ordeal with the now incarcerated Damian was a totally unrelated matter as far as Jasen was concerned. It had nothing to do with his infidelity. This was much different and they had to keep it secret.

But Jasen had resolved to tell Caitlyn that he was going to file for divorce and move out. For a long time the parting of ways had seemed inevitable for them. Although he could easily rationalize the reasons, he knew he would struggle to have the dreaded conversation. He was prepared to tell her the day after she returned—but she dropped her own bombshell first.

"Jasen," she started the conversation as he helped her dry the dinner dishes, "I've made up my mind. I can't live a lie anymore. I'm leaving you. I want a divorce."

His mouth dropped open and his heart began to race. What?! She wanted a divorce? *She* wanted a divorce? What lie had she been living? He was stunned. He could not muster a response. All the hand-wringing while debating how he would tell her of his decision, and now she was pre-empting him! He was both shocked and relieved.

"Well?" she snapped at him. "Are you just going to stare at me? Did you hear what I said? I want a divorce."

"Yes, yes. I heard you. It's just...just..."

"Just what? Surely you aren't surprised. We've been drifting apart for years. The love is gone. The flames burned out long ago. You are miserable. I am miserable. Why torture ourselves any longer? It's time to admit it. I want more." She sounded so matter-of-fact.

"Is there someone else?" He actually didn't really care.

"What difference does it make? But yes, there is. I've been seeing a wonderful man for some time. You don't know him."

Jasen's mind was agitating with mixed emotions like an off-balance washing machine. "What are your plans then?"

"I have a lawyer to help with all the legal stuff. You need your own. I'm moving out this weekend." She turned and walked away, leaving Jasen to get his bearings.

Just like that it was over. He knew Jade would not believe it. He wondered how much difference it would make in their relationship. With the attacker buried, would all of the chaos of the past few days change how she felt about him? He hoped not. He worried that she might blame herself.

***

As the plane leveled out for its final approach and landing at Hartsfield, he relived the past six months. Ending a marriage of nearly nineteen years was a challenge he was not fully prepared for. Yet it had not been as difficult as he had imagined. He knew how far apart he and Caitlyn had drifted over the past several years. She had moved out a few days after her confession. Nearly twenty years whisked away like the changing, fickle wind. Gone.

Jasen's thoughts shifted to his and Jade's secret and the narrow escape from their most recent disaster. He still felt anxious about his decision to cover up the killing. But he knew it could not be any other way. Going to the police at this point would only makes things more complicated, even though revealing his affair with Jade had become almost a moot point.

The cement truck had come a week after the storm and permanently sealed the evidence of that night. Jasen knew that the body would never be found. The secret would never be revealed.

Jasen and Jade had taken the stranger's car to an abandoned strip-mining pit that was filled with eighty feet of water. It was fifteen miles from where they lived and very isolated from everything. Jasen felt certain that he was not seen when, with a surge of inhuman strength, he pushed the old white Ford four-door sedan into the yawning jaws of the huge rock pit. As the bulk of steel and rubber tires tipped toward the inky abyss, he noticed that the car had Mississippi plates, Carroll County. He was sure then that the killer was from the Greenwood area.

The car plunged into the dark, water-filled pit and sank quickly. Jasen and Jade had been careful to leave no fingerprints on the car. Jade had parked a half mile from the pit so that her tire treads would not be found near the scene, if anything ever happened—a very unlikely possibility, Jasen thought. He walked, then ran back to her car and hugged her when he got in beside her. Relief spread across their faces as their eyes locked together in apparent victory.

That same night Jasen and Jade spent what would be their last time together for the next six months. He had told her about Caitlyn's shocking revelation, and as he had guessed, Jade blamed herself. She felt guilt and betrayal. She was uncertain of everything now. Confusion and doubt cast their shadows on her, and she felt sporadic waves of nausea and tightness in her gut.

"What about the attacker?" she speculated. "If he was after the rooster or me or both, there are probably others out there that know. I'm targeted. I can't stay here in Lawrenceville, Jasen, I have to leave."

Escape now, she thought. Now! She saw no other options.

She was right. Others would surely trace the dead man to her house. She had to leave. Time could be running out.

Within three days, Jade had resigned from her Bell South position and flown to New York City. She moved in with a former Atlanta girlfriend who had relocated there. With good references she found a similar job in NYC. Like a blinding flash of lightning she had illuminated Jasen's life with new and intense emotions, stories of survival against impossible odds, and irresistible desire, and then like a crashing God-to-ground thunderbolt, Jade was gone. Caitlyn was gone. Jasen was alone.

For six months, Jasen drifted back and forth between thoughts about what could have been and what should have been. The divorce was finalized in three months. Days became nights and nights, days. Jade had not communicated with him at all. She ignored his calls to her cell phone. She had slammed the door on their relationship.

He faded deeply into a paralyzing melancholia haunted by regret. He needed Jade. He needed to hold her and protect her. Their lives had become irreversibly intertwined, and it was surely not happenstance that had connected them. But he did not know what Jade would do or what she wanted. So many tragedies had rocked her life like unpredictable earthquakes. So many disappointments. So many demons. Now there were real threats against her very existence, and her past was quickly becoming her present.

Jasen clung to hope. He searched for answers to end the void in his life and convince Jade that he could protect her. He had to solve the bizarre puzzle and hidden secrets from Greenwood, Mississippi. He must find redemption for Jade's tears.

Jade had given the Malmaison rooster to him before she left. She told him that she was convinced that it portended danger and was surely the cause of all of her nightmarish encounters. She asked him to hide it or destroy it. He hid it behind a garage cabinet in a large box, concealed from any casual looker.

Then the proverbial light bulb flashed on! Why had he not thought of it before? He felt so stupid. His loneliness and thoughts of Jade had preempted his rational life and had made him forget about Greenwood

LeFlore's mysterious Venezuelan trophy. Neither he nor Jade had any idea of the bird's true past, but it seemed all too apparent that the rooster held the answers to everything. If he could solve the mystery, surely he could get Jade back into his life.

He retrieved the incredibly beautiful rooster with its evil, piercing stare from his secure hiding spot. He took it out of the box and went inside and sat down at the kitchen table. He sat the rooster in the center of the table, just as Jade had. The rooster stared at him as if it was alive, taunting him. Then he thought he saw its head move.

Jasen jerked back in a defensive reflex, almost expecting the bird to attack him. He hated the very sight of roosters and had always had a special distaste for this one. His imagination was out of control. But he stared back at Willie with a laser-like gaze and wondered about the bird's secret and its connection to Jake Luther, to the man with no name, to Calvin Caliban, and to who knew what other desperados from Greenwood, Mississippi, who might be stalking them.

He picked up the rooster cautiously and slowly began to examine it in anticipation of an answer. He looked and he looked. He felt the bird for any unusual bulges, anything that did not seem right. He even held the dead rooster to his ear and listened for sounds. Ridiculous, he thought. Nothing.

"Think!" he admonished himself. Would he have to destroy the rooster to satisfy his suspicions? He was tempted. Very tempted.

Finally he turned the bird over to inspect the twelve-inch-long piece of wooden fence post on which the rooster perched. Nothing unusual, just a piece of old wood. How was the bird attached to the post? He looked for a screw or something. Nothing caught his eye.

He turned the bird back to face him and looked at Willie, muttering out loud.

"What is your secret, you creepy barnyard creature? What are you protecting? Don't let this end here. Speak to me, for God's sake. Crow or something! Tell me! Speak!"

Willie was statue-of-stone silent. No Rooster of Barcelós miracle today. Jasen reached for Willie and held him beak to nose, staring with tempting thoughts of literally ripping the bird apart feather by feather. He sat him back down on the table.

He deduced that LeFlore—assuming that the crafty chief had hidden something in the rooster—would likely have a secret way to access the contents. On impulse Jasen tried pushing simultaneously on the opposite ends of the wooden post. It did not make sense, but, hey, nothing else was working, he reasoned.

Startled, he felt the right end give a bit, and he pushed it inward about a quarter of an inch. The now recessed end "clicked" into an apparently locked position. Nothing happened. He sat holding his breath in anticipation of something, anything. The bird sat idly, stubbornly protecting its mystery. Jasen deduced again that there must be a step two. He stared and stared and thought and pondered his next move. Was there another moveable part?

He looked at Willie perched on the post, and suddenly it came to him! He grasped the body of the rooster and starting turning. The bird moved! He turned Willie 180 degrees to his right to face the opposite direction. He heard a louder click, and the right recessed end piece popped outward. Jasen pulled the end piece out and off. The post seemed to be hollow. Surely this must be the secret hiding place for something. Had he found the Choctaw chief's lost secret?

Jasen peered into the opening. It was dark inside the hollow post, so he got his flashlight and inspected the opening again. He saw a piece of cloth. He couldn't reach it with his large fingers so he retrieved his needle nose pliers from a kitchen drawer. He reached in with the pliers and grasped the cloth and pulled it out very slowly.

It was a very thin piece of white cloth. Jasen sat back down holding the discovery in his hands. He could tell that the cloth was folded around something hard. He carefully unfolded each corner, cautiously protecting the unknown contents with care. And then he saw the apparent secret.

It was a key!

Anticipation of a great revelation suddenly deflated like air gushing out of a ruptured balloon as he plunged in a free fall from excitement to confused disappointment and puzzlement.

"A key?" he muttered to himself. "Great! A key is what this is all about? Come on!"

He held the small key and inspected it. It had the number "8" stamped into both sides of the top of the key, and he began to think that maybe this was *the* key to everything. A safe deposit box key? A storage locker key? A key to a home safe? A key to a cash box? Post office box, maybe?

He felt a gnawing knot in his gut. The mystery was not solved, only growing more mysterious. Jasen was not going to be anybody's hero today. Someone had hidden the secret key in Willie's perch, but who? What did the key open? He looked at Willie with his brown eyes pleading for answers. The rooster was silent.

Jasen sat back in his chair. He had come so close to unraveling a hidden century-and-a-half-old mystery and discovering the reason for the madness of decades of assaults and attacks on Jean, Jade, and now Jasen. Anger, frustration, and disappointment filled his thoughts. Something wasn't right. There must be more. But what?

He held the end of the fence post in his left hand and turned the rooster 180 degrees back to its original position. Leflore's ingenious locking mechanism intrigued him, but what about the left end of the post? Curious, he locked the right end again then turned the rooster 180 degrees, as before. The end popped open again. He decided to complete the full circle and turned the bird another 180 degrees. Abruptly the left end of the post clicked and popped out!

Jasen was suddenly pumped with surprise and renewed excitement. There *was* more! He pulled the end of the post out and saw a small piece of folded paper tucked into the tiny space that had been hidden from the opposite end. He reached into the tiny space and snagged the paper and slowly extracted it from its secret hiding place.

It was obviously old paper, faded and slightly brittle. He saw that something was written on the fragile paper in black ink that was quite irregular in clarity, faded apparently by age and darkness. The writing was a beautiful cursive, He leaned back, slowly exhaled, and read.

"old hickorys word was sworn by all on the banks of the long ears waters my nation must survive and the promised justice be served the creator will bless and protect us in fertile lands west of the father of waters the symbol of peace will be sealed till truth perpetual happiness and eternal peace bless all of my brothers and sisters a friend from a land afar has brought us good fortune and guards these words it rests beneath a cross for the one who redeems my brothers tears may god forgive me and forever protect my nation"

c.g.l. 1830 a.d.

Jasen read and reread the intriguing note.

"c.g.l." That had to be Colonel Greenwood LeFlore. Jasen remembered enough about the great Choctaw chief from his graduate school thesis to know the potential significance of the message. The friend mentioned in the note surely had to be none other than Willie! But what cross? And what rested beneath a cross? Cold, electrifying chills traversed his body from his head to the tips of his toes.

"Incredible !" was all he could think.

A mysterious message from 165 years in the past from the last great chief of the Choctaw Nation and a key to the secret. Jasen's mind churned with questions. Whatever the key opened had to be important, he concluded. The message would be another challenge. He had to tell Jade. He had to get in touch with her somehow. He was suddenly operating on adrenalin overdrive and exploded out of his chair to get his phone.

He left her multiple voice messages on her cell phone. She had not returned any of his previous calls.

"Jade! I *must* speak to you. I think I know the answers to your mysteries. I found something in Willie. You must come back. We need to do this together. I need you. I love you. Please call me. Please."

***

Jade listened to his latest message and a tear began to form in her eye. Her roommate, Beth Pendergass, was watching her as she had during so many of Jasen's previous calls. She saw a different Jade this time and noticed the tear tracking down Jade's right cheek.

"OK, let's have it, Jade. You listen to every one of his messages and then you delete them immediately. And you don't call him back. When is this little game of 'how to torture my boyfriend' going to stop? That man obviously loves you. You're driving him crazy and you've got to stop ignoring him!"

Beth could see the beginning of a tiny chink in the armor. "What did he say this time? I can tell he's getting desperate. What'd he say?"

Jade laid the phone down and looked at Beth but didn't speak.

"Tell me, Jade. What did he say? Are you going to call him? For God's sake, girlfriend, say something!"

Jade sat down and looked out the large picture window that showcased the concrete jungle below, skyscrapers of every shape and height, and brilliant city lights too numerous to count on Manhattan's East Side.

"I'm afraid, Beth. I'm not sure I can face more disappointments in my life. And I'm afraid that I'll end up just like Mom. It's too dangerous back there. But he's alone and he found something important that may answer a lot of questions that will let me get on with my life. And I miss him so much. He's the only man that I know I can really trust. I love him."

"OK, so what's the problem? He needs you. You need him. He loves you. You love him. You've got questions. He's got the answers. End of discussion. Don't let this guy get away! Get your butt in there and pack your stuff. And for God's sake, call him!"

The next evening she called him. He somehow sensed that she really wanted to be with him. She did not say it, but he knew she was smiling. She said she would let him know about her travel plans. He could meet her at Hartsfield.

But he honestly did not know if Jade would really come home or not. Her roommate Beth no doubt made staying in New York comfortable, safe, and secure. What he did not know was that Beth was on his side!

Destiny had inexplicably bonded Delta Jade Colton and Jasen Michael Prospero. Fate had entrusted them with a duty of conscience. The future was waiting for them. Jasen knew she must come back to him.

CHAPTER TWENTY-THREE

The Reunion

Two days later, as he waited near the gate for her flight to arrive, Jasen briefly and fondly remembered how she had described his early infatuation with her. She always had joked that "she must have bent over or something" or maybe a meteor fell out of the sky and hit him on the head. But to Jasen it was all about sincerity and honesty. Their brief times together had been about plain fun. No demands. No obligations. No expectations of anything in return. Just fun. Sharing a moment. A touch. A hug. A smile. A laugh. A cold beer on a hot afternoon. A brief, intimate encounter. A moment in time to feel good just for that moment only. Just a butterfly kiss. That's actually the way it was with Jade.

As he waited in nervous anticipation, he tried to dismiss thoughts of the worst-case scenario. But he remained hopeful. Jade had set a track record for ups and downs in their relationship, and Jasen was constantly remembering something she had told him more than once—she didn't stay in relationships. It wasn't her nature. Too many disappointments. Too difficult to trust anyone. So many heartaches.

The flight arrived ten minutes late, and the passengers began to orderly deplane. He didn't see her. It seemed that most of the passengers hurried past him on their way to catch a connecting flight or scurry to meet someone. He turned around and looked back down the terminal corridor in case he had missed her. Nothing. His heart sank and he bit his lip. He fought back the moisture in his eyes and wiped away a slight drip from his nose.

Two flight attendants were exiting from the skyway opening.

"Are there any more passengers still on board?" he asked.

"No, we are the last ones off. Are you looking for someone?" said one of the attendants.

"Well, yes, but maybe I missed her. Thank you anyway."

He was dejected and confused. Maybe he got the flight number wrong. Sure. That was it. He called her cell. No answer. He walked halfway down the terminal and stepped onto the escalator headed down to the subterranean train tunnels. As he reached the end of the escalator, he noticed quite a crowd of travelers waiting for the next train. Suddenly his eye focused on a sign that was being held above the travelers. It was just a plain white sign with numbers on it. At first glance, it didn't register. Then he knew.

The numbers were "411." As Jasen stepped off the escalator, a stunningly beautiful redhead turned around holding the sign above her head. The crowd seemed to move away from her on both sides like the Red Sea parting. She was smiling "her" smile. He ran the final twenty steps past the strangers on each side, put his arms around her, and lifted her off the ground. He gently lowered her back to the concrete floor and they kissed ever so softly. Someone in the crowd began clapping, then all joined in, knowing only that two people they did not know were reunited, content, and happy. Everyone loves a happy ending.

"I'm home," she whispered in his ear.

"I know," he smiled. "But we have to go to Greenwood."

CHAPTER TWENTY-FOUR
Return to Greenwood

As they drove the thirty miles from the airport back to Lawrenceville, Jasen gave Jade the details of his discovery inside the rooster's perch. They both speculated about what might be on the "other end" of that special key. Jasen showed it to her and she only partially agreed that it looked like a locker key. But it could be a key to anything, she said.

If the rooster, apparently stolen from the burning Malmaison and ending up in Jake Luther's possession, was what everyone was after, was the key Jake's? If so, then whatever the key opened had to be in Greenwood. Or had someone else hidden the key? Either way, they had to go to Greenwood.

Jasen opined on the importance of the key. Either the locker or whatever it opened had something very valuable in it or was potentially very damaging and incriminating to someone or something. Or maybe it was both! That would explain Jake's tracking down Jean in Jackson and following her to Eutaw and then the assault on Jasen and Jade by the deceased stranger. And what about Calvin Caliban's mad obsession with Willie? Regardless, the reunited lovers had plunged headfirst into something treacherous and at the same time dangerously alluring and adventurous.

Jade shared her reluctance to go to Greenwood. She could only see danger.

Jasen reassured her. "No one in Greenwood knows what you look like. They certainly don't know me. Besides, until we unravel this mystery and deal with this, we won't be able to sleep at night or feel safe wherever we go. We have no choice. We can do this, Jade."

"Jasen. Maybe we need to just go to the police. We have no earthly idea what we will find or what kind of people we are dealing with. This entire idea is insane!"

"Listen, Jade. No way we can bring the law in now. Don't forget, we *killed* a guy and then covered up the whole thing. Yes, it was self-defense. Yes, we acted on impulse. God, we were both in shock! And I didn't want to take the chance of revealing our affair. We're in this too far to turn back now. Stupid? Maybe, but, hey, something tells me that this will turn out fine. We have to find answers. We're going. End of discussion."

***

They talked a lot on the eight-hour drive from Lawrenceville to Greenwood as they listened to country music on the radio. Jade turned the dial occasionally to lock onto a new station as one after another lost its signal and faded. Jasen gave Jade all of the details of his sleuth-like deductive method of discovering Willie's secret compartments. They speculated and debated over the small key, Jade being the skeptic about ever finding what it might unlock.

Jasen asked Jade to read and reread the secret message from Greenwood LeFlore that had been hidden in the rooster for over 130 years. He told Jade that sooner or later they must share the note with historians or LeFlore's descendants. If he and Jade eventually solved the riddle and found something valuable or of historical significance and thus invaluable, it would be morally wrong to keep it for themselves, he said. Even keeping the rooster for so many years had fostered and perpetuated a real moral dilemma. Jade said that she had never thought about the rooster in that light.

Jasen told Jade again about his research thesis from his graduate school days. He told her that the basic premise of his paper was to explore Greenwood LeFlore's own moral dilemma and eventually to justify or validate LeFlore's ultimate position of "selling out" the Choctaw Nation to the US government. Jasen had discovered through extensive reading that LeFlore himself had questioned his own actions and had been inwardly tormented about what he had done until his death in 1865. He had shared privately that he feared being eternally labeled as a traitor to his own brethren. The "Trail of Tears" march to Oklahoma deeply saddened LeFlore, who felt personal ownership for the tragic relocation of his tribe. And now, with the secret note revealed, it was apparent that LeFlore had been looking for some kind of redemption.

Jasen said that his thesis had essentially done that, but of course it was not publicly shared for historical reference. It was just an academic exercise. Maybe, he told her, he could somehow resurrect his paper and publicly argue his conclusion. Jade couldn't even fathom his interest in "redeeming" someone who had been dead for 130 years. She admired his heart. Just one of many reasons to love him, she told herself.

As they passed through Birmingham, Jade told Jasen about the night she and Jean drove through the Iron City while escaping from Damian in Jackson and Jake Luther in Eutaw. She saw Vulcan, the huge iron statue atop Red Mountain, as they passed through the downtown area on Interstate 20/59 and remembered asking her mom about it on that journey of flight and fright so many years ago. Her mom's bravery and the memories of their special mother-daughter bond briefly brought a tear to her eye. So long ago. Yet the ordeal was not over. Somehow she knew it was not over and she was beginning to seriously dread what lay ahead in Greenwood.

It was late on a cloudy, dreary Saturday afternoon when they crossed into the Greenwood incorporated city limits on US Highway 82. The western skies in the distance had darkened, and the gray clouds were low and seemed to be swirling in all directions. The wind agitated the leaves in the groves of trees like clothes in a dryer and created miniature spirals of dust in the fields that bordered the highway.

"Great!" observed Jasen. "Of all the luck. Looks like there's a big, ugly storm moving in from the west. I hope the bottom doesn't fall out before we've checked out our targets—the train depot, the Greyhound terminal, and the downtown post office. I think they're all close to where you said your mom worked before she moved away with you when you were a baby, right?"

"Yes, but Jasen, I told you on the way over. That key could fit almost anything. We're stabbing in the dark, the consummate wild goose chase. I feel like we're on a scavenger hunt without any clues. If we don't find a match, what's next?" Jade was beginning to play the devil's advocate.

"I haven't thought that far ahead. One step at a time, please. Think positive, for heaven's sake! Maybe we should look for Jake Luther; he'll know for sure," Jasen said and chuckled.

"That's not even close to being funny, Jasen. Jake is dead. I killed him. We're on our own to solve this," Jade said, trying not to imagine the worst if Jake was by some chance still out there. "We need some good luck. Let's get this done and get out of here as soon as we can. I just don't feel safe here."

They turned right onto Main Street and followed it to Carrollton Avenue. Jasen had studied a map of the city and had circled the spot where the train depot was located. He wanted to first check out the depot for storage lockers.

They headed east on Carrollton for a few blocks past a row of retail shops and saw the depot on the right. Jasen pulled into the parking lot and pushed the gear shift of Jade's Maxima to "P" and killed the engine. They looked at each other and simultaneously took in a deep volume of Greenwood air.

"Do you want me to go in alone?" Jasen asked, anticipating her response.

"We're doing this together! Let's go," Jade said, and they exited, ready for their first test. They looked up at the threatening skies as they opened the door and entered the Amtrak depot.

Part Three

CHAPTER TWENTY-FIVE

The Summer Tempest

The rain began falling in a gentle, warm shower as they walked into the empty waiting room of the small train depot. Jasen scanned the room quickly for storage lockers. He saw none. A ticket counter was on the far wall, but no one seemed to be manning the post. Jasen looked at the arrival/departure board just above the ticket counter and noted only one train arrival each day. Arrive 2:20 p.m., depart 2:40 p.m. It was 4:10 by Jasen's watch, thus the empty waiting area.

Jade had also observed no apparent lockers, but wanted to be sure. She walked over to the counter and rang the desk bell. A thin, short, elderly agent wearing black, horn-rimmed glasses looked out toward the counter from a room behind it. He saw Jade and said, "I'll be right with you." He disappeared from view and in less than a minute had shuffled his way from the back office to his side of the ticket counter. He put on a black cap that was tagged "Ticket Agent."

"Yes, OK," he spoke to himself as he donned the cap. "No more trains today. Need a ticket for tomorrow? How may I be of assistance?"

"Good afternoon," Jade said politely. "We're not interested in a ticket. Just curious about something. Do you have any storage lockers here in the depot?"

"No, ma'am. No lockers here at all. Don't think we ever had any. Looking to store some luggage or something? I do have a baggage storage area if you need to leave some luggage here. I can give you a claim ticket." The agent looked puzzled as he pondered Jade's question. No one had ever requested lockers for his low passenger volume station.

Jasen had walked around the station waiting area while Jade investigated the locker question. He looked with curiosity at the black-and-white pictures on the walls. Framed prints of old trains and locomotives from many years past were all there was to break the monotony of the plain vanilla, aging station. The waiting room chairs were solid wood and looked older than the building.

Jade responded, "No, no thank you. We're just looking for storage lockers here in town. Thanks anyway."

"You two don't look familiar to me," said the agent, who now wanted to satisfy his own curiosity. "Not from around here, I figure." He peered over the top of his Buddy Holly-style glasses and studied Jade.

Jasen motioned to Jade with his head to move toward the exit. He did not really want to give away too much information. "No, actually we're not. Drove into town to visit some relatives. My, uh, my friend here was born in Greenwood."

Jasen had said more than he intended. "Thanks so much for your help. We need to be going before the rain gets heavier." They headed toward the door and heard the agent call out.

"You might want to check out the Greyhound station down on Main. I think they have a few lockers. Have a nice day." He wondered what these very polished-looking strangers were up to. He mumbled to himself as he shuffled to his back office, where he picked up the telephone and dialed a local number.

The rain had intensified and a few flashes of lightning and distant rumbles off to the west suggested a thunderstorm moving in. Jade and Jasen ran to her Maxima and dove into their respective sides, trying to dodge the larger raindrops.

"Strike one," quipped Jasen. "I'm not surprised that that old depot didn't have lockers. Obviously Greenwood doesn't get much train traffic, especially the passenger kind."

Jade was still mulling over the ticket agent. "Did he seem a little creepy to you? I didn't feel very comfortable with the way he stared a hole through me. Did you notice it?"

"You're paranoid, Jade. No, I wasn't really paying much attention to him. Maybe you reminded him of someone."

A sickening thought suddenly filled Jade's head. Did Jasen realize what he just said? She was the spitting image of her mother. They could have passed for twin sisters instead of mother and daughter. What if the agent had known Jean? What if he had known Jake Luther? Cold chills made her tremble slightly and she hoped Jasen had not noticed.

He had. "You OK, Jade?"

"Yes, I'm fine. Just got a little chilled from the rain. Crank this thing up and let's get to the Greyhound station." She smiled at him as she affectionately rubbed his upper arm.

"You got it. Cross your fingers. It sounds like we may be getting warmer." He headed back west on Carrollton and turned right onto Main Street.

The rain was falling harder, and large puddles of water were already filling the low spots on the streets. The black, leaden clouds had dimmed all hints of sunlight, and lightning flashes danced like electrified shadows erratically across the late afternoon skies. Loud booms of thunder were closer now, only a few seconds behind each jagged lightning bolt. Signs on posts and buildings were flapping and whipping around in the storm's gusty winds.

"Just when we're on the verge, I hope, of success, the heavens open up and torment us!" Jasen said as he slowed the car to a crawl, trying to see through the sheets of rain pounding against the windshield. The wiper blades could not keep up with the volume of water pouring from the clouds like a mountain waterfall in spring. "I think we're in for quite a storm."

"I can't see a thing, Jasen. Why don't you pull over and let's wait this one out?" Jade said anxiously.

"You may be right, Jade, but the Greyhound terminal is just another block or two up Main. I'll inch along. I think Church Street may actually be the next intersection." Jasen leaned forward in his seat trying to see between the huge raindrops and held the steering wheel tightly.

It was a classic "cats, dogs, and frogs" deluge as Jasen caught a glimpse of the East Church Street sign and crawled past the violently swaying traffic light, which was green.

"I see it!" On his right, Jasen had spied the small Greyhound Lines station, a white building with blue trim, and he pulled into the partially flooded parking lot. Shifting into park, he turned off the ignition and looked at Jade, who was clutching the passenger door rest. "OK. We'll wait until this tempest settles down. Wow! I can't remember the last time I saw it rain this hard."

"I just hope this storm isn't a bad omen. This is *not* making me a happy camper, Jasen," Jade said.

"Relax, please, Jade. It's late summer. It's the South. It's what happens this time of year," Jasen said calmly, effectively hiding his own nervousness.

"As soon as it eases a bit, I'll run inside and check the lockers; that is, if that Amtrak ticket agent was correct. We're close, Jade, so close. I can feel it."

Neither he nor Jade noticed the late model black sedan that pulled into the parking lot behind them and stopped just off the edge of Main Street.

The torrential rain had created obvious flash flooding in downtown Greenwood, as Jasen could see that the terminal parking lot now resembled an outdoor swimming pool. He noticed that lights were still on inside the bus terminal and he silently was glad that so far there was no power outage downtown. Minutes passed and the rain refused to slow. Finally, after a long forty minutes, visibility improved and the storm took a breath. But it was not done. The black sedan had maneuvered around the side of the terminal without being noticed. Only the back bumper was visible to any casual observer. The heavy rain had provided distraction and cover for the unknown stalker.

Jasen was past patience as they waited out the storm. "Jade, I'm going in before the rain picks up again." He didn't give her a chance to respond as he opened the driver's door and darted toward the front entrance, his arms forming an ineffective umbrella above his head. The water was up to his ankles, filling his shoes and soaking his feet. Jade resisted the urge to join him; it was still coming down too hard for her comfort. She watched as he disappeared into the small building.

Minutes passed that to Jade seemed like an hour. "Where is he?" she asked aloud. She was tempted to brave the rain, which was getting harder again, and go after him, but she decided to give him a little more time. Her nerves were frazzled and her pulse raced. Had he found it? What was going on? Jasen, come on! She was on the precipice of losing it.

As she strained to see the front door of the Greyhound station through the rain, she was oblivious to a dark figure in a slick black raincoat and rain hat who was creeping up behind her Maxima. Now even with the back bumper of her car, he could see only one passenger silhouette and no one in the driver's seat. He crouched down to conceal his approach.

Jade had lost all patience and now put her hand on the door handle, waffling between waiting and going after Jasen. The man in the raincoat peeked from behind the back bumper and saw the passenger door beginning to open. He had to make his move...now! He stood and took a step toward Jade, who had put one leg out of the car, ready to run toward the station door. Jade was thinking only of dodging the pounding rain and did not notice that someone was coming up behind her.

Suddenly the door of the terminal opened and Jasen appeared. When he saw Jade on the verge of exiting the car he shouted, "Get back in the car! I'm coming." He raced to the driver's side as Jade pulled her wet leg back in and closed the passenger door. The stalker had heard Jasen and quickly ducked out of sight behind the Maxima, his task thwarted by Jasen's (un)timely return. He kept low and faded into the rain as he backtracked to his partially hidden sedan on the side of the terminal. He was confident that Jasen and Jade had not seen him.

As Jasen closed his door, Jade breathed an anxious sigh of relief. "OK, let's have it. Did you find it? What took so long? Tell me!"

"Sorry. Strike two. No luck. The waiting room did have ten lockers. No number eight. I tried the key on all of them anyway. Nothing. Then I chatted with the woman at the ticket counter. She asked me a lot of questions that I evaded. Folks in this town sure seem nosey, kind of like the colonel and Rose. Anyway, I tried to pick her brain about other places in town where you might find lockers. No YMCA or anything that she could think of. I did ask her about the post office. It's one block over and the outer lobby where the PO boxes are should be open, she said."

"Just like I told you, sweetie. We're on one wild, wacky, and now stormy goose chase. I'm going in the post office with you, by the way. Waiting for you really rattled me. To heck with this rain." Jade was gathering her strength but losing any hope of success.

Jasen started the car and backed slowly out of the parking lot and headed one block over to East Washington Street. "One more chance. Cross your fingers *and* your toes!" He reached over and squeezed Jade's hand. She looked at him with a guarded smile.

Jasen parked in front of the redbrick Federal Building and saw the door to the US Post Office. He was ready and anxious. "OK. Let's do it. Let's go." They both opened their doors simultaneously and charged through the rain and into the front foyer of the post office.

"I see them," Jasen said as he opened the next set of double glass doors and waited for Jade to enter in front of him. They saw a wall of post office boxes, all numbered. Jasen had a sinking feeling as he noticed the numbers were all four digits beginning with 1000. No single numbers. No number "8." They looked at each other with sagging faces of defeat.

Jade broke the silence of disappointment. "I think we may have struck out. This is not looking good."

"Now, now. Don't give up yet." Jasen was the eternal optimist. "Let me try the key first."

He tried it on all the boxes that had the number "8," starting with 1008. The key was not a good fit on any. Jade was correct. Strike three. No luck. They were back to square one.

What next? They looked at each other and felt empty and weary. Jasen took her hand and led her out the door and opened the passenger side door of the car for her. He plopped into the driver's seat, closed his door, and held the steering wheel with both hands, leaning forward and looking out the front windshield into the rain.

"I'm hungry. How about you?" Jasen needed to clear his head and tame the growl in his belly. "I saw an eatery, I think it was the Crystal Grill, across from the Amtrak station. What do you say?"

Jade looked at him blankly. "Not sure I can eat but, hey, go for it."

They didn't talk as Jasen drove back over to Carrollton Street and pulled up in front of the Crystal Grill. The storm had diminished, but a light sprinkle continued to fall. They went inside and were escorted to a table near the front window. The restaurant was only about half filled with early dinner patrons, probably due to the nasty storm that had kept some diners leery of venturing out. A young and attractive African American waitress came up to them with menus and a warm smile. Her name badge said "Maisha."

"Good evening," she said. "Welcome to the Crystal Grill. Have you been here before?"

Jade responded first. "No, actually, it's our first trip to Greenwood. Well, no, not exactly. I was born here but moved away when I was a baby. Anyway, first time here at the Crystal Grill."

"Well, I think you won't be sorry. We're known for our 'Southern comfort' food. The fried chicken and fried green tomatoes are to die for, and our lemon icebox pie is outstanding. What can I get you to drink?"

She took their drink orders and disappeared into the kitchen area in the back.

"Very nice young lady, don't you think?" Jasen observed to Jade.

"Umm hmm," she hummed and nodded in agreement as she studied the menu.

They looked up from their menus when an elderly black man approached. They looked quickly at each other, then back at the stranger who was now almost at their table. He was tall, with short, graying hair and had several moles on his face.

He nodded politely and, looking directly at Jade, said, "Excuse me for interrupting, but I must ask you a question."

She had heard that voice before. Jade looked into his gentle eyes, and a chilling sense of déjà vu flashed in her head. "Of course," she responded.

"I saw you come in and suddenly had a memory flashback. I think I know you. You look so familiar. Are you from around here?"

Jade felt unusually calm as she answered, "Well, I was born here. My parents are from here and my grandparents. I moved away with my mother when I was just an infant."

The elderly gentleman with nonthreatening eyes smiled and knew at once. "You're Jade, aren't you?" It had been nearly forty years. He was face to face with Jean Colton's daughter, almost a clone of her mother.

"My name is Willie Campbell. I knew your mother, Jean, and I knew you too. May I sit down?" He didn't wait for an answer. He sat down beside Jade and took her hand with a gentle hold rather than a shake. "I can't believe after all of these years that our paths have crossed again." Jade was spellbound. Their eyes were locked for the second time in a lifetime.

Jasen observed the unexpected reunion with keen interest. Could this be the same Willie that the controversial rooster was named after? He was tweaked with curiosity.

Willie looked over at Jasen and apologized. "Oh, I'm sorry." He reached for Jasen's hand and shook it. "I didn't mean to be rude. You are...?"

"Jasen, Jasen Prospero. Jade and I are, uh, good friends. Neighbors, to be exact. We're here on a, well, kind of a treasure hunt of sorts." Willie looked puzzled. "It's a long story." Jasen was still in his caution mode.

Maisha had returned with their sweet iced tea and sat the glasses on the table.

"I see you two met my granddaughter, Maisha," Willie said, looking up at her. "We have a family-run business here. I am the owner of the Crystal Grill. Come a long, long way since I worked with your mother over at the Cotton Exchange." He grinned proudly. "Farmhand, to janitor, to restaurant owner. Quite a journey for an old black man in the Mississippi Delta."

They gave their dinner order to Maisha as Willie continued to fondly recount and relive his friendship with Jean and little Jade so many years ago. He even confessed his role in helping Jean escape from his old boss, the slippery Jake Luther. When he told them about Jean's crazy idea of stealing Jake's stuffed rooster, they looked at each other, dumbfounded. Jasen could see it in Jade's eyes. Willie had been Jean's ally. He would be their ally too. They would tell him about the rooster and their true reason for their return to Greenwood. Maybe he could help with the mystery of the key.

Jade told Willie most of her remembered events from her Jackson, Mississippi, days to the present, touching superficially on the encounter with Jake Luther in Eutaw, Alabama. Willie did not give any indication that he knew what happened to Jake and listened politely. He was still in awe and hypnotized by Jade's uncanny resemblance to Jean. He seemed very proud of Jean's risky friendship with him, especially during the heyday of KKK activity in Greenwood and other areas of the South. It was obvious that the two had had a very special relationship with sincere trust and mutual respect. Jade could easily see how her mom could like Willie.

Jasen shared the story of the rooster Willie with the restaurant owner Willie, who shared the legend of the Malmaison rooster that had belonged to the family of Chief LeFlore. Willie was one of the few who suspected that Jake had stolen the rooster during the chaos of the devastating 1942 fire that had destroyed the mansion. When Jasen told Willie about the mysterious message from LeFlore that he had discovered in the rooster's base, Willie pursed his lips and said, "hmmmmmmm." He thought it was strange that none of LeFlore's descendants had ever suspected the significance of the rooster or even knew that the chief may have hidden secrets that he carried with him to his grave up on LeFlore Point east of town.

Jade and Jasen continued their sharing of their sleuth-like adventures with Willie between bites of savory, perfectly seasoned fried chicken, speckled butter beans, and gravy-topped mashed potatoes. Jasen told Willie that the cornbread was the best he had ever had. He mentioned his family's Greek restaurant in Atlanta and their excellent Greek dishes, but admitted that the Crystal Grill's comfort food was incredible too. Willie smiled, pleased, and watched both of them enjoy every bite.

Willie wanted to help in any way he could. "Let me take a look at the key that you say was hidden in the rooster," he said.

Jasen replied, "Of course." He felt in his trouser pocket, first right, then left. He patted his shirt pocket. He looked at Jade. "Jade, do you have the key?"

"No," she answered. "You had it when we were in the post office. I never touched it."

Jasen was not worried. "Probably in the car. I may have laid it on the center console when we jumped back in the car. Let me go check. I'll be right back."

He stood up and headed out the front door of the grill. Jade followed him with her eyes then turned her head and looked out the window. The rain had stopped.

Willie had obviously committed to them by now. "I don't know if I can help with the key, Miss Jade, but I'll take a look. You two seem to have opened up more than one ugly can of worms. I think you need some help in solving this puzzle. And I agree with you. You may be in more danger."

Jade had taken her eyes off Jasen as Willie spoke, but turned to see him open the driver's door and lean in. Willie had his back to the window and was not focused on the outside. In the next beat of her heart, Jade saw a long, black sedan speed up and then suddenly stop right next to her Maxima. Jasen was still leaning over into the car and had not seen the approaching car. Before Jade could digest, comprehend, or filter what was happening, two men in long black coats bolted from the passenger side of the sedan and immediately surrounded Jasen. Each of them grabbed an arm, and a stunned and off-guard Jasen was forcefully shoved head first into the back seat of the vehicle. The two men jumped in behind their victim, and the sedan sped off, its rear end fishtailing slightly on the wet street. It disappeared down Carrollton Avenue into the soggy darkness.

Jade had jumped up with a look of helpless horror as she saw her partner and lover being abducted right before her startled green eyes. Willie had followed her gaze and her sudden look of shock and caught a brief glimpse of the fleeing car.

"Oh my God! Jasen!" Jade shouted it loud enough to cause other patrons to turn and look at her. "Willie, did you see that! What just happened? Who were those guys? Why are they doing this? Willie, call the police or something, now!"

She was in panic mode and visions of past demons flooded her mind. The summer tempest had calmed but a new tempest had consumed Jasen like a tsunami swallowing a sleeping victim. He was gone.

CHAPTER TWENTY-SIX

Swan Lake

It was up to Willie now to be her protector. He had heard enough about the years of ordeals experienced by Jean and now Jade to know who was behind the intrigue and revengeful pursuit. He had recognized the black sedan.

"Miss Jade, it looks like you two have stirred the wrath of some mean dude evildoers, and I think I know who they are. Please, calm down and I'll explain. But first let's go back to my office. We need to get out of the public eye." He looked at several gawking patrons and smiled at them as Jade rose from her seat and followed him to the back office. He closed the door as she settled into a chair in front of his desk.

"Willie, I'm afraid. Someone has already tried to kill both of us. If these are the same people, Jasen is in extreme danger. We have to do something. Please! What are we going to do?" Jade was usually stronger than this, but Jasen was her life now. She had to find him and save him. Willie had helped her mother. Now he was *her* only hope.

"Maybe we should call the police? Or the FBI? I mean, we need help!" Jade was one step from meltdown.

Willie was already two steps ahead of her. He told her that calling the police was not an option because of who the abductors were. He picked up the phone on his desk and dialed. Someone on the other end answered after one ring.

"Junior? It's Dad. I've got a friend here at the Grill that needs our help. Get your brothers and meet me in thirty minutes where County Road 462 crosses 166. We have some 'business' to take care of at the old Swan Lake cabin. Bring some 'artillery' and some rope just in case. OK?" He paused for an answer. "Great. OK, thirty minutes."

Willie smiled confidently as he replaced the receiver. "My sons will meet us. I have a good idea where the guys in the black sedan took Jasen. I'll fill you in on the way. That is, if you want to tag along. This could get real nasty. These scoundrels are known for violence and are totally unpredictable."

Jade did not hesitate. "I'm coming! I got Jasen into this mess and I need to get him out. I just hope we're not too late." She tried to reach down into her emotional armamentarium to find her Choctaw lineage courage and strength. The caption on her gifted T-shirt would be her rallying cry.

They headed out the back door of the Grill, and Willie pointed Jade toward his maroon-colored Buick LeSabre. From memories of his own personal brushes with Greenwood violence, Willie was familiar with his town's shadowy characters and had already guessed at the abductors' modus operandi.

Willie continued as they got into the car, "They may make him uncomfortable, but they won't kill him until they get the information they're after. I don't know what Jake Luther hid in that rooster, but I can pretty much guess that it had something to do with his Klan organization. And I really doubt that Jake would hide a key like that. Had to be something more valuable. Or something very secretive that he didn't want anyone else to know. Jake was the treasurer here for the local KKK and in cahoots with some of Greenwood's more prominent figures, including the sheriff. That's why we can't call the police yet. There's still a tight-knit gang of dastardly thugs in this county. I don't trust anybody 'cept my boys."

Willie watched as Jade fastened her seat belt and then started the engine and headed west to Main Street and then turned south back to US 82. Willie drove cautiously on the still very wet roadway, occasionally swerving to dodge small tree limbs and debris blown about by the storm.

"How far is Swan Lake? Jade asked Willie as they headed east on Highway 82.

"Just a few miles, but we're going in the back way, down an old fisherman's dirt road. Probably more like a mud road after that storm. I just hope we don't get stuck. But the back road is best. Don't want to announce our presence. We'll meet up with my boys in about fifteen more minutes."

As Willie was signaling to make the right turn off 82 onto CR 462, Jade's eyes were drawn to a car with a raised hood that was stalled off the shoulder on the opposite side of 82. It wasn't the car that drew her attention. It was the young woman, illuminated by the car's headlights, who had turned to look at Willie's car approaching the intersection.

"Willie, pull over! Stop the car. Now!" Jade was nearly screaming.

Willie looked at Jade and knew better than to argue with a determined woman with green eyes! He slowed, pulled off the highway, and stopped.

"What is it, Ms. Jade? Did I do something? What is it?"

Jade did not answer. She was already opening her passenger door and stepping out into the night's damp air and right into a puddle of muddy water. She ignored her wet feet and couldn't believe her eyes. The young woman across the road was looking their way, and suddenly her eyes and Jade's locked. The stranded motorist jumped up and down and began to wave energetically. It was Ariel!

"Jade! Jade! It's Ariel! I need some help," she shouted excitedly from across the highway. Ariel was not going to question her dumb luck or what Jade was up to riding in a car with an elderly black man, after dark, a long way from home in Lawrenceville, Georgia. She was focused only on being rescued in a foreign land, of sorts. Relief flowed across her unblemished youthful face.

"Willie," Jade said, looking into the car's window. "That's Jasen's daughter over there! Don't ask me what she's doing here. I can only guess. Come on, let's get over there and help her."

They both crossed the highway, and Jade hurried to Ariel, giving her a comforting, warm hug. She pushed away slightly and looked at Ariel's shirt. She laughed aloud and hugged her again.

"I am beginning to think that you really believe what's on that shirt, young lady. Maybe we need to change it to 'Strong *and* Lucky Women...'" They both laughed.

Willie was standing behind them admiring the warm exchange. Now he stepped toward them and said, "Hi. I'm Willie Campbell. Jade's friend."

"My goodness. I'm sorry, Willie," Jade said. "I was so shocked and surprised, I lost my manners. But we need to postpone getting acquainted until later. Willie, we have to get going. Your boys will be waiting."

"Waiting for what?" Ariel asked, her mind spinning with imagination.

Jade took charge. "It's complicated, Ariel. Your dad may be in danger, and it's all my fault." She did not want to use the word "abduction." "We're on our way to find him. I don't know what we'll find. It may be dangerous. Willie and his sons are helping."

"My God!" Ariel held her hand over her mouth. "Jade, it's *my* dad and I'm going with you! Please!"

Jade and Willie looked at each other then back at Ariel. Minutes were becoming critical. There was no time to argue. Jade needed to find Jasen, and soon!

"What the heck," she acquiesced. "Willie, please close the hood. Ariel, get your purse or billfold and your keys and lock your car. Come on. We have a wonderful man waiting on us somewhere down that dark road."

***

The old abandoned cabin on the north end of Swan Lake was conveniently isolated and had been used only by a few local fishermen many years ago and long since forgotten by everyone else. Jake Luther and his band of racist Klansmen had used the cabin on more than one occasion as a secret rendezvous site to plot their evil deeds. It was also a perfect venue for harassing, torturing, and even killing their victims of hate and extreme prejudice.

Willie had been taken there by Big Jake years before and beaten severely just after Jean disappeared from Greenwood. Jake had accused Willie of aiding Jean's escape and of forbidden fraternization with a white woman. Willie never understood why Big Jake had not killed him. The hooded men in the room had taunted Jake to finish Willie off, but Jake stopped the pummeling just as Willie was losing consciousness. He faintly heard Jake's warning that his family would be killed if he ever spoke to another white woman again. He awoke several hours later bloody, bruised severely, with muscles and bones searing with pain, and several teeth broken. His attackers were gone. Willie had vowed that night to one day find justice for himself and all who had suffered at the hands of the despicable Klan and the monster Big Jake Luther.

***

As he sat in a hard wooden chair with his arms tied behind his back and his feet bound painfully tight by nylon rope, Jasen was still trying to orient himself to the events of the past hour. One minute he was searching for the key in Jade's car and the next he was lassoed, corralled, and thrust into the back seat of someone's car, and suddenly a black hood shut out all light and the world from him. An unseen voice told him to keep quiet or he would be shot.

His head was still covered by the hood, and he had no clue as to his location or the identity of his abductors. He only knew that he and Jade had stumbled into a raging pit of vengeful, venomous, and determined enemies. But he was more concerned about Jade than his own dilemma. He hoped she was safe.

He had not confronted such extreme danger in his life since that snowy night in Jade's bedroom. That nightmare had driven him to a new plateau of survival instincts and confidence. The college professor now had to dig deep within himself and find the spirit, courage, and strength to rival a trained and seasoned secret agent. He had to find a way to survive, again.

As his entire life flashed through his mind, someone suddenly yanked the black hood from over his head, and he struggled to focus his constricting pupils as they were shocked by a brilliant light that temporarily blinded him. He turned his head defensively and closed his lids. He slowly opened his eyes again and tried to look away from the light that seemed as bright as a midday summer sun.

He could not see the person holding the light but scanned the darkened room and could see three white-hooded figures surrounding him and staring at him. The one holding the light spoke first.

"Welcome to Swan Lake, Mr. Prospero." Jasen could not see him, but the voice was eerily familiar. He realized he had encountered another snollygoster like this back in Lawrenceville.

"I had a feeling that you and your fair, redheaded girlfriend would be coming to Greenwood. Funny how, what's the saying, everything that goes around, comes around? Yeah, I think that's it. Ms. Colton started here, and I think it's going to end here for her. Too bad you got in the way. Looks like you two have reached the end of your little road trip!"

His voice was gravelly and menacing. Jasen strained to look beyond the blinding light. Who was this psycho and what were his intentions? Jasen was struggling to put all the pieces together. The voice haunted him. He had heard it before.

Jasen's pulse suddenly quickened. "What have you done with Jade? What do you want? We haven't done anything to you. What's this all about? Untie me!" he demanded despite knowing he had no bargaining chips in this game of good guys versus bad guys. The bad guys were winning.

"Come, come, Mr. Prospero. You know full well what this is about. You two have something that belongs to us and we want it back. Simple. You give me what you found, we let you go. Doesn't that sound fair?" The leader of the abductors was not convincing, and without a plan, Jasen did not see things ending well for him. He'd play dumb.

"Listen, whoever you are. I don't know what in the world you're talking about. And can you please stop blinding me with that light. I'm just a dull, uninteresting college professor from Georgia. I have nothing of yours. Jade and I came to Greenwood to visit her aging grandparents. That's all. We haven't found anything. And I hope you realize that kidnapping is a federal offense. I suggest you let me go while you're ahead." Jasen was not sounding very convincing either.

The leader quipped back, "Yeah, well, murder is a federal offense too, so who's keeping score? I have a suggestion for you too. Tell me what I want to know or kiss your sweet college professor ass good-bye. You've got exactly sixty seconds to hand over what you have or what you know. And the clock starts now! This conversation is over." He lowered the light and looked at his watch.

Jason now saw that the leader's head was also covered by a white hood. He was sure that he had recognized the voice. If only he could rip the hood off of the cowardly ruffian. He was obviously the master trepan of this band of gangsters.

Perspiring profusely, he felt his racing heart pound painfully against his sternum. Jasen prepared for the worst. He had no idea where Jade was; did they have her too? Was she being interrogated at another location? Jade had no information to turn over to them. They were wasting their time. Whatever the secret was, Jade and Jasen knew nothing more than they had when they got to Greenwood. These hooligans thought otherwise. Jasen wished that they had brought the rooster, either to offer it up to the bad guys or maybe to bring himself and Jade the long overdue good fortune that Willie the rooster had so far not delivered. He wished now that he had trashed the bird.

Jasen had nothing to confess. Was this his swan song at, of all places, Swan Lake? If he could only have one last look at Jade's smile…

"Time's up." The leader was ready for his next step. "OK, if that's the way you prefer it, Mr. Prospero." He motioned to the largest of the three hooded thugs. "My friend here is very resourceful when it comes to encouraging resistors to talk. This will be your last opportunity, Mr. Prospero." Fortunately his vicious grin was invisible to Jasen.

The heavyweight thug walked over to Jasen and briefly looked away. In the next second, he turned back toward Jasen, catching him totally off guard. His extra-large fist slammed into Jasen's exposed jaw and snapped Jasen's head violently to one side. Blood-tinged saliva spewed from Jasen's mouth as he moaned loudly from the force of the punch.

Without giving Jasen a moment to process the pain and damage, the brute followed up with a smash of his fisted hand into Jasen's abdomen. Jasen doubled over from the assault to his gut as a wave of sharp, knife-like nausea spread across his midsection. The pain in his face and stomach were battling for which was worse. Jasen immediately realized that his nightmare was just getting started.

"OK, Professor. My colleague here is merely getting warmed up." The leader was obviously enjoying the show. "Do yourself a favor. Tell me what you know, and we'll stop right here. How about it?"

Jasen was still lost in the fog of pain that shrouded him and could only look up helplessly at his tormentor.

The leader motioned for the heavyweight to back off and waved his hand at a second man to move toward Jasen. Number two pulled an electric cattle prod from his coat. He jerked Jasen's shirt tail out and exposed his sweaty, tight abdomen. The wet skin would be an excellent conductor.

"Last chance, Mr. Prospero. My next friend here usually gets very 'shocking' results!" He laughed deviously.

Jasen said nothing.

"Do it!" The leader backed away.

The initial assault with the hot prod sent waves of electricity across Jasen's abdomen, causing his already bruised and painful abdominal muscles to tighten into a steel-like hardness, then violently spasm in rhythmic waves of piercing pain. Jasen tightened his jaws with clenched teeth and pushed against his bound feet as his body thrust upward, lifting him several inches off the chair. When the attacker stopped the current after seconds that seemed like minutes, Jasen's body settled back into the chair. Jasen had not screamed out.

"Very impressive, Mr. Prospero. Most of the time we get at least an 'ouch' with the first round. Seems you have a high tolerance for pain. Or do you? We can go to the next level, if you are game. Unless you would prefer to turn over the information and we can all go home. What's your call, Mr. Prospero?"

Jasen tried to maintain his Mel Gibson *Braveheart* bravado. He kept mum.

"Have it your way then." He gestured at the heavyweight enforcer, who turned the dial on the end of the prod up two more notches. Stepping up to Jasen, he pushed the tip of the hot electric rod into Jasen's wet abdomen for the second time.

Jasen's body surged upward from his chair and arched backward in convulsive jerking. The charge burned ten times hotter than acciden-tally sticking your wet finger into a live electric socket. This time Jasen screamed from the sharp, shooting pains that charged up and down his torso. He fell back into his chair again when the prod was removed from his singed skin. The smell of burnt flesh scented the dimly lit room.

Jasen was now convinced that the villains would stop at nothing, and he had not yet come up with plan "B." He then soberly realized he didn't even have a plan "A." He was physically strong from his body building habit but had been unsuccessful at subtle attempts to loosen the tight ropes binding his hands behind his back. He knew that even if he could somehow free himself, it was four against one. He was not a superman; he accepted that. He began to fantasize and thought of all of those James Bond movies and 007's seemingly impossible escapes from similar dilemmas. But that was Hollywood. This was real. There was no beauti-ful CIA agent to save him just in the nick of time, was there?

Time was running out. He could not deal with more torture. His thoughts flickered back to all of the "could-have-beens" in his life. He had to tell the determined leader something. But what? He had only found a key. The key was lost or in Jade's car. But what did the key open? Was there something else in the rooster that had been discovered and removed long before he cleverly opened the rooster's perch? More questions than stars in the heavens. All without answers.

"OK now, Mr. Prospero. What do you have to share with me? Or would you enjoy a little more 'entertainment' from my friends here?" the leader asked, nodding at his three accomplices.

Jasen knew that no matter what he told the sadist, he was close to breathing his last gasp of Mississippi Delta air. His face remained blank as perspiration flowed down his forehead and temples.

His evil nemesis had only touched on his resources for extracting information from his victims. Now he turned to a small table and reached for a trifold leather case that was tied loosely by a string. He untied the case and revealed a pocketed array of apparent instruments of torture—razor-sharp knives of varying lengths, surgical scalpels, surgical snips and pliers, a small bone saw, a small hammer, and some thin steel surgical wire. Even in the darkened room, Jasen could see enough to get his attention. He was incredulous. This could not be happening to him! What would be the maniacal leader's next step?

"Just shoot me," he said to himself. "No more torture, please." But he kept silent as the leader walked over to him with the open instrument case and stared coldly at his bound and totally helpless prey. He seemed to be humming. He picked up one instrument at a time, examining each one methodically. He started with the knives.

"This particular knife is perfect for stabbing deep into a muscle; twisting it tends to trigger immediate nerve conduction and violent spasms." He replaced it in its assigned pocket. He withdrew a smaller knife with a serrated blade. "I love this one. It tends to beautifully slice thin layers of skin from the face better than a plastic surgeon's scalpel, which, oh by the way, I just happen to have right here." He withdrew it from its pocket and passed it slowly back and forth in front of Jasen's eyes.

He continued to withdraw each instrument one by one, detailing its purpose and then placing each one back in its assigned pocket. The pliers were for extracting teeth, the surgical snips for removing parts of fingers and toes, the surgical wire for wrapping around earlobes and twisting tighter and tighter until the ears fell off, and the saw for removing anything too thick for the snips. It was obvious to Jasen that the sadistic, evil leader relished his show-and-tell charade.

Jasen's imagination was spinning out of control like a broken gyroscope, and he tried to block visuals of what might be next. He sat with tensed muscles but said nothing.

The leader had lost all patience. Either Mr. Prospero was the most stupid college professor he had ever met or he knew nothing. He refused to credit his courage and could not possibly understand Jasen's feelings for Jade. The hour was getting late. He was ready to end the nonsense and go after Jade.

He looked at his companions and said, "Seems like we're wasting our time with this idiot. He's either stupid or so love struck or both that he can't even comprehend what's happening. I've had enough of him. Take care of him. I'll be outside. He's making me sick to my stomach just to look at him." The leader turned and walked out the cabin's front door into the pitch-black night.

The heavyweight with the electrified cattle prod backed away, and a third thug walked toward Jasen. He pulled a 9 mm semiautomatic Luger from his belt and stopped only a foot away from his tightly bound victim. He pulled his hood off so that Jasen could see his face before he completed his assigned task. The face was unknown to Jasen.

The gunman stood with the Luger aimed at Jasen's forehead, waiting for the fear or horror to appear on Jasen's bruised face. It did not come. There was no pleading or begging. Jasen was ready. He hoped Jade knew how much he loved her.

CHAPTER TWENTY-SEVEN
Delta Justice

As promised, William Jr. and his three brothers were waiting at the intersection of County Roads 462 and 166. Willie pulled behind their dark green Ford pickup, stopped, and got out. He talked to them, gesturing toward Swan Lake off to the west while Jade and Ariel stayed in the car. Jade turned her head to speak to Ariel, who was on the edge of her seat in the back of Willie's Buick LeSabre.

"Ariel. I am so sorry that I got your dad into this situation. We were both determined to once and for all solve a lot of mysteries and answer a lot of questions— that stupid rooster, a key Jasen found, a 130-year-old note from an Indian chief, trying to figure out who had been stalking my mother and now me for so many years—it smacks of some gloomy, sordid, fictional spy novel, not real life. I know all of this is confusing to you." Jade was firing thoughts at Ariel without taking a breath.

"I haven't even asked you what in the world you are doing here. You can tell me later, by the way. And Ariel, uh, why do you have that golf club with you?"

Willie returned to the car before Ariel could answer and got back into the driver's side. He restarted the engine and turned his head in Jade's direction.

"My boys are going in first. We'll follow. We'll have to turn off the head-lights before we get too close. You two stay low and keep your heads down. I doubt that they will have a lookout, but it's better to not look like sitting ducks. They probably feel invulnerable down this back road; it's a perfect place for a hideout. I think I'm one of the few living non-Klansmen to even know about the cabin."

The road was muddy and unfriendly, just as Willie had predicted. Both the Campbell sons' truck and Willie's Buick zigzagged around low spots and washed-out ruts filled with thick, muddy water. They rounded a blind curve, and the pickup in the lead came to a sudden stop. Willie could not see what was ahead of his son's truck, but Junior got out and walked back to the Buick.

"There's a downed pine tree blocking the road up ahead," said Junior. "We'll have to go the rest of the way on foot. Put on your mud boots!"

"Ha ha," responded Willie. "My Sunday shoes will have to do. Your mother will kill me!"

"Better her than whoever is in that cabin," Junior joked, trying to sup-press thoughts of the danger ahead.

The Campbell boys led the way as they moved to the right side of the road to avoid the muddiest areas in the middle. In less than ten minutes, Junior motioned for everyone to halt. They all crouched low, straining to see the faint light in the windows of the wood-framed cabin a hundred yards ahead.

Willie kept his voice low and said, "Me and my sons are going in first. There's a front and back entrance, so we'll cover both in case they try to escape."

Willie looked back at Jade and Ariel. "This might get real messy. You ladies are better off waiting here." He could tell they weren't buying it.

"Really," he cautioned, "stay right here. We'll bring Jasen back to you. I promise." His look was only half convincing.

The men kept low as they headed toward the cabin in single file. Meanwhile Jade and Ariel looked at each other and smiled. They had not come along just to cower in the woods. Jade and Ariel, her Great Big Bertha driver in tow, followed the Campbells, staying a few yards behind them.

As Willie and his sons approached the cabin, they could not see any posted guard. Junior gave hand signals for Samuel and Joe to circle around to the back side of the cabin, and he knew that they would be prepared for anything. Junior, Willie, and Thomas silently made their way to the windows on either side of the front door, keeping low and below the windows. Willie carefully eased upward to the window's edge so that he could see inside the poorly lit interior. He saw someone bound to a chair in the center of the room and four hooded figures standing around him. Jasen was alive.

He held up four fingers, indicating the number of hostiles. He noticed that one of the captors was holding some kind of case in front of his victim. Suddenly he placed the case on a table, turned, and then headed toward the door. Willie ducked down quickly and motioned for his sons to retreat out of sight.

The cabin door opened, and from their undetected positions behind trees and brushy landscape, they saw a white-hooded figure enter the night and remove his hooded mask. It was too dark to make out the man's identity. He walked twenty feet and stopped near the front of a black sedan that was parked close to the hideaway's front door. He reached into his front shirt pocket and pulled out a cigarette from a concealed pack and lit one. He did not appear to have a gun or other weapon.

Because the hopeful and confident rescuers had no rehearsed plan and were relying on instinct and impromptu luck, Willie decided to make the first move. It was risky, but he knew that Junior and Thomas were ready.

Willie stood and revealed his hiding spot. The idea, he thought, was to distract the man and let the element of surprise do the rest. He approached the unsuspecting abductor and said, "Mister, can you help me? I'm lost and my car's stuck back there in the mud."

The leader looked up with shock and disbelief that anyone could have happened upon the cabin and the dastardly events unfolding inside.

"Who the hell are you?" he demanded, straining to see who was walking toward him in the darkness. At the same time he dropped the cigarette and reached inside his jacket pocket and exposed a revolver. Before he could take aim at Willie, his head jerked violently to his left and he toppled onto the hood of the sedan.

The gun dropped from his trigger hand as he rolled across the hood and fell to the ground in front of the car. He was on his back, stunned by the surprise stealth force of the power-packed impact to the right side of his head. He raised his throbbing head, struggling to see through the stars and fogginess created from the painful collision with what seemed like a wrecking ball. He focused and tried to look at his attacker, then, in a cat-like move, he suddenly rolled to one side and used his arms to attempt to get up and defend himself. Before he could stand, another sledgehammer blow connected, this time with his occiput. It was more effective than the first strike, and he fell back to the ground, his body limp.

Jade, holding Ariel's huge-headed golf club, stood over him and looked up at Willie. "You know, I never knew I was so good at golf. If that creep's head had been a golf ball, I think it would have gone over three hundred yards!" She grinned and then looked back at the bad guy on the ground. The moonless night was dim, but Jade recognized her fallen prey easily. It was Calvin Caliban!

Willie, Junior, and Thomas had surrounded the leader's body after Jade's lightning attack. Thomas handed her a rope and whispered, "Tie him up before he comes to, *if* he comes to. We still have work to do."

The Campbells regrouped, hunched down, and crept back over to the cabin, Junior first stooping to pick up the leader's white hood.

From their posts on the cabin's backside, Samuel and Joe were unaware of Jade's takedown of the leader. Samuel had peeked inside the cabin through a back window just as the leader was exiting the front door. He watched as another man who seemed to be removing his hood walked over to the bound Jasen and pointed a gun at his forehead. Samuel knew that if they were going to save Jasen, they had to do something and do it quickly. He was counting on his father and brothers on the front side to follow his next move. He pounded loudly on the cabin's back door and yelled out.

"Help! Help me! Please, I need help! Open up the door! Please help me!" Then he pounded again, louder this time.

The executioner with his locked and loaded revolver was temporarily frozen in a paralysis of confusion. All three hooded thugs looked at the back door at the same time as they mentally sorted their options. Had their leader confronted trouble? Was that him pounding on the back door? What was going down?

The gunman turned back to Jasen and aimed again for his head. Jasen was not sure what was happening either, and his eyes darted frantically around the room.

The man with the gun motioned with his head for the other two to go check the back door. As they approached the back door, the front door of the cabin flew open. The three henchmen saw a white-hooded man standing in the open doorway. Assuming that their leader was OK and coming back in, they stopped in their tracks and for a second were lulled back into a secure mental mode. That second was all the time that Junior needed.

"Hold it!" shouted Junior in a disguised voice from under his borrowed hood. "Change of plans."

The leader's voice sounded strange. Quickly the gunman turned the Luger toward him but then hesitated. The hesitation cost him.

Junior had already raised his own Smith & Wesson Dirty Harry-style.44 magnum revolver, which he had hidden behind his back, and in the split second of the gunman's delay, he fired at the man's gun hand with sharpshooter accuracy. The missile shattered the gunman's hand, sending torn skin, bone fragments, and blood across the room and the 9 mm Luger to the floor. The now unarmed executioner screamed in agony. Grabbing his mangled hand, he staggered to the side of the room where he dropped to his knees. He stared at his unrecognizable hand and the blood gushing from his wound.

Samuel and Joe had crashed through the back door just as Junior's bullet found its target. The remaining hooded men, stunned and reeling with uncertainty at the sight of the hooded Junior to their right with his gun blazing and two unknown blacks erupting through the back door, suddenly resembled newborn fawns cornered by three starving coyotes. One of the men, aware of his suddenly limited options, pulled a long-bladed Jim Bowie hunting knife from its belted holster and waved it at Samuel and Joe.

Samuel stopped just out of the knife's reach and stood his ground. "I don't think that knife is going to get you out of here, Mr. Klansman." Junior was pulling the leader's borrowed hood off his head as Samuel gestured toward him. "My brother over there never misses. Drop the knife or your hand is going to end up either missing or maimed just like your friend over there. Your choice."

The three thugs were whipped and now outnumbered as Willie, Thomas, Jade, and Ariel all charged into the cabin. Jade still clutched the golf club and waved it at the two now being subdued by Samuel and Joe. The wounded man was still trying to stop the blood spurting from his hand with each heart beat. Junior's shot had apparently ripped open an artery.

Suddenly Jade saw Jasen still hogtied to the wooden chair, and she handed the golf club to Ariel and hurried to Jasen's side. Green eyes locked onto brown eyes and she hugged him tightly.

"I'm so sorry, Jasen. It's all my fault. It's all my fault. Are you OK?"

"Well, let's put it this way." He was trying to conceal his harrowing encounter and latest brush with death with levity. "Delta Jade always comes through. But I think you have a habit of cutting it a wee bit close." He winked and their lips met in a soft "I love you" moment. "By the way," he said, "you aren't really a CIA agent, are you?"

"I will say this, my love. I am definitely considering a career change!" They both chuckled softly.

Willie cut the ropes free from Jasen's hands and feet and the couple embraced. Jasen stood, rubbing his very sore wrists, and looked over Jade's shoulders at a young woman leaning on a golf club and smiling at him.

"Ariel! What in heaven's name are you doing here? Did you miss the exit at Starkville or something?" He was sure that he would hear all about it when they were far removed from the evening's chaos. Ariel rushed to him and hugged him tightly.

"I'm so glad you're safe, Dad. I love you."

"I love you too, Ariel."

Tears of relief flowed. The Campbells looked on with satisfaction and an ironic sense of justice. No mysteries had been solved. But Jade and Jasen were safe for now.

CHAPTER TWENTY-EIGHT

Retreat

The drive back to Georgia for Jade and Jasen was a mixture of celebrating Jasen's last-second rescue and extreme frustration over their failed quest for Willie the rooster's secrets. Willie Campbell and sons had securely bound Calvin and his Klansmen. Jade and Jasen were not completely surprised to learn that Calvin Caliban was actually Calvin Luther, nephew of the one and only Jake Luther. That explained his stalking and obsession with the rooster. But, who was the man in Jade's bedroom on that wintry night six months ago?

Willie explained that Calvin had an ample covey of hit men. Calvin never did the dirty deeds himself, so he had probably sent one of his hired guns. And what about Big Jake Luther? Was he indeed a fatal victim of young Jade's scissor attack back in Eutaw so many years ago? Willie hesitated as he offered only that there were many rumors around Greenwood about Big Jake Luther's real fate. Jade and Jasen had stared at each other wide-eyed, not getting the answer they wanted so much to hear.

Willie had reluctantly put a tourniquet around the arm of the bleeding gunman in the cabin, preferring to let the monster bleed to death. Instead, all four of the vicious villians were left bound and gagged, hanging upside down by their feet from the exposed central wood beam in the cabin.

His sons wanted to finish the job, but Willie vetoed that. He was not a killer, though he admitted that some bad guys simply deserved it. Willie knew he could not call the LeFlore County sheriff, a cousin of the late Sheriff John Thomas Rodgers, one of Jake Luther's original henchmen. And the local judge had been paid off by the Klan to ignore their activities or refuse to prosecute for the right price.

He had a third cousin, Darrell Washington, who was a rookie Mississippi Highway Patrolman, so he called him with a tip about some Klansmen that had gotten themselves into some trouble when they kidnaped an unknown out-of-towner. It seems, he told Darrell, that the victim had outsmarted the gang and got the draw on them. Willie said that he heard that one of the gang accidentally shot himself in the hand. The victim must have been quite a man to take on four Klansmen, Willie speculated.

Regardless, he told Darrell, he should check it out and make the collar over at a small cabin on the northeast side of Swan Lake off CR 462. Darrell said he had heard stories of a secret cabin used by the KKK years ago. Willie said the "discovery" may just get him an early promotion. Willie told him that the contents of the cabin—the hoods, the torture tools, guns—would be evidence enough of what the gang was up to. Finally he told Darrell to avoid the local judge who "might be" on the Klan's "payroll." Darrell understood.

The Campbells led the way as they all left Swan Lake and its unsavory victims neatly wrapped and tied and ready for Darrell and the MHP. Willie was sure that Darrell would find the cabin and clean up the mess they had left behind. Jade and Jasen felt safe for the moment but wondered how many more Calvins, Jakes, and other creeps were lurking around the shadowy haunts of LeFlore County.

Willie drove them back to Ariel's stalled Honda, and Jasen had no problem getting it running again. It had apparently stalled when she drove through a flooded intersection. Willie asked them to come back to the Crystal Grill, even though it was late. He was sure that he could round up some of the Grill's famous lemon icebox pie. Somehow the incredibly delicious pie helped all of them temporarily forget the shootout at Swan Lake. Willie insisted that they spend the night at his place. He argued that it was simply too late and too dangerous to travel until the bad guys were behind bars. None of them disagreed. Willie spent the rest of the unforgettable evening entertaining everyone with folktales about Greenwood LeFlore and rumors of his treasures that were never found.

Early the next day, Jade and Jasen left Greenwood and memories that seemed more like a bad dream than reality. They followed Ariel eastward on US 82 and escorted her to her dorm on the MSU campus in Starkville. Fears of the Swan Lake gang seeking retribution were not unfounded, but if the justice criminal process was allowed to work, Jasen felt that they would be safe. He told Jade that the ultimate solution was to discover what was so important to the Klan that they would risk kidnaping, torture, and even murder. Together, he told her, they would find the secrets.

CHAPTER TWENTY-NINE

Girls Love Secrets

They left Starkville and headed on to Lawrenceville, Jasen driving. "What exactly did those murderous gargoyles do to you back there, Jasen?" Jade asked, knowing that it was probably too ghastly to rehash.

"Actually I'd rather not revisit it. But, since you asked…" He looked at her intensity and felt more loved than ever in his life. "I tried to mentally block most of it. I kept thinking of you and if you were safe and how much I love you and if only I could see you once more before…"

She squeezed his arm and leaned toward him and kissed him on the cheek. Her hand accidentally pushed on his abdomen.

He winched in pain. "Easy, easy, sweetheart. My stomach is a tad bit sore."

She reached over and raised his untucked shirt tail.

"Jasen! My God! You're bruised and have burn marks. Those monstrous beasts! Are you hurting?" She felt helpless and guilty all over again.

"Only when I laugh, or when someone leans on me!" He smiled and tried not to laugh.

Jade pushed away and said, "Oh, I'm so sorry. I didn't know your stomach looked so bad. Your face is black, blue, and swollen too. I need to get you home and pull out my jar of TLC," she joked.

"I can't wait!" Jasen responded. "But first we've got some mysteries to solve. Let's start from the beginning and put all of the pieces together."

Jasen started in his logical and deductive professor style. "We know for sure that Jake Luther was a big shot with the local KKK. I think Willie said that he was the treasurer. So if he knew the secret way to open LeFlore's rooster, then we can assume he likely hid money or something related to money. Possibly records of money flow, laundering, and financial transactions between Klan members. And again, if Willie is correct about today's Klansmen being in positions of power, then it stands to reason that similar hatemongers were in cahoots with Jake back in the fifties and sixties. I would bet that none of them, if still alive, or their relatives, would like that kind of information made public.

"While you were in New York, I researched KKK activity in the Delta area back in the early civil rights era. There were a lot of unsolved crimes like hangings, torture, and assorted injustices against minorities. If Jake and his cronies were involved in any of them, there may be hidden documents that would incriminate them. Jade, we have waded up to our necks in a pool of vicious, vengeful criminals. We have to get some authorities involved, somehow. We're amateurs trying to pretend we know what we're doing."

Jade was listening and admiring Jasen's calm and logical demeanor. Even after his near miss with death, he was strong and determined. And handsome too, she thought, even with a black and blue, puffy face.

"Well, I've thought about going to the FBI or someone, but we have to be prepared to deal with our buried attacker cover-up, no pun intended. Plus the whole Jake Luther mystery," Jade reasoned. "First I think we need to understand why we've been targeted. Jasen, put in your Sherlock Holmes brain and let's figure this out!"

"OK, Dr. Watson. I'm trying. I'm trying! Let's see, where did I stop?"

"You were reliving the Jake era," Jade reminded him.

"Oh, Jake. Yes. Let's agree that something valuable, incriminating, mysterious—or all of the above—was hidden in the rooster. You mom took the rooster. Jake tracked you down to Jackson and followed you to Eutaw. His persistence speaks for itself. Also, it appears to have been his downfall. After you apparently 'took care' of Jake, the rooster seemed to lose its importance, or Jake's followers took an awfully long time tracing you and your mom to Georgia. Throw in the Damian factor, just for argument's sake, and you two have been stalked for years. I'm still debating Damian's connection to Greenwood. He is a bona fide, certified nut case, for sure."

Jasen continued, "I never trusted Calvin, even before he tried to kill me, so it's no surprise to me that he and Jake are related. In some ways, Calvin is more of a ruthless monster than Jake. He had his chance many times to harm you or steal the rooster. To me, he's a spineless coward, psychopathic racist that has to delegate the nasty deeds to his bozo thugs. If we want final justice for him, you know we'll have to go back to LeFlore County and testify. And that, frankly, my dear, scares the hell out of me. I lived my entire life over and over back there in that cabin."

Jade was soaking it all in but getting impatient. "Jasen, we've been over this multiple times. We're no closer to the answers than when we started this awful trip. What's our next step?" She was pleading.

"Jade, I know this is a sensitive subject, but let's talk about your mom." He hoped that she could go there.

She smiled sadly. "It's OK."

"OK. Now I think this is what happened. It's the only thing that makes sense. Your mom must have stumbled upon the secret compartment in Willie's perch. That's why I didn't find any of Jake's secrets when I discovered the trick to opening the hollow perch. I'm an idiot for not putting this together sooner. The key did *not* belong to Jake. It had to be your mom's! Jade, are you sure she never said anything to you about discovering Jake's secret? Think. Maybe when you were much younger?"

Jade shook her head. "No, no. Don't you think I would remember secrets? Girls love their secrets! My gut tells me that Mom discovered something that she thought would further endanger both of us and kept it to herself, in case I was ever put in a predicament like you were in last night. I think she must have been protecting me, in her own way. Mom went to her grave with her secret, but I don't think she intended to. Her passing was untimely, thanks to the other psycho in my life, Damian. But I think she gave me a clue one day when we were talking about the future, dying, and other gloomy things that we all avoid talking about sometimes until it's too late."

"What clue? What did she say?" Jasen pressed.

"Well, the first clue is obvious. She said that I must never, ever part ways with the rooster. She said that I had to protect it, no matter what happened. I think I've honored that wish for sure!"

"OK," said Jasen. "What else?"

"Well, it didn't make sense when she said it, but she said that if I ever ran out of time, to keep her cuckoo clock close. That time heals everything. Stupid me! I thought she was just being existential. Jasen, do you remember hanging the cuckoo and we talked about it being broken? I asked you if you could fix it, remember?"

"Yes, of course I remember," Jasen answered, still trying to see where this was going.

"Jasen, the cuckoo clock is another clue. Maybe the clock doesn't work because Mom hid something inside it. Which means that the key probably opens the clock! If so, I've been living with the answer right under my nose all these years and didn't even realize it. Jasen, we have to find that key or else we're busting that clock open!"

"I can't believe I forgot about the key," Jasen said as he refocused. "That's what got me kidnaped and tortured. I thought it might be right here in the center console, which I was searching right before I was grabbed and the lights went out. I never checked the seat or the floorboard." He reached behind his back and felt down in the recess between the seat and back rest.

"Jasen?" Jade was fixed on his expression. "Why are you grinning like Sylvester the cat when he finally caught Tweetie Bird?"

Jasen pulled his left arm back in front of him, his hand in a fist. He turned his hand over and opened it.

Jade saw the key resting in his palm. "Well, I'll be damned!" She almost jumped out of her seat and reached across to hug him.

"Careful! You'll make me lose control." Jasen felt he was overdue for some good fortune. "Now," he said. "If your mom was pointing you in the right direction, then we may be on our way to the correct lock box." The trip back home had suddenly turned sunny. The tempests were fading away in the rearview mirror.

***

They pulled into Jade's driveway by midafternoon on a cloudless day. The low pressure system that had brought the violent storms to the South had moved eastward, and high pressure was creeping in. Neither hesitated as they bolted from the car and raced each other to the front door. As Jade opened the door, she laughed and said, "After you, sweetie."

Jasen almost ran to the cuckoo clock and took it off the wall. They sat side by side on the sofa as Jasen turned the clock over and inspected the back. He smiled with sweet success at Jade as they saw a keyhole with a number "8" just above it.

"Do you want the honor or shall I open it?" he asked her.

Jade smiled back. "You earned it back there in Greenwood. Please, be my guest."

He inserted the key. Perfect fit. It turned easily, and the back panel loosened. Jasen removed it, set it aside, and peered into the back of the clock that was missing the guts of its gears, motor, and mechanics. A large manila envelope was stuffed securely into the empty clock motor housing. Jasen removed it and handed it to Jade.

"OK," he said. He took a beep breath. "Let's see why those sickos have been trying to kill us. You open it."

CHAPTER THIRTY

The Envelope

Jade took the envelope from Jasen, opened it, and reached inside.

Her eyes were off the Richter scale with anticipation. "OK, here goes." She pulled out some triple-folded papers and carefully unfolded them.

"What are they, Jade?" Jasen leaned in to get a look.

"It looks like several pages from some kind of accounting journal. Here. You read it." She handed it to Jasen.

"Well, there are a lot of entries of very large sums of money, dates, and what appears to be initials of the recepients. A lot of JLs, some JTRs, and an assortment of others. All dated different times in 1954 and 1955. My guess is that this documents dirty payoffs to Klansmen for who knows what all evils and crimes against humanity." He shuffled to another sheet.

"Hey, look at this. It says 'Swan Lake' at the top. A list of names. Might be the victims that they targeted and took to the cabin.

"Geez! Would you look at this! Name number eight is none other than Willie Campbell, our rescuer! This is incredible! Gives me shivers to imagine what may have happened to these poor souls."

Jade shared her conversation that she had had with Willie on the way to the cabin the night before. He had been in that torture chamber before, but as a victim like Jasen. He was beaten by Jake Luther himself, but his life was spared for reasons he never understood. His recounting of the brutal beating was bone-chilling and extremely uncomfortable to Jade.

Jasen continued, "I have a feeling that this stuff would be of major interest to the FBI. No wonder we've had a noose around our necks and one foot in the grave! We've been sitting on a powder keg. All of these years you and you mom had no idea what she had stolen. This can't be all. What else is in there?" Jasen asked, pointing to the envelope.

Jade reached in the envelope again and looked at Jasen with wild, "I can't believe this" eyes. In her extracted hand she tightly held a very fat roll of currency bound by a flimsy, deteriorating rubber band.

"I think we hit the mother lode, Jasen!" She reached in the envelope again and pulled out a second and a third and then a fourth enormous roll of currency, all bound by cracking rubber bands.

Jasen was debating with his conscious as he took the rolls of money from Jade and could see only blood and death written all over the discovered spoils, hidden away for so many years. It had to be KKK money—Jake's cache that he had cleverly hidden in the rooster. No wonder he had come after Jean. Jasen snapped off the rubber bands and counted. Every bill was a one-hundred-dollar note. Two hundred and fifty per roll. They were staring at $100,000 in cold, hard cash!

"I can't believe Mom hid this from me for so many years." Jade was trying to process what may have motivated Jean to secretly stash away such a large sum of money and the KKK secrets and keep it all completely to herself.

"Fear," Jasen concluded. "She knew what might happen if she revealed her discovery, even to you. No doubt in my mind. And obviously her clue about 'time healing all things' was about the money. But whose money is it now? What do we do with it? With Jake dead, we're the only living souls that know about this. It's our money. Do we have to tell anybody?"

Jade rested her hand on Jasen's, which was holding one roll of $25,000, and looked for honest answers in his eyes. He had none.

"Look, Jade. We don't have to decide about the money this minute or even today. We need to get it to a safe place. I'm taking it to the bank and putting it in a safe deposit box, along with those ledger documents. We also need to check with Willie back in Greenwood about the status of Calvin and company. I feel like we still have a target on our backs. I'm ready to go to the authorities."

Jade wasn't so sure. "Maybe—I mean of course—but we need to decide what, with whom, or how much we share. I mean, *we* may look more like the crooks than the Greenwood mobsters! Let's check with Willie. I'm not sure we go to his cousin Darrell; but this all started in Greenwood, so maybe the Mississippi Bureau of Investigation makes sense.

"We also haven't solved all of the mystery. What about LeFlore's coded message? I think you may be the first one since the chief hid it who actually saw it. I don't think Jake Luther or Mom ever knew about the post's other end in which you found the note. Do you realize that for 130 years that note was lost to eternity until you stumbled on it?"

"From what Willie told me, everyone in the LeFlore family assumed that the rooster and basically everything else was consumed in the 1942 Malmaison fire. If LeFlore never told anyone about hidden treasures, no one would have even looked for them. Historians say that the fire destroyed everything except for a few pieces of drawing room furniture and silverware. We are the only two people that know that LeFlore had secrets he never revealed to anyone."

Jade looked down sadly and said, "Speaking of secrets, I almost cried myself when Willie told me what happened to Chief LeFlore after his death. He was apparently very proud to be a US citizen and very proud of his country. He was wrapped, at his request to his children, in a US flag when he was buried in the family plot near his mansion. Quite an honor for an Indian chief. But LeFlore still had many enemies among the Choctaw tribe. The Trail of Tears only rubbed salt into their wounds. Willie said that, as the legend goes, several years after LeFlore died, his body was exhumed by a group of still resentful Choctaws. They removed him from the site near Point LeFlore and reburied him, this time face down, at an unknown location in an unmarked grave. To this day, no one knows where they buried him. Such a sad ending for him when you consider that most felt that he was a very great man in the history of American Choctaws. Many Choctaw history books barely mention him.

"Jasen, I think we may be on the verge of righting a wrong. LeFlore somehow held out hope or sensed that someone would discover his secret and redeem his good name with the Choctaws. Jasen, you're that person! You are LeFlore's redeemer! The redeemer of the Choctaws' tears."

Jason looked stunned. "Gives me goose flesh when you put it that way, Jade. But I am not a redeemer. Redemption is spiritual, something God does. You're making me seem a little sacreligious or not of this earth."

Jasen collected his thoughts and continued, "We're talking about two separate issues here. One, the Jake Luther intrigue with his KKK shenanigans and hooligans,and two, finding Greenwood LeFlore's long-forgotten secrets and treasures. Who would have ever imagined that a college professor from Georgia would end up in the middle of KKK cold case crimes and at the same time be picked by fate or some divine power, like you suggest, to be the 'redeemer' for the last great Choctaw Indian chief? I am beginning to feel a little overwhelmed and uncomfortable. Please pinch me and wake me up from this out-of-body experience!"

"You are definitely not dreaming. Jasen, this is incredible. I mean, do you really believe in coincidence? None of this would have ever happened if we hadn't become neighbors. I'm reeling here with just trying to wrap my head around the past eighteen months of my life. I think I need something strong to drink! I mean, wow!"

Jade leaned back on the sofa and closed her eyes as she thought about her mom and all of the crossroads and forks in the roads along her life's journey. Take the other fork and you end up in a totally different place and time. Complete strangers suddenly meet at a crossroad. Choices. Life is simply about choices, she thought. Why did she choose Jasen? Why did he choose her? It didn't matter, really. They had to get prepared for the next fork to choose.

CHAPTER THIRTY-ONE
French Camp, Mississippi

"Willie? This is Jasen Prospero."

Willie was pleased to hear his voice. "How are you two doing? Everything OK?"

"Yes, yes, Jade and I are fine. Still looking over our shoulders at every turn but we're OK. But look, Willie, I need your help again. It sounds like your cousin Darrell has Calvin and his three thugs locked up and hopefully getting a taste of real Delta justice. We owe you big time, Willie. And you're not going to believe what we found!"

Willie responded, "The key? You found the key?"

"Yes, yes. And we found what the key unlocked. However, it's way too sensitive to share with you on the telephone, but I'll say this. Jade's mom took more than Jake Luther's rooster with her when she moved to Jackson! It was plenty of motive for the relentless pursuit of Jean and Jade, believe me.

"But that's not why I called. Remember that note I told you I found in the base of the rooster—the one apparently hidden by Chief LeFlore so many years ago? Well, Jade and I are determined to decode it and bring some final closure to the legendary debate about LeFlore the Patriot versus LeFlore the Traitor. Can I pick your brain? Jade said you're quite the historian on the Mississippi Choctaws. We need some help."

Willie was the same gracious and kind listener as he was their rescuer. He said he would give it his best shot. "You sure seem unusually interested in preserving the good name of Greenwood LeFlore, Jasen. He's been dead for such a long time. Really, what difference does it make now?"

"Let's just say that I'm on a personal mission. Plus, his family needs to know the truth." Jasen pulled out the secret message and read it again to Willie.

> "old hickorys word was sworn by all on the banks of the long ears waters my nation must survive and the promised justice be served the creator will bless and protect us in fertile lands west of the father of waters the symbol of peace will be sealed till truth perpetual happiness and eternal peace bless all of my brothers and sisters a friend from a land afar has brought us good fortune and guards these words it rests beneath a cross for the one who redeems my brothers tears may god forgive me and forever protect my nation"
>
> c.g.l. 1830 a.d.

"OK, that's it. What do you think, Willie?" Jasen asked even though he had his ideas about most of the message but was stuck on the "cross" reference.

Willie asked Jasen to reread the message three times as he was writing it down verbatim, exact punctuation, exactly the way LeFlore wrote it; and then he began to read between the lines.

"Legend has it that LeFlore made a secret deal with the US Indian commissioners over at Dancing Rabbit Creek. No one ever knew how much truth there was to that rumor, so I wonder if he left some documents with evidence of the 'deal.' I think that may be the 'truth' reference. Just guessing, you understand? It's definitely a fact that the Choctaws were relocated to the most fertile part of Oklahoma, as he mentions. That might have been part of LeFlore's demands. Regardless, the Choctaws were relocated to the best possible land, considering the other choices.

"It's well documented in the treaty council proceedings that LeFlore orchestrated the smoking of a sacred gold peace pipe at Dancing Rabbit, so that has to be the symbol of peace. But it was never seen again by anyone after that treaty signing. If LeFlore had it, it either burned up or melted in the fire years after his death or he 'sealed' it or hid it some-where. I think this note is simply a reference to where he hid the pipe and maybe other important treasures or documents. The real puzzle to me is why he never told anyone else, or it seems he never did. Maybe he intended to but died unexpectedly before he could. We'll never know.

"The friend from afar is, most certainly, the rooster. Because legend also has it that LeFlore had a 'magical' rooster from South America. Everyone forgot about it after the fire. How and why Jake Luther made off with it is anyone's guess. Ironic, isn't it? He never really realized the rooster's true value. Or maybe he believed those stories about the 'magi-cal rooster.' I think the rooster got his revenge though, ha!

"Which brings us back to the 'cross' reference. I must admit that this is quite vague. There are hundreds and hundreds of crosses in the Greenwood area. I can't believe that LeFlore would be that general about a resting place. He has to be saying something more specific. Help me here, Jasen. The answer is right here in front of our eyes. Think! What do you see? It's here. It has to be!"

The silence was deafening on both ends of the phone call as neurons fired and synapses connected and were routed and rerouted into memory banks. A minute passed, then two. Neither man said anything. Suddenly Edison's invention lit up Willie's mind.

He wisely gave Jasen the next clue. "Do you notice anything unusual about LeFlore's note? Errors, punctuation, word case? Do you see what I see?"

"Well, yes. I see some minor omissions. No punctuation. I see 'god' not capitalized. In fact, nothing is in caps, all lowercase words. Interesting, but what does that prove, Willie?"

Willie answered, "Nothing, nothing by itself. I've read some of his writings before. He was not the grammar chief, for sure. But what if 'a cross' is not referring to a cross but to a person 'A. Cross'? Was there someone he knew by that name? Hold on a minute, Jasen. Let me grab the book I have on the history of Mississippi Choctaws and LeFlore." He returned to the line in less than thirty seconds.

"OK. There's some information here about his family, some of his Malmaison staff, his last will and testament, his two grand carriages, and wait! You won't believe this, Jasen! Under his staff, it lists his coachman's name—Aaron Cross. Well, bless me, Jesus! Jasen, we may be on to something. 'A cross' has to be Aaron Cross, his driver.

"Uh-oh. It lists Cross's death as 1870. LeFlore died in 1865, before Cross. 'Beneath a cross' can't be right. I mean, what was he saying 'beneath a cross'? Can't be beneath his body or his grave marker. What's he saying? Think, Willie, think!" he admonished himself.

Jasen couldn't believe what Willie had found. "Beneath Aaron Cross. Hmmm. OK, let me see. You said that the documents list Aaron Cross as LeFlore's coachman. Was there another? You said he had two carriages, right?"

"Correct, but the staff roster only lists one coachman—Cross. And yes, he had two carriages—the grand carriage was his favorite. It actually survived the 1942 fire; the other one burned up with the mansion."

"Willie," Jasen responded, "we're making this harder than it is. Beneath a cross—Aaron drove the carriages. He was LeFlore's only driver. Willie, I think Mr. Cross was sitting on the hidden treasures and never knew it! I think LeFlore's secret hiding place was under Cross's carriage seat.

Nothing else makes sense. But which carriage—the one that survived or the one that burned up?"

"Mr. Prospero, I think LeFlore is speaking to you from his grave. I think you may have nailed it! Hopefully it's the surviving coach."

"Which is where, Willie?" Jasen asked anxiously.

"Well, it was on display in a historic district with some other Choctaw relics in, of all places, a small town east of here along the Natchez Trace and a little north of Kosciusko—it's called French Camp. LeFlore's father had a trading post at French Camp. I have no earthly idea if the carriage is still there or not."

"Only one way to find out! Jade and I will meet you there tomorrow. Will that work for you? Three o'clock. Can you be there?" Jasen asked, now pacing in circles in his den like a restless cat.

"Works for me, Jasen. I'll be there. Three sharp. And Jasen, be careful." Willie's mind was speeding like a spinning top at the thought of changing Mississippi Indian legends. And he could not miss this opportunity to help his new friends again.

***

It was half past two in the afternoon of a warm and humid August day when Jasen and Jade turned onto Le Fleur Circle in French Camp and followed the signage to the historic district. Their level of anticipation was eleven on a scale of ten.

When they pulled in front of the carriage house, Willie Campbell was relaxing in the porch swing at the entrance to the wood-framed front addition of the B & B cabin that had large plate glass windows that showcased the famous LeFlore carriage.

"Let's do this," Jasen said as he shook hands with Willie.

"Ms. Jade," Willie said as he stood, nodding politely. He hugged Jade affectionately. "Hope your drive was a good one."

"No problems, Willie. Thanks for all you've done," Jade said.

They entered the display room and stopped and stared at the beautifully preserved carriage. They looked at each other and took in a deep breath of the stuffy old cabin air.

An elderly white-haired male volunteer attendant came into the room to greet the visitors, something they had not anticipated. But they weren't thieves. They told the attendant the intriguing story of LeFlore's secret note and that their visit was honorable and intended to exonerate the chief's past. The attendant was understanding but said that he did not have the authority to allow anyone to inspect the carriage or possibly deface it. Jasen was not prepared to accept a "no," so he decided to share LeFlore's note with the volunteer. It did the trick. He was a retired Mississippi history teacher and was almost as curious now as his visitors. He would take the chance. He said that he could get fired, but what the heck. It wouldn't affect his pay! He chuckled and then allowed them to inspect the coachman's bench seat on the carriage.

Jasen climbed up on the seat and carefully inspected its design and construction. He could see that the seat was boxed out and could definitely have a hidden compartment. He needed some tools to pry open the top of the wooden seat that had been painted black. The attendant left the room and returned with a hammer, a flat-head screwdriver, and a small crowbar.

The attendant, knowing the risk he was taking, cautioned Jasen. "You had better not leave any scars or signs of tampering. Understand?"

Jasen nodded his head and said, "Sure, no problem." He winked at Willie.

The top of the old seat had apparently been both nailed and glued into place. It was over 150 years old, and the wood was soft and the glue had deteriorated. Jasen easily pried loose the three-foot-long seat with almost no visible damage. The volunteer was looking on nervously and wringing his hands. He knew he should not have allowed the tampering but was now well beyond curiosity.

Jasen lifted the old seat and laid it gently onto the top of the carriage. He looked down into the revealed compartment and stared motionless, not speaking.

Jade was past patience from the palpitating suspense. "Jasen! For God's sake! Say something. Is anything there?"

Willie and the attendant had moved to the side of carriage, both wide-eyed and holding their breath.

Jasen stooped down and reached into LeFlore's secret hiding spot. He raised his arms and was holding a metal box that was approximately twelve inches wide by five inches deep. He leaned down and handed it to Willie. Willie turned and looked at Jade.

"You open it, Jade."

"No, Willie. This is for Jasen. Greenwood LeFlore left it for his 'redeemer.' As spiritual as this sounds, and trust me, I have never been that spiritual, I told Jasen that I believe he was destined by a higher power to do this. Jasen." She looked up at him.

Jasen had reached back down into the seat box and was now holding with both hands a beautiful sword with a brilliant blue steel blade and gold-mounted handle. The attendant gasped when he saw it.

"That's Leflore's sword that was given to him when he was elected Western District chief at age twenty-two! Legend had it that President

Thomas Jefferson had actually bestowed that sword upon a former chief before LeFlore," he said in astonishment. "Everyone thought it was lost for eternity. Please, hand it down to me, very carefully."

Jasen gave it to the volunteer who cradled it gently, awed at the discovery of such a treasure.

Jasen climbed down off the carriage and accepted the metal box from Jade. He sat it down on a nearby desk and glanced at Jade, who was now by his side. She smiled and placed her hand affectionately on his arm.

Jasen carefully opened the mysterious box to which Willie the rooster had led them. Willie—was he the demon bird or the purveyor of good fortune?

LeFlore's secrets had been preserved and protected for this moment in history.

First, a leather portfolio tied tightly with thin crimson braided silk rope. Then two different oiled cloths that were wrapped around hard objects. Lastly, a small leather pouch that was closed tightly by a leather purse string.

Jasen elected to open the portfolio first. It contained what appeared to be some of LeFlore's memoirs and his personal accounting of the treaty signed at Dancing Rabbit Creek in 1830. Jasen passed the portfolio of papers, apparently all in LeFlore's own handwriting, to the retired Mississippi history teacher, who eagerly and immediately began reading the treaty accounting.

Next Jasen unfolded the oiled cloths, one at a time. They all looked on with hypnotic fixation at the unwrapped objects. The first to be exposed was Nacoochee, the gold effigy pipe, the securer of Andrew Jackson's justice for all Choctaws. And the second was LeFlore's ornate solid silver medal, over four inches in diameter, another item bestowed by Thomas Jefferson on Choctaw chiefs. Both had also been assumed lost forever when LeFlore died without mentioning them in his will. The attendant said that they were both symbolic of the peace and goodwill that existed between the United States and the Choctaw Nation and that they were of unimaginable historical importance.

Willie thought to himself, "What an understatement!"

Finally Jasen took the leather pouch and gingerly loosened the leather purse string. He poured the contents into his open palm.

Jade saw them first. "Wow! Double wow! Triple wow! Incredible! Jasen! Those have to be the largest pearls I've ever laid eyes on. Six of them, and so beautiful! Where could they have come from? Why would he hide such precious gems?"

Jasen said, "Well, maybe this will explain it." He had pulled a small folded paper from the bottom of the pouch.

He unfolded the paper and read aloud.

"these magnificent pearls were given to me by my good friend manuel sanz the rooster and these pearls from sanz's pearl islands were his last worldly possessions when he came to america i was humbled to receive these gifts from a poor negro who had lost everything i have promised my god to preserve these treasures for the one he chooses to redeem my brothers and sisters trail of tears and grant me pardon heaven will bless the redeemer"

Jasen looked intently at LeFlore's handwritten message. "He's consistent," he said, rolling his eyes and looking over at Willie. "No caps, no punctuation."

Jasen flushed red with humble embarrassment when Jade and Willie both said, "Jasen, that's you he is referring to. You were chosen. You are the redeemer."

"Well, maybe, maybe not, but let's not get carried away with all of this redeemer talk. This is just too crazy and a little overwhelming. I need to sit down." He found a chair and plopped into it. "I think I need a drink!"

The history teacher had gleaned enough from LeFlore's memoirs to conclude that Colonel Greenwood LeFlore's position in Mississippi history would have to be rewritten. The accounting of the secret deal with the US commissioners at Dancing Rabbit Creek would convince any skeptical Choctaw of the impossible task that LeFlore had faced in trying to protect his Indian nation. No one would argue about his loyalty to his race. His stature among Indian chiefs would be redeemed hopefully forever. Jasen's discovery was destined to set straight all the wrongs that had been slammed against LeFlore's noble name. The teacher said that the world would now see LeFlore as one of the greatest patriots of his time and the Choctaws' greatest leader. He said that he hoped LeFlore would now turn over in his unknown grave and no longer be face down.

As Willie, Jasen, and Jade left the carriage house and the grand carriage still in pristine condition, the retired volunteer assured them that he would explain the findings and events of the day to the French Camp Academy (the official custodian of the carriage) and to the Mississippi Historical Society. He might lose his attendant position, but he would be a hero to historians looking for the truth.

He recommended that the three of them stop by the Council House Café before they left French Camp. He said that the building was once a place where Chief LeFlore met with other chiefs during tribal negotiations. He recommended that they try the famous "Big Willie" BLT. All three looked at each other and erupted with laughter. The attendant looked a little puzzled; he didn't get the joke.

Finally he insisted that Jasen take the pearls. There was no doubt that he had earned the gems. No one needed to know about their existence. Except the four of them and Greenwood Leflore. Justice was finally done.

Epilogue

CHAPTER THIRTY-TWO

Tropical Sun

Somewhere in the Caribbean

The tropical sun was warm and bright as they held hands lying on their chaise lounge beside each other on the white sandy beach dotted with tall royal palms. The gentle Caribbean ocean breeze evaporated the perspiration from Jasen's brow as he turned to see her famous smile once again. The white bikini, her silky smooth auburn hair, and her lively jade eyes accentuated her beauty.

He had speculated more than he should have about their lives back on Windermere Cove fortuitously colliding like celestial bodies that had been separated by light years in the darkness of space. Did he believe that everything happens for a reason? he had asked himself. Are our lives already planned for us before we're born? He tried to suppress his academic, spiritual, and philosophical analyses and just enjoy the moment.

Jade broke the silence of the blissful afternoon and brought him mentally back to the resort's beach. "Did I ever tell you how much I love you?"

He grinned warmly and said, "Well, lately I keep hearing that from you, and you know, I think you mean it. I mean, you have traveled some rocky roads to get to this spot. I was always afraid that you would never open up to me and let me in. Whatever I did, I'm glad. I think we make a great team. Fate or luck doesn't matter. We're here. We're happy. And we've made a difference in a few lives. What more could we ask for?"

"Oh, believe me, my dear," Jade said, hoping he was on the same page. "There's one more thing I could ask for!"

He knew what she wanted. "Let's not get too far ahead of ourselves, Jade. I want what you want, but when we get back to reality in Georgia, there are a lot of loose ends dangling out there. The Greenwood danger hasn't gone away, I don't think. I hope it has, but I'm not convinced. Then, there's the money. We have to decide what we do with someone else's one hundred thousand dollars. Even though no one alive save us knows about it."

"Jasen, finders keepers is the way I see it. Just like you 'earned' the pearls, I think we both 'earned' the money, if for no other reason than for my mom's sake. Maybe you'll come around. Loosen up, Mr. Ethics Professor."

"I'll try," he said. They turned their heads and looked up at the cloudless turquoise sky and then closed their eyes. He squeezed her hand tightly and said softly, "I love you too."

They had their backs to the resort's white high-rise building, which overlooked a magnificent sparkling blue pool. The freeform pool was surrounded by mostly female sun worshipers who were decked out in colorful, skimpy string bikinis and relaxing in cabana-style chaise loungers. Some were reading the latest best sellers by their favorite writer like Grisham, Brown, King, Steele, and Cravatt.

On an eighth-floor balcony high above the pool, a lone figure dressed in white linen trousers and a loud, tropical-patterned shirt stood looking out over the perfectly landscaped resort. He focused his binoculars past the pool and to the smooth sandy beach of the coral-green Caribbean Sea. He scanned several rows of beach chairs and loungers then suddenly stopped. He adjusted the focus and stared intently. Holding the binoculars in one hand, he reached in his trouser pocket and retrieved a flip phone. He hit "1" on the speed dial setting. He heard a "Yes?" after two rings.

"I found them."

end book one